Books by Niki Livingston

Theia's Moons Series
Eyes Wide Shut
Enyo's Warrior
Protectors of the Stars
Guardian

The Chaos Awakened Saga
Marked Chaos
Expanded Chaos
Transformed Chaos

Novels
Be My Leprechaun

Novellas
Wrong Side of the Mirror

Novelettes
A Web Through Time
Wicked Heart
Wicked Soul
Jolly Old Monster
Unable to Wake

THEIA'S MOONS

Enyo's Warrior

NIKI LIVINGSTON

Enyo's Warrior

This book is a work of fiction, including, but not limited to, characters, events, and features. They are all the imagination of the author and any resemblance of any aspect of persons, living or dead, is entirely circumstantial.

To mom.

Thank you for showing me how

to be my own warrior.

Fate whispers to the warrior, "You cannot withstand the storm."

The warrior whispers back, "I am the storm."

-Unknown

ONE
Childhood Fantasies

Twenty-Four years in the Past

IT WAS ANOTHER conversation Malkia didn't understand. Hearing her parents fight wasn't unusual but grasping why it was usually about her was hard for her young mind. She crouched behind the seating, her back pressed against the back of the sofa, cringing at the sound of her name.

"Thane, we have worked tirelessly for this, and we gave up a great deal to ensure Malkia was engineered properly. Hiding her away is the only option," Haltia badgered her mate. Her piercing green eyes stared him down and her resonant voice grew, as she leaned in toward Malkia's father. "*She* will be electrifying when the time comes. The Artemisians will be annihilated with a swoop of her hand, and we will finally enjoy all that we've worked so hard to create. Please don't back out on this now. These meek second thoughts make you look small."

Malkia watched her father's forehead furrow and his eyes crinkle, as he stared at her mother standing above him. She could see from her hiding spot his muscles tense up and knew his large stature would tower over her mother, if he was standing.

"I'm not questioning our goals or even the idea of hiding her away. What I don't like, is leaving her with such meager beings. The people of Esaki are lowly and unintelligent," Thane bolstered. His hands balled up and he closed his eyes before he continued, his strong voice penetrating the air around Malkia. "Their abilities are trifling and inadequate, and Malkia will destroy them if she doesn't learn how to control what she has. Her powers generate too easily for her, and the warlocks never intended for the children to leave our sides, until they were prepared. I'm not sure why you are making calls without including me. We need more time."

Malkia's mother smiled wickedly at Thane, her voice bubbling with enthusiasm. "Silly man, I have this under control. The warlocks have already devised a spell which will guard Malkia's and the other children's memories from them. They won't be able to remember their powers, let alone use them. This will be for the best, and Palma will be there with her. When it is time to retrieve them, they will be ready to train and finish this nonsense, once and for all."

Thane wiped his forehead, growling under his breath. "Woman, you need to communicate better. I don't agree with leaving the girls with that filth of a people, however, I'm done arguing with you. Summon Asha and let's discuss the details. You and that witch are no longer going to exclude me from these plans."

Malkia peeked from behind the seating again as her mother's smile stretched across her face and her father's forehead remained creased in an angry scowl.

The eating area and the sitting room were connected into one large room, allowing Malkia to observe from the far end. She kept herself hidden, afraid her parents would be angry if they knew she was eavesdropping. The couch was her shield and as she peered around the corner of the seat, she could see her father stand up from the wooden chair and glare at her mother. As usual her mother ignored his rough edges, and smiled at her mate, before skipping out of the room.

Malkia used the distraction to move spryly out of her hiding spot. She whirled around the corner where her father couldn't see her and was careful to keep her feet above the ground as she floated down the stairs and out the silent door.

Palma was sitting in their tree house, far above the dirt ground, waiting for her sister to return.

"What took you so long?" Palma demanded. Her sullen face staring at her sister. "I was becoming bored out here."

"Mother and father were having one of their battles again," Malkia replied, keeping her voice low. "Mother, as usual, is winning." She hesitated before continuing. "Do you know what engineered means?"

Palma looked at her, dumbfounded, shaking her head. "Who cares? Let's play with our koukla's before we have to go in for supper."

Malkia smiled as she grabbed her koukla. Palma and she combed their hair and put beautiful jewels and decorations on their bodies and in their hair. When they were done, the koukla's looked like royalty. Giggling, the girls dreamed that they would wear such jewels one day.

"Mother says we were created to do amazing things. I bet, that means, we will rule the universe and be the queens, who all people bow down to," Malkia's sweet voice sang. "We will be priviledged to wear all the jewels and crowns that we want and be as radiant as our koukla's."

The giggling grew louder as Palma tackled Malkia and they rolled over to the side of the tree house. As they tumbled over the edge, their bodies glided to the ground pinning Malkia underneath Palma's knees. Malkia's lavender light enveloped them, and Palma laughed out loud.

"Not fair! Your light always tickles me." Palma giggled as she pulled away from her sister and attempted to escape the light.

"You're my prisoner, little lady. We will fly to the land of Esaki, and I will keep you prisoner there forever."

"*Malkia*," her father's voice boomed behind her.

The light crumbled and the girls jumped up from their play. Malkia whipped around to see her father's cheeks and forehead flushed crimson red as if the top of his head was going to explode. Her mother looked like she had seen a ghost, her face drained of all color. Malkia hung her head and sulked over to her parents.

"Where did you hear the word Esaki?" Haltia asked, before her mate could berate the child. Her hand rested on the metal stair railing leading to their fields.

Malkia didn't look up, her legs trembling beneath her.

"Look at your mother when she speaks to you," Thane hissed. He folded his arms over his chest, standing tall as he peered down at her. "Where did you hear that word?"

Malkia peeked upwards, staring at her parents through her eyelashes, as she unconsciously reached over and grabbed Palma's hand. Her sister was shaking but gave Malkia's hand a squeeze of encouragement.

"I...I...I heard it when I came in earlier for a drink," Malkia stammered, a fat tear slipping down her cheek. "I tried not to listen, but you were so loud. It was hard for me."

Haltia glanced over at Thane and then back at Malkia, her silvery voice reassuring. "No worries, my dear child. You did nothing wrong. We will need you to keep that word to yourself for a while, as it contains a surprise for many of our friends."

"Yes Mother. I promise, I'll never say it again."

"Good girl," Haltia murmured, her voice was sweet as honey. "Now you two run along and cause some mischief. We will call you in shortly for supper."

Malkia wiped away her tears and smiled up at her parents, as Palma yanked her toward the lavender and rose flowers. The glee in their laughter echoed throughout the yard. They ran through the flowers and eventually rolled in the vegetation around them, admiring the colors of the sky and pointing at the beautiful features of Theia.

Her vibrant glow shone in the sunlight and gave her heavenly features. There were rumors of exquisite beings, who walked the lands of Theia and Malkia dreamt of strolling among them.

The two girls laughed and wrestled, talking about going to Theia when they were the queens of the universe. It seemed like the only reasonable place where two queens would rule their people. Malkia's laughter froze midstream noticing a small figure hovering in the trees.

She gasped, pointing. "Palma, someone is watching us!"

Palma whipped around, but whatever or whoever it was had disappeared. Malkia blinked several times, stepping toward the trees. Now she was wondering if she had been seeing things. She had never seen any person so lovely and dazzling as the one in the trees.

Maybe it is one of Theia's beings, Malkia thought inquisitively to herself. *What are you talking about?* Palma replied in her head.

"*Get out of my thoughts,*" Malkia snapped out loud. She glared at her sister.

Palma glowered at Malkia with irritation, before turning around and stomping off. Malkia sat back down and examined the place in the trees. The purple flowers swayed in the soft wind and Malkia realized she could have been seeing flowers dancing with the breeze. She frowned, and reclined once more on the vegetation, gazing at Theia and thinking of the small being.

"Malkia dear, wake up. You need to come in for supper."

She could hear her mother's voice from the blackness of her sleep. At first, she didn't realize she was napping, but after a few moments she opened her eyes with much hesitancy to see her mother hovering over her. She sat up quickly and squinted at her surroundings. The first sun was setting on the horizon, creating dark shadows in the trees.

Her stomach grumbled. "I'm starving, Mother. Can we go eat now?" Malkia mumbled. She yawned, stretching her arms up to the sky.

"Yes, baby. Come here and give me some snuggles. I will carry you," her mother said, holding out her arms.

Malkia glided to her mother and felt the warmth of her arms encircle her. The embrace was warm and safe, as she nestled into her mother's neck. Haltia strolled toward their home, humming a soft tune to Malkia. At times like this, Malkia never wanted to be away from her parents. No dream of being on Theia would keep her away from them.

Supper was full of laughter and loud conversation as Malkia's family conversed about their day. The three adults put on a good show for Malkia and her sister, but the darted glances between her mother and father put her on edge. She bit at her fingernails, wishing she had the ability to hear anyone's thoughts.

Palma took that opportunity to interrupt her, trying to find out what she was thinking herself. Malkia glared at her sister across the table and blocked her from entering her head. It annoyed her when Palma did it so often. She never felt safe in her own mind.

She was excited to go to bed tonight and contemplate her parent's earlier discussion. She just wanted to know what was going on, but they used words she didn't understand, and it was hard to follow.

She slouched in her chair, twirling the end of her hair with her finger as she studied her parents and Asha. Palma jumped into the conversation here and there, acting as if she knew what they were all talking about. The adults laughed and teased her, before returning to their conversation.

As the evening dragged on, Malkia became bored of her sister and parents. She asked to be excused, saying she was tired from the hot day. Haltia bounced out of her chair, kissing and hugging Malkia, before sending her to Thane for a goodnight hug. Thane, as usual, was stiff as he reached down and pecked Malkia on the top of the head. He didn't notice her disappointment as he turned away and continued his conversation with Asha.

Malkia gazed at the back of his head for a moment, before spinning around and lumbering to her room, feeling the weight of the day. Palma ran past her giggling, beating her down the hallway. She searched Malkia's face and then slammed her bedroom door. Malkia could hear her laughing but couldn't understand what she thought was so funny. Her thoughts remained blocked, which made it hard to hear Palma's.

She looked at the closed door for a moment, shrugging as she moved toward her own bedroom. Malkia was more interested in her parent's plan and whether she had really seen the Being in the trees. Her mind wandered back to the beauty of the small, winged person, wishing she could speak to whomever it was.

She burrowed into her pillow, imagining the Being and what it would say to her. As the different scenes raced through her mind, her eyelids grew heavy. Her yawn took over her face, and she snuggled closer to her pillow, allowing her eyes to close completely.

In the morning, the wind was raging, and startled young Malkia awake. The first sun was stretching its rays across the horizon as she watched from her warm bed. Her thoughts went back to the day before and the strange conversation of her parents. The winged being had been in her dreams, along with whisperings of Esaki. Malkia's budding mind was racing with worry and the uneasiness was making her anxious for her family.

She sat up in bed and peered around her room. The walls were filled with shadows and Malkia felt goosebumps traveling up her neck. Quietly she slipped out of bed, running over to the doorway. There were figures moving in the direction of the sitting room and she was glad to know someone else was awake.

Malkia drifted down the hallway and peeked around the corner. She watched as her parents, Asha and three other adults whispered frantically about something Malkia couldn't hear. The whispers of the strangers in her house merged into a soft hum that grated on her nerves.

There was some rustling in the far corner of the room and Malkia could see a smaller figure sitting on a chair, fidgeting in the seat. Malkia strained her eyes to see who this mystery person was, when he moved out of the shadows and stared straight at her. She took a quick step backward and bumped into a warm, soft body.

Malkia jumped and glared at the person standing behind her. The woman was shorter than most adult women, but stood over her, nonetheless. Her smile was sweet like a dragon, showing her bright white teeth. Gawking at the woman's teeth, she noticed how sharp they were at the ends.

"You must be Malkia," the woman said. Her smile widened when she observed Malkia's eyes on her teeth.

Malkia's head bobbed up and down, glancing behind her to see the rest of the adults and the boy child staring at them. Haltia motioned for Malkia to come over by her as she eyed the stout woman like a hawk. Shuffling softly over to her mother, she burrowed into her lap with her face turned toward the boy. He gave her a sheepish smile, his eyes glistening with admiration. It unnerved Malkia as she buried her face into her mother's neck.

"Malkia, you need to look at me," her mother muttered into her ear. "We need to tell you what is happening, and what we expect of you."

Pulling away from her mother, she searched her worried face. Her watery eyes scared Malkia and she became concerned with her parent's actions. She looked around at the other adults in the room and noticed how quiet it had become. All eyes had focused on Malkia, her pulse quickening from the stares of all the strangers. It was unusual to have her parents appear frightened, especially surrounded by other people.

Thane reached over to Malkia, his behavior more tender than usual. He peered into her eyes, addressing her concerns with his low voice, "Dear girl, we have an important mission for you and your sister. Damon over here, will be helping as well." He pointed at the boy and then sat back as he continued, "We have told you about the Artemis demons. Do you remember me explaining how frightening these creatures are?"

Malkia nodded at her father, staring at his dark eyes. She thought back to his description of their red serpent eyes and green scaly skin. The detail that had scared her the most was their hands. He had described long talon-like fingers, which had the strength to rip a person to shreds.

"These creatures want to take you away. They know we have children who have powers far greater than their own, and they desire your enslavement," her father's voice was thick with emotion. "We have a plan to protect you and the other children. You won't have to do anything while you are under this protection, except be a child. We will return for you as soon as it is safe to do so."

Malkia couldn't understand why they were even talking about this. They were acting like they wouldn't be there. She tuned them out, as they continued to explain the moon Esaki. Her eyes wandered over to the boy sitting in the corner, his eyes wide with concern. He shot her an annoyed look when he noticed Malkia's gaze and lack of interest.

"Malkia, have you been listening?" She heard her father's stern voice. It pulled her attention back to the adults.

"Yes, Father," she began, but then noticed the disappointed expression on his face and finished sheepishly with, "No, Father I'm too tired to understand all you are saying."

Her father nodded, turning his attention back to the other people in the room. "We need to hide the three children away by the end of the day. The others must follow as soon as they can. We can stop this take-over and prevent our most valuable possessions from being stolen, but we must act quickly." Her father rose quickly, directing the rest to do the same before continuing, "If there are any more issues or questions, they will have to wait. For now our main focus is protecting these children."

The adults in the room nodded in unison and began gathering up personal items. Malkia watched as they filed out of the house, along with the boy they called Damon. She felt sad and confused and just wanted her mother to hold her again.

Her parents said their good-byes, and then migrated into the kitchen, keeping their voices soft as they began to argue. Malkia stared at them from the couch, growing anxious from the confusion. She thought of the small, winged person she spotted yesterday, the talk about Esaki, the strangers in her house and the little boy who seemed too serious. She stood up, making her way out of the sitting room and heading to the safety of her bed.

As she walked to her room, her father bellowed down the hall,

"Little lady, we need to talk."

Malkia abruptly halted, slowly turning around and facing them with a puzzled expression. Her mother's long legs brought her quickly to her side, giving her a quick hug before swooping Malkia up into her arms.

Her father lumbered past the two of them, knocking on Palma's door. The door creaked open as he twisted the knob. "Palma, please get out of bed and come into the kitchen. Your mother and I need to speak to you and your sister. Please be quick," his voice shuddered, as is if he had the weight of the moon on his shoulders and it made her pulse quicken.

Haltia carried Malkia into the kitchen and sat her on one of the barstools. Her father followed them in and sat down on the barstool farthest away from her. A few moments later a tired eyed Palma came stumbling in. Thane picked her up and placed her on the barstool next to him, as she rubbed her eyes and yawned.

Palma had always been his favorite and he made it painfully obvious at many points in their lives. Malkia did her best to not let her heart hurt when she witnessed how tender he was with her sister, but her heart was weak at this moment.

Haltia put her hand on Malkia's back, eyeing her mate with contempt. "Thane, please hurry."

"Girls, we have a mission for both of you," Thane's tremulous voice began. He stared intently at Palma and ignored Malkia. "We have to leave you for some time on one of Theia's other moons. The Artemis creatures want to take you two away from us and destroy our home. We need to put you some where safe, while we halt their attacks."

Palma stared at her father in surprise as the sobs rose in her throat. Malkia focused on their father as he pulled Palma into his arms, whispering into her ear. Haltia put her hands on Malkia's cheeks, steering her eyes toward her.

"Baby, you need to be brave." Her mother's eyes stared intently at her. "We will always be with you. Even when you cannot see or remember us. Please know we are doing this to protect you," Haltia whispered softly.

Malkia could feel the tears welling up in her eyes and as they spilled over, she snuggled her face into her mother's chest and pretended this disaster wasn't happening.

It was then Malkia heard the drumming overhead approach of engines, and as they grew closer, their thundering mechanics shook the house. She glanced up at her mother and then over at her father as their faces turned from concern to terror.

"We are out of time," Haltia sputtered loudly.

"Let's go," Thane yelled. He grabbed the two girls, running toward the basement stairs that led to their ship.

Malkia watched her mother sprinting behind them, closing the bay door as their father boarded their craft and set the girls down. Their mother raced onto the ship, latching the door behind her. She cursed loudly when the bolt slashed her arm, and Malkia eyeballed her mother's bloody arm as she pivoted toward them.

Her mother ushered them forward. "You two need to lie down in the beds. We have a long trip ahead of us and it will be better if you rest before we arrive to your new home," Her mother ordered, leading them to another room in the ship.

Handing her a small cup filled with liquid to drink, Malkia gagged as the syrup slid down her throat. Her mother provided a cup of water to chase down the medicine and then helped her onto her bed.

As she stretched out on the hard pad, Haltia kissed her on the forehead and wiped the tears from Malkia's face. She did the same to Palma, covering them both with the soft blanket.

"When you wake, we will be on Esaki. Sleep now my loves."

Malkia glanced over at her sister and watched as Palma drifted into a peaceful slumber. She felt the ship jolt forward as she watched the back of her mother move away. She wanted to resist the sleep, but within moments her eyes closed, and she drifted into the blackness.

"Malkia, we will be back to retrieve you as soon as we can. Please, please forgive us."

Her mother's eyes brimmed with tears and Malkia watched as they slipped down her cheeks. She was pulled into her mother's chest and held tightly. Out of the blue, her father was there with his arms wrapped tightly around both of them. Palma was nowhere to be seen and Malkia couldn't remember where she had gone. The situation was confusing, and her mind was cloudy.

"Malkia," her mother's voice quivered as she gazed down at her. "I wish we could allow you remember us. It's just not safe. You will be in my heart always and as soon as we can, we will return."

TWO

Attack on Domesca

Present Day

MALKIA STOOD ON the edge of the cliff and examined the shadowed valley before her. The memory of the day she came to this moon was still fresh in her mind, as well as the pain of being left by her parents. Her thoughts had shifted back to that moment many times over the past few weeks, going over different details and attempting to understand why her parents had chosen this path for her.

Her sister Palma had been her best friend here on Esaki. She had always felt an odd connection to her sister but could never put her finger on it. As she recalled that day and her father's disdain for her, while he showered Palma with love and affection, she ached for the fog to be put back on her memories.

Her parents had brought her to Esaki, left her with strangers, blocked her memories and powers and when it had been time to fetch her, she had been left behind. Malkia wondered if she had been left on purpose. If she was as important as they say, why would they wait so long to reunite with her? The heartache filled her body and she trembled from the sting.

After seeing her father in the woods, Malkia had united her people with Damon's group. Damon had been willing to negotiate and Malkia had forgiven him for his offenses. Dario despised the man, but he was tolerant for her sake. The last mutt had been banished and the dragons had chased him off. The rest of his group had been given the choice to go back to their old lives or stay in Domesca. It had been a friendly truce and Malkia was grateful it hadn't ended in a blood bath.

Calming down from her heightened emotions, she gazed mindlessly at Jasper's castle and town below her. The world stretched on around it, and the enchanting vegetation nestled her bare feet, as she watched the first sun begin to drench the valley with its light. Being in solitude helped her connect with herself, and she needed these quiet moments to ground her soul.

Her dragon, Tantiana, stood just behind her and she could feel her heated breath on her neck. Parowan, her winged horse, had stomped off a number of times because of the dragon. However, over the past couple of days she had become more tolerant having her around.

The joys of raising two adolescent creatures. Malkia chuckled softly.

Tantiana had become fiercely loyal and remained with Malkia whenever she was outside. The Domesca residents had been afraid at first but had come around once they could see the dragons were there to protect them. At least a dozen more beasts had shown up outside the castle walls and had made their homes in the caves surrounding the city. Malkia remained the sole communicator with them, although the dragon's playful connection with each other could be heard throughout the valley.

The day was just beginning and Malkia was enjoying the rise of the suns as they lit up the world and brought the creatures and people out of their slumbers. She gazed at the scene before her as she rubbed Tantiana's neck, listening to the beast purr.

"I guess we should return to town, baby," Malkia whispered sweetly to her dragon, continuing to scratch and rub the itchy crevice behind her ear.

Tantiana bobbed her head up and down and shot Malkia a sideways look.

As Malkia climbed onto Tantiana's back, an ear-piercing scream interrupted her thoughts, spiraling her back to reality. Glancing over at the fortress she now called home, she saw the town's people running toward a dwelling on the edge of town. She settled into her seat as Tantiana dove into the brisk morning air, sensing her master's mind become anxious for the people below.

It didn't take long for Tantiana to reach the home where the people were crowded around like busy bees. Malkia landed on the dirt below with a soft thud. Her purple light surrounded her as she floated into the home, where she was met by Jasper. His face had paled to an ashen gray, with his trembling hand held over his mouth.

"What happened?" Malkia's voice remained steady.

"Take a look. They are both in the kitchen," Jasper whispered, avoiding Malkia's stare.

Malkia could sense the tragedy before she walked into the kitchen. Whoever had maliciously taken these people's lives, wanted her to see it. Her father was *not* above barbarism.

Her eyes scanned the room from the doorway, first noticing the woman placed on the chair next to the cleaning sink. Her head had been propped back onto the edge of the sink, her eyes wide, but drained of all life. The hushed dripping of blood in the basin, grew deafening as she stared into the dead eyes. Malkia followed the direction of the woman's stare and her stomach churned as she turned to see the staged scene.

The man was hanging from the wall. Several long swords had been plowed through his flesh and bones, embedded into the wall behind him. His mouth gaped wide, and his eyes were noticeably forced closed. His body was contorted as if he was in mid scream upon his death but was silenced before anyone could hear his cries.

Malkia examined the room and the two people whose lives were taken. She could feel the connection with their souls, which sent chills shooting through her body. She looked around to see if anyone else noticed the strong energy, but the three other people in the room continued to examine the bodies, attempting to remove them from their poses.

Malkia stood under the man while the others worked on the woman. She jumped when she felt someone touch her shoulder. Whipping her head around, her eyes then narrowed, when she realized no one was near her. The room felt claustrophobic, although it was open and large.

"Father?" she whispered into the empty air around her. *He wouldn't dare to show himself,* Malkia thought, her heart aching for the one man whom she had craved love from. What or who she sensed, wasn't her father. Nor was it her mother or anyone else she had felt before. She shook her head, determined to clear her mind and focus on the matter at hand.

At that moment, the chilly breeze from the open windows slithered against the back of her neck. Her body crawled with goose bumps, and the hair at the nape of her neck stood on end. She glanced around again, her mind growing anxious as Damon came racing into the room his eyes wild with worry. They darted around the room at the corpses, finally resting on Malkia.

"Are you okay? Did they hurt you?" His voice climbed an octave as he skimmed over her body with a clenched his jaw, his eyes checking for any injuries.

"Damon, calm down," she demanded, raking her hand through her hair. "I arrived after the fact. I'm fine. Although, I have a feeling this was meant for me. Probably for both of us." Her voice became a whisper as she spoke the last sentence. There was dread filling her heart and mind.

Damon glanced around at the scene in the kitchen and nodded as he realized the war was beginning. The others in the room laid the woman on blankets and wrapped her body tightly. They approached Malkia and Damon, nodding as they began their work on the man.

Malkia moved toward the door, just as Dario and Jasper entered.

"They have found three more homes in the same disarray. Something is happening and we need to protect these people, before your people extinguish them all," Dario ordered, glaring at Damon.

Malkia and Damon's gazes met just as they heard more screams coming from the direction of the castle. Malkia jumped, flying past the men. Already knowing what she was going to find, she had to see it.

She came upon the house and was overtaken by the pain that surrounded the small dwelling. Tears welled up in her eyes as she entered the front door and inspected the massacre before her.

The older child had been beheaded, but not before his parents were disemboweled. Malkia could see the torment that had set into their eyes knowing their child was witnessing a horrifying moment. Their organs were exposed, while their dead eyes stared bewildered at the child's head which had been deposited on the mantel.

Malkia's face flushed with anger, as her rage began to build. Her father had stepped over a line that could not be erased and as she examined the gruesome scene, she cried out in frustration. Her angry tears flooded her eyes and she quickly wiped them away, leaning against the wall for support.

Damon walked into the room behind her and gasped with disbelief. Jasper's cry was not far behind, and Malkia guessed Dario must be writhing inside with his silent response.

The war with her people was beginning and she had no idea how they were moving so quickly. She was more powerful than they were. She had the ability to stop them, but not when she had no idea what their next move was. Her head spun with doubt as she studied the heartbreak before her. These people didn't have to die. They didn't deserve to experience the pain and heartache they had felt before their last breath.

Malkia slowly followed the three men out of the dwelling and accompanied them to each of the three other bloodbaths. The townspeople cried out in shock and anger as each home was inspected and the bodies were wrapped and moved to the morgue. They would be delivered to the stars after the suns set tonight.

Malkia left the last residence in a fury and raced toward the castle walls. She had to know her sister was safe. She flew through the hallways, not blinking as she disappeared through her sisters' door.

The room was deathly still. She glanced over at Mataya's bed and noticed it was undisturbed. Her nightgown remained on the edge of the bed, unworn. Malkia bolted over to Mataya's powder room and yanked open the door to a dark and empty room.

Tears ran down her face as she dashed through the castle, asking everyone she encountered if they had seen her sister recently. One by one they each shook their heads, but when she spoke to the last person, they remembered seeing her with Justin. Malkia was feeling the fear build in her heart as she frantically searched every inch of the manor. Making her way through the fortress, cringing at the necessity of entering their private conversations, it became obvious no one knew where her sister was.

Just when she was on the verge of faltering, she stumbled upon Justin. His body was hidden in a dark corner closet at the farthest north end of the castle. At first, he appeared to be dead, but Malkia found a faint heartbeat. She pulled him into her light and darted back to Bella's room.

Bella and she had become fast friends and now she needed her more than ever. She hammered frantically on the door with her fist, sagging against the frame with lightheaded relief when Bella answered. They positioned Justin on Bella's bed, and she began a healing spell, as Malkia watched in desperation.

The day wore on as Bella's spell was slowly bringing Justin's dark chocolate skin back from the ashen gray it had been. His heart became stronger, and his breathing was deep and full.

"Bella, I need to inform Dario and Jasper about this. I won't be long. If he wakes let him know I will be back, and to stay put," Malkia said, as she strode quickly toward the door.

Bella nodded, her hands directly over Justin's chest, "Please hurry. Mataya could be anywhere by now."

"The monsters who took her and killed those innocent people, will pay," Malkia muttered under her breath, hastening toward the meeting hall.

The leaders and guards were standing in the hall, along with several dozen concerned citizens. The noise from their chatter thundered, reaching Malkia before she entered. She peered around for Jasper and Dario, finally seeing Damon wave at her from across the room. She bolted through the crowd. The three men watched her as she stopped in front of them, noticing the worried expression on her face.

"Did something else happen?" Jasper asked first, his brows furrowed with concern.

"Mataya is missing," Malkia exhaled, biting her lip.

"Are you sure?" Dario questioned.

Her hands balled up and her shoulders stiffened, as she snapped back at Dario. "Of course, I'm sure. I searched the entire castle. I've asked everyone I could find, and no one has seen her since last night." She inhaled quickly, catching her breath. "On top of all of that, I found Justin in a nook at the far end of the castle. I thought he was dead, but Bella has been healing him. Is that enough certainty for you?" Dario's eyes fell, and Malkia regretted the words as soon as she finished.

Jasper moved in between them, and put both of his hands on Malkia's shoulders, peering into her eyes. "Malkia, we need to lock down the town and the castle. Can you focus on that for a moment?"

"What? What about Mataya? What about the monsters who have done this?" Malkia sputtered, wiping the beads of sweat from her forehead with the back of her hand.

Jasper took a step closer, forcing her to focus on him. "We need to stop and secure the town. I'm worried for Mataya and we'll look for her, but you have to barricade these people from either leaving or from coming back. Can you protect us?" Jasper asked again, his tone firm.

Malkia was stunned by his request, but her thoughts returned to the murdered families in the town. "Yes, I can," she replied, nodding her head. She reclined into the closest chair, glancing up at the group before settling back.

She closed her eyes and focused on the fortress and the town around it. Communicating to the dragons, she had them check the outer areas of the town. Once she knew everyone was safely in the town boundaries, she enveloped the whole area in her protective light. The dragons remained inside the town boundaries and took their places as guards.

When Malkia opened her eyes, several people had stopped to watch her. Damon had stayed by her side, as Dario had moved away. His hatred for Damon showed in his expression.

"It's done." She rose from the chair, moving into the midst of the group. "The people are safe as long as the murderers have left. If they haven't, they will be unable to leave. I need to return to Bella and Justin, and I could use some assistance. Any volunteers?"

"I will come," Damon spoke first.

Dario narrowed his eyes at Damon, as he whirled around and stomped off toward Bella's room. "I will go, as well," he muttered.

Malkia and Damon caught up to Dario, silently making their way to Bella and Justin.

As they entered her room, the first thing Malkia noticed was Justin propped up on Bella's bed. His eyes drooped and his body remained motionless as he attempted to make eye contact.

"Have you found Mataya?" Justin whispered, his voice shaking.

Malkia rushed to his side. "No, Justin," she stammered. "Can you tell us what happened?"

Justin's eyes closed, tears spilling over as he shook his head. "We were arguing. She was upset with this war, and your family, and I couldn't convince her to calm down. She was yelling at me, as if I had been the one to cause the war between the moons and then without any warning, some kind of lightning shot out of her." He reached up and wiped the tears from his face, his voice shaking with emotion. "It hit the wall behind me, shattering the stones. She froze, staring at what she had done and then I heard her scream just when my head was smashed. The next thing I remember is waking up to Bella."

"Someone has taken her," Bella spoke up from the shadows. She moved toward Malkia, placing her hand on the bedpost. "I completed a spell just before you arrived that enabled me to view the scene. It appears as if I was watching from under water, so the view isn't perfect. However, I was able to see a figure sneak up behind Justin." She paused, glancing around at the other men. "It was fast and if I didn't have the ability to slow it down, I probably wouldn't have seen it.

Whoever it was, they were privy to magic and honestly, because Mataya observed this figure, I believe she has power." She focused her attention back to Malkia. "Did your family descend from witches?"

"I don't think so." Malkia inhaled a deep breath, anxiety swirling within her. "My Mom never showed any kind of abilities. My Dad possessed significant strength and speed, but never used magic to my knowledge. Don't you think they would have done something to prevent the war if they were witches?"

Bella strolled back to her table, rubbing her thumb over her lips. She glanced over at the others as she said, "The kind of magic we possess wouldn't have stopped the war. Maybe if the witches had united, we could have prevented the bulk of the damage. However, we didn't even realize the strength of our numbers." She sat down in her chair, thumbing through a book. "The persecution kept us hidden for so many years, even from each other."

"Honestly Bella, I have no idea if my family are descendants of witches. After everything that has transpired over the past few weeks, I would be foolish to say it wasn't a possibility." Malkia sighed, leaning against the bed post as she shook her head. "My birth parents chose them for a reason. Being witches could have had a play in their choosing. If Mataya is a witch and didn't know it, why would anyone want her? Were they watching her? Have they been following us? It seems so coincidental at this point, but then nothing is what it seems these days."

Dario curled his arm around Malkia, wiping her long hair away from her eyes. "We will find Mataya. We will piece together this mess and put an end to this war. Don't overwhelm your head with the past and what might have been."

Malkia nodded, glancing up at Dario. "We need to go back and speak with Jasper. Then we need to begin searching the area for Mataya."

"My protection will only last for so long," Malkia announced to the group around her, wringing her hands together. "The energy I manifest is resilient, but I cannot keep my light surrounding the whole city, and at the same time search for my sister. As well, I must devise a plan to return to my home moon and stop my parents." She pivoted in her seat, looking at each individual as she finished speaking. "For now, no one can come into the city, and no one can leave. However, if we don't find Mataya inside my light, then I will have to end the protection and broaden my search. We need to formulate another plan to keep all these people safe."

Jasper's head hung in defeat as he muttered, "I have no ideas on how to protect them. Our people have gone above and beyond what they said they would do to regain you and Damon. Maybe it's time to give up and go back to them."

Malkia's face twitched with irritation as she scrutinized the man whom she had grown to admire. "Jasper, they used me. My father is an awful man, who never loved me and is, at this moment, holding my daughter hostage. Give me one good reason why I would ever want to work for him?" She leaned forward in her chair, her brows rising as she ridiculed him. "I don't have the energy to keep you focused as well. If you're ready to give up, then leave. Don't think for a moment I'm giving that man an ounce of my powers."

Jasper's eyes glazed over as he turned his head away from the group. "I feel weak, because I'm exhausted. I just examined over a dozen murders in the town for which I'm responsible to protect. Perhaps this is defeat talking." He shrugged his shoulders, keeping his head low. "I don't really want to give up, but my heart bleeds for my people, and that is bound to show up in some way."

"Understandable," Dario put his hand on Jasper's shoulder, his eyes narrowing at Malkia. "We are all friends, and we'll stand by each other. You should rest. We can take this shift and pull together some ideas."

Malkia rose from her seat and surveyed the faces in the room. "Dario is right. If we divide now, we have already lost." She turned to Jasper, lowering her voice. "I apologize for my rude comments. They're inexcusable. Let's take a moment to gather our thoughts, search for my sister, as well as rest and eat. Then we can bring it together. What do you all say?"

The weary group nodded slowly and filed out of the room. Malkia needed some time by herself as she quietly glided out of the room, and away from the group. She knew they weren't as worried about Mataya, but she didn't care. Although, the townspeople were important, and she would do what she could to keep them safe, her prime objective was finding her sister.

THREE

Broken Trust

MALKIA SAT BACK on her bed and examined the room she resided in. Dario had his own room, but he stayed with her most nights. Their commitment to one another had been the talk of the town for a few days, but now they were comfortably together, and no one seemed to notice any more.

Her mind shifted to her daughter, and she wished Esta and Palma were there as well. As if summoned by her longing, her sister appeared before her.

"*Malkia*," Palma exclaimed, bouncing onto her bed. "I've been waiting for your channel. When are you returning home?"

Malkia gazed at her sister before she said anything. It was surreal to see her sitting there, as if nothing had happened. Palma had not seen the destruction of Esaki, by the Eris people. She hadn't known the fear of the unknown and the heartbreak of loss. She had been returned to the safety of their birth moon and did not seem the slightest concerned in all the events which had transpired.

Her golden hair hung long to her waist, looking as breathtaking as ever. Boys and girls alike had always been drawn to her exquisite sister.

Her green eyes were large like Malkia's, but they had an emerald glisten to them that made her entrancing. Malkia had never felt envious of her sister but seeing her radiant white teeth as she smiled wide and enchanting, she sensed a sudden twinge of jealousy.

"Palma," Malkia's eyes widened as she sat straighter, biting her bottom lip. "Why can I channel you? I thought I was cut off. I haven't been able to channel anyone from home for weeks."

Palma shot Malkia a wicked smile. "I have my ways, dear sister." She clapped her hands together, bringing them to her smiling face. "Did you really think I would let father keep me from you? Once I knew you were alive, I have done everything I can to talk to you. I just needed the final piece. I needed you to think of me."

"It doesn't seem that easy." Malkia's lips pressed together as she shook her head. "I've thought of you many times, as well as Esta. How did you break through? Is it really as easy as thinking of that person?"

Palma shook her head, moving to the edge of her bed. "No, not really that easy. However, it is quite simple. It's a push to see us in your mind's eye. If you just think of us, you cannot channel." She shrugged her shoulders. "And if you wish to see us, then it happens as long as the one on the other end is open to being channeled. It seems there is a stronger block going out, then coming in. I just had to wait for the right moment to help you break through. Anyway, it won't be long before they realize their barricade has been shattered. I need to talk to you, my sweet sister." Palma leaned forward as if she was giving Malkia a secret. "Father is furious. He cannot believe you stood up to him. He said, if your Esaki parents were still alive, he would stangle them with his two hands for making you soft. They were supposed to teach you to be strong and he says, they failed. Malkia, please come home. Forget your revenge. What happened, happened. Esta is here. She's safe and extremely tenacious and yearns to be reunited with her mother. And I want you to come home. I miss you terribly."

Malkia whimpered at the thought of seeing Esta again. Her voice shook as she spoke, "Palma, how can I return? They used me! Our parents planned this revenge and abandoned me until they could use me for their benefit. How can I ever come back to that?"

"Malkia, they need you to finish this war. It has to end. The Artemisians are vicious and cruel and the Enyoans are inadequate and weak. Our parents need you and honestly, so do the rest of us." Palma tried to reason with her. She shifted her body, moving closer to her sister. "Did you know you and Damon were betrothed at birth? They always intended for you two to be united. Something happened, preventing Damon from coming to your town. Someone knew the plan and made sure he didn't make the journey. It was about a year later when you met Raul. From what I understand, Damon would have given you dynamically powerful children. They would have been unstoppable," Palma whispered the last few sentences and glanced at her door, before making eye contact with Malkia again.

As soon as their gazes met, Palma's door opened up behind her and both Malkia and she jumped. Malkia nearly lost the vision of her sister, until she realized it was Esta.

"*Esta*," Malkia exclaimed. She stood up from her bed. "Baby girl."

"Mom?" Esta whispered. She closed the door soundlessly. "Is that you?"

The nine-year-old beauty crept closer to the vision of her mother and reached out to touch Malkia. The empty air brought tears to the child's eyes, and she gazed at her mother behind the watery stream.

"Please come home mom," Esta begged. Her inky irises brimmed with longing.

Malkia stepped forward, aching to hold her child. "I want to, my sweet little angel. I want to come right now. I promise, when the time is right, I will be there to whisk you away from those people."

Esta's eyes fell as Malkia said, "when the time is right" and glanced over at Palma. She sobbed and hiccoughed gently in her dejection, turning to leave as Palma glared at Malkia.

"*Wait Esta!*" Malkia cried. She put her arm out as to stop her daughter. "I'm not leaving you there. These people aren't looking for our best interest. They want to use me as a weapon, and I cannot allow that. I will come rescue you. I'll be with you again." Her voice rose in desperation. "*They stole you from me!*"

Esta gazed back at Malkia and then over at Palma. "I don't want to leave, Mother. These people are my family, too, and I know they love me."

Without another word she floated soundlessly out of the room and never looked back. Malkia fell back onto her bed in defeat. She glanced at Palma and could see the same scorn her father had worn. She was in on it. They had arranged this charade to set her up to look like the enemy to her daughter.

"Palma, I will be there to pick up my daughter," she snarled, her face crimson with fury. "You cannot stop me." Malkia cut off the vision and melted into her bed.

The tears flooded down her face, as the fits of grief moved through her body. She felt hopeless, thinking of the obstacles she was going to have to overcome in order to reach her daughter. Her father was determined to break her.

It was then that she realized her father probably had Mataya abducted and would use her to force Malkia back to Eris. He was not too far off with his thinking, as she thought of ways to surprise attack her parents. Her mind wandered over different options, and then she remembered the small ship down in the sublevel of Jasper's castle. Her hair whipped around her body, as she sat up quickly. Sprinting out of her room, she raced down the stairs.

When she reached the main floor, the silence was deafening. There was no one to be seen and the dead air lingered, sending an eerie sensation surging through her body. She peered around the corners and hustled toward the staircase at the far end of the hall.

The guard wasn't at the door and his absence caused Malkia to hesitate, for a moment. She enclosed herself with her purple light and walked right through the door. Her light illuminated the stairway before her, while she glided down the staircase and the corridor as quickly as she could. The sweat on her forehead trickled down the side of her face, as she grew closer to the switch of electricity.

The lights crackled when they came to life and Malkia inspected the room that held the flying machine. Silence enveloped the room, aside from the quiet hum of the power. Although the noise was comforting as she hustled toward the ship. She glided cautiously around the machine and examined the area where Jasper had opened the door. He had touched a certain spot, but when Malkia inspected the area, the smooth exterior appeared to be the same no matter where she looked. She pushed where she thought Jasper had done so, but nothing happened.

She tapped it again, but the ship didn't make a sound. Smacking her hand against the side and forgetting her strength, she left a slight dent in the ship.

"This is ridiculous," she yelled out loud. She stared down the machine as if it was a living thing.

"*Malkia*!" Dario's loud voice came from behind, startling her.

She jumped, glancing over at him and then back at the flying machine. "Go away, Dario. I need to do this on my own." She continued to run her hand along the exterior, searching for a way in. "They have my daughter and have no intentions of giving her back. I have to retrieve her."

Dario stepped over to Malkia and gently encircled his hand around her arm. "You cannot do this alone," he said, squeezing her skin slightly. "You asked us all to stand by you and save your daughter, but ever since that moment you have continuously shut us out and kept us in the dark. When are you going to start trusting me to be your ally?"

Malkia stared at the man she loved most. "Dario I'm not sure I will ever fully trust anyone again. Out of everyone I know, you and Mataya are the only ones I come close to trusting." She paused, trying to move around Dario. As he blocked her way, she said in exasperation, "If I do this on my own, then I won't put you in harm's way. After the morning murders, I am not sure anyone will be safe as long as my parents are plotting to have me return."

"Then let me help you," Dario pleaded. He tightened his grip on her arm. "We can go right now. Leave the rest of the Esaki people, safe from your people, and go find your daughter."

Malkia eyed Dario, feeling suspicious of his sudden desire to leave at that moment. He had been against doing anything for weeks and had fought her on almost every idea to retrieve Esta. Now he wanted to leave on the spur of the moment, without informing Jasper or their other friends.

"Why the sudden change of heart?" Malkia scrutinized him.

"Malkia, over a dozen people were murdered today. *Maliciously murdered*," he enunciated the last two words, his eyes widening in frustration. "Seeing what your people are willing to do has changed my mind. We need to act now. The fewer people involved, the safer everyone will be."

She was not convinced. It had been a long few weeks, but Dario had spoken the loudest in favor of staying put and letting her people come to them. He had insisted on waiting for their play, as if he had known they would make one.

Her mind began to race, as she glared at her best friend. *"You knew,"* she spat the words venomously at him, shaking off his grip and stepping back. Her voice grew into a scream, as her eyes narrowed to crinkled slits. "You knew they were going to make a move and you knew it was going to be horrifying. Who *are* you?"

Dario stared back, wide-eyed with shock. "Malkia, I have no idea what you're talking about. I did not know they would murder anyone, and I have no role that includes helping your people." He moved closer to Malkia, reaching out to touch her face. "You must be tired. You haven't been acting like yourself for days now and I think this responsibility is wearing you down. Please don't turn your back on me now when I need you the most."

His words screeched like an alarm inside her skull as if the apparent manipulation was weaved with a dangerous ulterior motive. When his fingers touched her face, he quickly closed the gap, pulling her into his comforting embrace. Her body tensed, as her mind screamed it was a trap. Then the prick to the back of her neck told her she was too late. Pulling away from Dario, the haze quickly drifted over her thoughts, and she noticed his contrite expression.

"I'm sorry, my sweet Malkia." He held her body, as it relaxed. "I have to finish what I came here to do. It has been too many years away from my people and they are waiting for my return. You're the only one who can stop the Artemisians, and your people from destroying all of us." His expression turned into a sneer, as he muttered, "I have spent too many years waiting for you to have your powers restored. Sleep now and when we talk again, I'll make you understand why coming with me is so important."

Malkia's mind gave out on her, as the drug oozed through her veins, forcing the blackness to take over her body.

FOUR

Captive

MALKIA GROANED AS she slowly returned to consciousness. Her head was pounding as if drums had been implanted into her head and the beat only worsened when she pried open her eyes.

She squinted into the darkness of her room and noticed she was lying on a hard platform. Her back ached from the unyielding pad and the coarseness of the blanket made her skin itch. As her eyes adjusted, she could see the outline of the door and the light beyond. She noticed the small room was similar to the one her and Palma slept in on their way to Esaki.

She was in the flying machine.

She began to sit up but thought better of it as the blood rushed to her brain and her eyes welled with tears of vertigo and pain. Whatever Dario had given her, the effects churned her stomach, and she was unable to move in her accustomed matter. She examined the room with her head on the padding and wondered how he planned on keeping her locked away. She was stronger than he. She would have no issues breaking through the door and taking over the ship.

I just need to clear my head, so I can stand. Her cynical thoughts raced through her head.

She reclined on the stiff bed for as long as she dared, then slowly inched her legs over the edge so her feet were nearly touching the ground. Gingerly, she lifted her head and moved her body into a sitting position. Her head began to swim, but the pain was gone, and the nausea had subsided. She sat on the edge of the bed, easing her mind, and forcing herself to focus on moving. The drug he had given her was blocking her abilities. She couldn't illuminate her purple light, nor will herself to fly. The only thing she could do was focus on standing up and having the strength to knock him out once she solved the problem of the closed door.

Easing her feet onto the floor, her toes quickly curled away from the icy surface. Malkia stared at the door and willed her feet to stay firm on the floor as she inched her body off the bed and stood. She reached forward to steady her shaky legs, and nearly tumbled forward when her left ankle folded beneath her weight, sending pain radiating throughout her body.

The nausea returned with a vengeance, and she began to cry as the vomit wormed its way up her throat, a noxious fountain pooling on the floor below her. The splatter hit her ankles, dripping down her legs and the wall she was using to steady herself. Her body rocked back and forth as she lost control of herself and began to weep desperate tears. Her stomach threatened her again with an urge to let go of whatever was sitting in her gut, but somehow, she willed it to remain calm. Instead, she let the tears roll down her face and land among the bile below her, as she frantically examined her situation.

"*Damn you, Dario,*" Malkia cursed the man she had loved—still loved. The one man she had trusted with her whole being. Now, she was being taken away by him, to Theia knows where and she had no idea how to stop him.

Malkia's body continued to shake but her legs remained steady. After a few moments, she was able to straighten her upper body, wiping away the tears and bile from her face. She grabbed hold of the rough blanket and reached down to wipe off her legs. It was then she realized she was not wearing her tattered long pants and shirt she had been wearing earlier. She was dressed in a bulky shirt and her legs were bare.

She scoured the room, hoping to find her clothes and boots, but there was nothing lying out in the open. She slowly moved to the closet at the far end of the room and pulled it open, breathing a sigh of relief when she saw her clothes hanging.

Malkia slipped the large shirt over her head, flinching at a sharp pain in her left shoulder. She tried to look at what it was, but the pain came from the back of her shoulder and the dim light seeping underneath the door, wasn't enough for her to examine the area. She moved her fingers over the sight of the pain and felt a bump beneath her skin. Pressing down, she yelped out loud as the searing pain nearly sent her to her knees. She quickly put her hands over her mouth, at the same time realizing the damage was already done.

She rammed her bare feet into her pants, yanking them up over her hips. Despite the pain in her shoulder intensifying, she pulled her shirt over her head. She knew she had been too loud, and Dario would be coming to retrieve her, if he had heard. Sitting down on the bed, she tugged her boots on, feeling the panic rise in her chest. Her purple light had still not returned, and the drums in her head were pounding to a ferocious beat.

She leaned her head up against the wall next to the bed and watched the light underneath the door. It remained steady and she wondered why Dario hadn't come running, after she had yelled.

Maybe he's sleeping. Maybe he was hurt and couldn't move, she thought. The latter would work far better for her, as long as no one else was expecting them or looking for her.

Malkia, is that you? The thought was faint but was most definitely Misty.

Malkia nearly jumped out of her boots. *Misty?!?* She feared Dario had hurt the little girl.

Malkia, where am I? It's so dark and cold in here.

Malkia paused and listened for Dario before communicating back to Misty. *I think we're in a flying ship, Misty. I'm not sure where we are going, but I have an idea of who has us. Stay put. I'll find you as soon as I can escape this room. Is there anyone else with you?*

No. Misty began. *I was playing hide and go seek with my friends and then I woke up here. I can't remember what happened.*

Okay. Stay still. If anyone comes to take you, pretend you're sleeping. Don't give them any reason to bring you out of your room. I will find you as soon as I can. Most importantly, stay in contact with me. Don't let go of my thoughts.

Malkia examined her room, searching for a weapon from the view of her small bed. Aside from the closet, there was no other storage area and there was nothing out in the open that could be used.

Misty's thoughts were shaking, as she replied. *I'm scared, Malkia. I just want to go back to my mom.*

I'm scared too. Stay strong. You have to be my rock. You and I are in this together.

I'll try.

You'll do great, Misty. You're much tougher than you know.

Thanks Malkia. I promise to do my best.

Good girl, Malkia praised the child. *I'll find you soon enough.*

Standing up from her bed, she ignored her shaky body and the pain spreading in her shoulder and down her back. Whatever was causing that bump, didn't want to be touched and at this moment she had no intention of setting it off again. She focused on moving toward the door, keeping the shuffle of her unsteady feet as quiet as possible.

The door pushed open with barely a squeak and Malkia peered into the lighted room. The mysterious silence disturbed her, as she glanced around the door. There was no one to be seen.

The room appeared to be an eating area. There were a couple of tables with chairs and what appeared to be a large ice chest. She moved deliberately toward the chest, hoping to find some water. The chest door was heavy and didn't pull open smoothly as she yanked at the handle and nearly tumbled backwards, the door giving way, and the stench of rotting flesh inundated the room.

The ache in Malkia's stomach returned as she stared back at the decapitated head of Jasper. She shoved the door shut, bile threatening to crawl back up her throat and tears tumbling down her cheeks.

She wanted nothing more than to give up, as she felt her body slump to the ground and did nothing to arrest the motion. She laid motionless, frozen in her soul, unforgiving tears creating a puddle next to her face. Her thoughts were murderous, and her heart was shattered. Everything inside of her crumbled, with the image of Jasper's frozen expression flashing through her mind.

Malkia? Misty's desperate thoughts interrupted her plans of revenge. *What happened?*

Malkia's mind jumped back to the situation at hand.

Oh Misty! Malkia's thoughts cried out. *I forgot you were there. Stay with me and keep me going. This isn't going to be as easy as I had hoped.*

I won't leave you, but you were thinking some awful thoughts. The images were blurred, but they scared me. Are we going to survive? Misty's thoughts were moving quickly through Malkia's and she understood the terror the girl was going through, as her own thoughts reflected back to her.

Misty, we are only going to endure this, if you keep reminding me to move. I won't submit, if I know I can save you.

Misty's thoughts were shaking, as if she was crying. *Okay, I will keep doing what I can. I won't leave you, Malkia.*

Thank you, my dear.

Malkia rose from the floor and began her journey down the hallway, away from Jasper's dead eyes. The next room was empty as well, with the door wide open. There was a large bed and drawers with a closet lining the walls around it. Nothing in there held any clues or value, so Malkia kept moving.

The next room was a bathroom and Malkia stared at herself in the mirror. Her hair was matted down on one side and the other was stringy and messy. She contemplated brushing it but noticed pieces of bile throughout the ends. She used a little bit of water to wash out what she could and ran her hands through her hair, but in the end, it remained a tangled mess.

"Oh well, my appearance is insignificant," she mumbled to herself, noticing her eyes were swollen from crying, before turning and leaving the room.

The next door had a window in it and was on the opposite side of the corridor. Malkia peeked through and observed stairs leading up with a door at the top.

She nudged the door open and winced when it creaked with age. Pausing for a moment, she waited for Dario to come rushing through the other door, but it remained still.

Malkia tiptoed through the doorway and slowly shut it, breathing a sigh of relief when it did not squeal again. She looked up the stairs and could see a light beaming through the window. She willed her purple light to manifest, sighing when it refused.

Misty, are you there?

I am. It's so quiet, Misty replied.

I'm heading up a flight of stairs. There was nothing else down by me. Just stay with me and I'll find you.

Malkia, I feel so cold. Misty's thoughts shook. *I can't move my body and it's still so dark. No light anywhere.*

Malkia couldn't imagine where they were imprisoning the poor girl. Maybe she was tied up with something over her eyes. Everywhere she looked there was some kind of light, but maybe they had put her in another part of the ship. However, Malkia didn't believe it was a very large ship, and there weren't many more areas in which to hide. *I'll find you, Misty,* she reassured the young child.

She crept up the stairs, doing everything she could to stay light on her feet. As she reached the platform, she peered cautiously through the window, gasping from the horrific scene in front of her. Quickly glancing away, she feared Misty had seen the view.

Malkia that was me! Misty screamed in her mind.

Misty, calm down. Stop. Malkia tried to reason with the frightened girl. *I'll figure this out. Leave my thoughts, right now!*

Misty didn't hear Malkia's demands. *What are they doing to me?*

I don't know. Malkia sobbed, not daring to look again. *I do not know, but I'm about to find out.*

Misty seemed to understand before Malkia could think it again. *Good-bye Malkia. Please save me.* Her tone was weeping with desperation.

Misty blocked her thoughts and Malkia didn't try to intrude. They were using her. Dario was hurting a little girl.

The rage was building up in Malkia, as the heat from her body increased and her heart sped up to a point of madness. The image of Misty twisted in her mind, and she bit back a scream, searching for a way to rescue the child. Cradling her face in her hands, she inhaled deep breaths and hoped for some sanity to return. Her pulse was deafening in her head, and as much as she needed to calm down, she could not contain the hysteria. It surrounded her as she willed herself to turn and face the window.

FIVE

Farewell Esaki

MISTY'S BODY FLOATED in the clear liquid, her eyes covered and tubes snaking from her body and head to areas in the back of the glass cage. Malkia gulped as she thought of the fear Misty was experiencing at that moment. It broke her heart, knowing she had brought this upon the poor child.

For a moment Malkia watched Misty's comatose body, contemplating how she was going to end this problem. The pulsating ache remained in her body, and she was unable to use her powers. She backed up against the wall and slid to the floor. Cradling her head between her knees, she focused desperately on her powers, but nothing happened.

Her mind wandered back to Dario and all the memories they had created together. Years of being by her side, assisting her, guiding her and lying about his love for her. It had all been planned. Orchestrated for the moment her powers were restored.

The memories created a bubble of fury, rising out of her heartbreak. As she willed her body to heal, she felt a heat rise from her toes and spread ferociously up to her face. She bounded up from her seated position, as her purple light burst from her body. Without hesitation she willed herself through the door, stopping short when her power fizzled, and she collided with the handle.

"Ugh," she moaned, grabbing her side.

She peered through the window and saw Dario racing toward her. Her protective light was flickering in and out and as he yanked open the door, it extinguished completely.

She gritted her teeth as he lumbered toward her. Bringing her elbow back, she balled up her fist and sent it straight into his throat. Clutching his neck, his eyes widened as he wheezed and stumbled back through the doorway. Malkia followed him over the threshold, still concentrating on her weak protective light. She brought her fist up again, slamming it directly into Dario's nose. He scrunched his face in pain as his knees slammed into the ground.

"That's for Misty, you bastard," Malkia growled, clenching her fists and spatting in disgust.

"Malkia, stop," Dario sputtered, blood oozing from his flared nostrils. "You don't understand. Please let me explain."

Malkia stared at him, watching his eyes plead for mercy. She glanced up at Misty floating in the glass prison before she connected her knee to Dario's chin. His body flew backward and struck the floor a few feet away.

"And that was for Jasper," she said, rubbing her knee from the collision.

She was just about to go after him again, when strong arms encircled her torso and held her arms tight against her body. She squirmed to look behind her but recognized the strength of the body holding her hostage.

Her heart fell into her stomach. "*You monster,*" Malkia screamed at Dario. "You were working with the mutts all along, weren't you?"

Dario had picked himself up off the floor, wiping the blood from his mouth. He glared at Malkia and nodded at the wolf-man holding her. She felt his grip loosen and the moment she was free, she twisted around and brought her elbow up to meet the mutt's face.

He grabbed her arm and yanked it behind her back. "She's too much trouble," the mutt barked, tightening his hold on her arms.

"I didn't waste all those years on Esaki just to end her now. Give her the shot and let's return to our planning," Dario instructed the wolf-man. "Kelsey, once she's subdued, we need to go over all the details of your visions. The little information you gave to Ginny, was not satisfying."

Malkia twisted her neck to see who Dario was speaking to, and gasped when she spotted Kelsey standing behind the mutt. "You were in on this?"

Kelsey frowned, standing with her hands on her hips. "Malkia, you have no idea how big "this" is. Being under your thumb for all those years, knowing you had no idea what you were even talking about, was comical to say the least. Irritating as well. Do *not* claim authority over me, when you're the one who has been in the dark all along." Turning her back on the three of them, she strolled over to a large table.

Malkia refocused her attention on Dario. Seeing the blood smeared down his face, had a gratifying sensation, but she quivered at the thought of not being able to escape. She felt the sting of the needle in her neck and winced knowing she was going to lose her ability to do anything useful in a few moments.

"Who are you?" Malkia stammered. She felt those damn tears welling up into her eyes again.

Dario glanced at Malkia as if she was a pest under his foot. He appeared to contemplate her question and then shook his head, before strolling over to Kelsey. The wolf-man holding Malkia, picked her up and laid her on a hard surface. He tied her hands together and hovered over her as her body relax.

"What is happening to me?" Malkia felt the effects of the drug, slide down her body.

"You will be unable to move again," the mutt said, with a devilish grin. "It's not the same concoction you had earlier, but it will dismantle all your abilities, except your telepathy. We need you to dive into Misty's mind, and the sooner you find your way past her blockade, the better it will be for both of you." He leaned closer, as he whispered, "My tolerance level for you has been depleted. Ripping Misty apart, just like I did with Jasper, will be a pleasure."

He snickered out loud as he sauntered away and joined the other two at the table. Watching them from across the room, she was unable to hear their hushed conversation and without an idea of how the drug works, she didn't know if she had a chance. Her body was limp and her abilities non-existent. She refused to intrude on Misty, but she was also afraid of what would happen if she didn't do what they asked.

From the angle she had been placed, she was able to see the table with her three abductors. She observed a portion of the glass cage and Misty's legs dangling in the liquid. Sections of the control panels for maneuvering the ship were visible, along with the door that led to the stairway. She circled her eyes back as far as they would go but was unable to see anything else.

She did her best to take in as many details as she could and study anything her abductors did. Someone always seemed to be watching her, but knowing she couldn't move, kept them on low alert.

After what seemed like an eternity, Dario moved away from the other three and strolled over to Malkia. She wanted to spit in his face but had a feeling her saliva was instead drooling down the side of her cheek. This was the worst prison she had ever experienced. She had zero feeling in her body and only had her mind to entertain her. The inability to show any expression or move any part of her body, created dread and utter frustration throughout her mind.

"Malkia," Dario whispered as he took a seat in front of her. "I know you don't understand this now, but I'm doing this for the good of my people. I have to save them, and you and Misty are the keys."

She stared at him, willing herself to at least glare at him, but her facial muscles refused to budge. In her mind, she cursed herself for being so weak.

"Baby, if you had just given me one more day, I would have been able to convince you to come willingly. Jasper would be alive, Damon would not be dying, and those villagers would have perished for a good cause." He stared intently at her face, as he rubbed the dark stubble underneath his chin. "As well, Misty and you would be riding safely and comfortably next to us on this voyage, but you had to go ruin it by not communicating with me. You were going to leave without me and that was just not an option." He leaned toward her, a twinkle in his eyes. "We are really going to have to work on our communication skills."

He studied her eyes and she hoped he could see the hatred embedded in them. *How dare he call me baby. Damon was never the crazy one; Dario was.*

"We have a moon to save." His brows knitted in a frown. "My moon. Your people from Eris and the creatures from Artemis have been battling between each other for far too long, and my moon has been caught right in the middle. They have all but destroyed what is good of my moon and it took patience to discover how to crush them, as well as stay in character until you received your powers back. I was worried when it was taking so long. That was when I had my men begin their influence on Damon. He was so easily manipulated." Dario chuckled out loud, winking as he leaned back in his chair. "And all that time he thought he was the one manipulating."

Dario grinned, pivoting in his chair to check on the other two. The mutt was staring back at Dario and Malkia, while Kelsey was checking the controls.

Malkia was astounded she was so easily duped, again. First by her parents and now by Dario. Everyone was using her and now they were taking advantage of Misty. She wanted her rage to build again, but the drug must have incapacitated that as well. She only felt hatred in her mind and heart.

Dario swiveled back, sneering at Malkia. "The best part about Damon, is he has no idea who really murdered his children. He has no idea he was being played from the moment we found out his identity. Both of you were." His eyes glazed over, as a smile dangled on the edge of lips. "It was a good thing your parents retrieved your baby, or we would have had to eliminate her as well. Kids are a nuisance."

That was his first mistake. He threatened Esta. Malkia's powers were brewing inside her, a spark of light igniting. She willed it to strengthen and build, as she thought of strangling Dario with her bare hands. He stared off into his own thoughts, his cocky smile etched on his face. As she scrutinized him, her energy slowly flourished, thanks to his arrogance and attempt of intimidation toward her daughter. However, waiting for the tide of her rage to swell was like watching snail's race.

While lying in her forced position, she couldn't help but wonder how she ever loved Dario. Was he really that good of a showman or was she simply, easily manipulated?

The mutt ambled toward them, and Malkia was afraid he would notice the drug was wearing thin. She willed her rage to grow faster, but it ignored her. The wolf-man stood next to Dario and smirked down at Malkia.

"You killed my brothers," he growled deep in his throat. "Dario, I would really love a chance to tear her limbs from her body."

Dario put his hand on the mutt's arm. "Balbo, stop. You know I wouldn't have allowed it to happen if it weren't for the sake of the mission. Leave her be. She will save the rest of our people."

Balbo snorted and glared at Malkia. "She'd better."

He turned as if to leave, but abruptly, he swung around and brought his fist into Malkia's stomach. Her unresisting body crashed against the wall behind her, her head cracking sharply against the hard surface. She couldn't feel any of the pain, but she knew once the drug wore off, she would be hurting. Her head remained bent in an awkward position, and she could not see what Dario was doing, but she heard him yelling.

"What's wrong with you?" Dario shouted. "Why do you have so much hostility toward her? She was never in the wrong and as Kelsey said, she was none the wiser on our plans. Give her a break already?"

"Why? Because you love her?" Balbo's bellow echoed throughout the room. "She killed my brothers. She gave the orders to burn Branton's body and then ripped Bexton's heart right out of his chest. We have nothing left of them, and you think because you have feelings for her, I'm going to give her a break?" There was a pause and Malkia was anxious to see what was happening. When he spoke again, his tone was calmer. "I will break her bones one by one before I ever ease up on her. She better save our people, or she will have to face me."

The room grew quiet, and Malkia detected an arm move past her face, gently shifted her body and head where it had been. She could see the mutt and Kelsey watching from afar. Balbo had put some space in between himself and Dario. Kelsey stood between the two parties, glaring at them both.

"You are *both* idiots. We spent all those years working hard to accomplish this feat, and this is how you both are acting?" She focused on Dario, frustration crinkling her eyes. "Dario, mother would be furious." She then turned to face the mutt, as she lectured him. "Balbo, we all knew the risks, so control your emotions. There is nothing wrong with mourning your brothers, but it won't fix the present situation. We have to find a way to leave this moon and continue our journey. Stop your bickering and return to your work." Kelsey pointed to Balbo. "Rory requires your assistance, to repair the ship."

We haven't left, Malkia thought, her pulse accelerating with excitement.

She watched as her three abductors put aside their differences and continued their discussion around the table. Her rage had flickered out, but the excitement was stirring up her powers and she could feel them inside once again. She only wished they would appear before Balbo decided to rip her apart.

The mutt left the room through an airlock door, just out of Malkia's field of vision. The other two stood by the table, conversing quietly. Malkia strained her ears to hear what was being said, but only heard occasional words. They spoke of Eris often and mentioned another name of Enyo. Artemis was thrown out into the discussion, along with "destruction", "revenge" and "hate". That was the most Malkia could gather from the hushed conversation.

It seemed as if the day had passed by, before the two stopped talking. Kelsey returned to the controls and Dario appeared caught up in his own thoughts, as he watched Kelsey speak through the microphone. A strange voice returned her calls, but Malkia could not understand what was being said.

The back of her head began to throb, and excitement returned, knowing the drug effect was waning. She willed herself to heal faster, a sense of elation building inside.

Dario strolled over to Misty's glass cage and examined the tubes in the back. Malkia could now tilt her head enough to watch as he adjusted some knobs and examined each tube. Although her head was pounding from the earlier collision with the wall and her stomach was aching from Balbo's fist, she was happy to know her body would be functioning again.

She carefully watched her two old friends and waited for that moment she could move again. Time ticked on by and no one came to speak with her. As her mind became clearer, she felt it would be a good time to communicate with Misty and see why they needed the little girl so desperately.

Misty. Are you there? Malkia pushed at the barrier in the girl's mind.

After a few moments, Malkia pressed again. *Misty?*

Her mind was silent.

Misty, I need to speak with you. Can you hear me? Please talk to me.

The interior silence was deafening and it intensified Malkia's anxiety. She could feel her powers stirring inside of her and she urged them to blossom fully. She imagined her protective light, pushing it out of her. It was there, but it needed more time. She could feel the drug oozing through her system, willing her body to heal itself, as she knew it could. In her mind she could see the thick black sludge smothering her light, and she continued to resist, urging the light to swell within her.

Malkia, I am here. Misty's sorrowful thoughts whispered in her mind.

Misty. Baby girl. I wanted to tell you what I have learned. You need to be prepared. They have you in that glass cage and they need you, and me to do something. I'm not sure what it is, but it's important to them that I be here. It is even more important you are locked away, only in your mind. There has to be a reason. They must know something we don't know. Does any of this make sense to you?

Misty was quiet again and the silence felt like a drum against Malkia's ears.

I do understand. Misty finally responded. *But I don't know why they need me. What would make me so important?*

I'm not sure. Malkia thought. *They know something. They have known about my abilities for years now. They came to Esaki with a mission, and they seem to have more information than anyone I've met. I want you to block me again, but while we aren't communicating, I want you to think back to any conversations your mother had with anyone of interest. Maybe she knew something. Maybe your father had some information that she was holding onto, anything that seems even slightly strange. Can you do that for me?*

Yes, Malkia. I can't think of anything right now. If I remember, I will let you know.

Thanks, sweetheart. Malkia responded. *Now put up that block and stay strong.*

I don't have a choice. Misty replied.

The silence returned to Malkia's mind, as Misty retreated within herself.

Malkia had watched the duo continue to work in their individual areas and no one even glanced in her direction. It concerned her that they had planned to leave her alone, in order for her to have time to communicate with Misty. Their absence raised her suspicions of their means of manipulation.

Turning her focus inward once more, she realized that her light had continued to vanquish the oozing darkness of the drug and was growing more vibrant by the moment.

The door from the stairway swung open and the mutt, along with a strange man strolled into the room. "The ship is fixed," the stranger announced. His smile stretched over his face. "It's an old beast, but it will fly us off Thalassa, and back to Enyo."

Dario slapped the man on the back. "I knew you could figure it out, Rory."

Rory glanced over at the glass cage and then threw a look in

Malkia's direction. There was relief on his face and Malkia wondered where he fit into the mold of this mission.

Kelsey interrupted her thoughts. "Let's go, then. Dario, please strap in Malkia, so we can take off."

As Dario lifted Malkia, she fought to maintain the charade of her limp body, hoping he wouldn't suspect she was gaining her strength and powers back. He set her in a chair, which was slightly reclined and fastened the restraints around her.

She watched the four others find seats, with Kelsey at the controls. As she watched, she remembered what Rory had said about Thalassa and realized she was no longer on Esaki. Thalassa was another moon mentioned in stories from her childhood. The realization she was no longer home, made her heart plummet into her stomach.

How am I going to escape? Malkia wondered, seeing the added complication to her situation.

She kept her eyes on the others and felt the pull of gravity as they rushed into the air. Moments later, when gravity's pull dissipated, she could see the stars ahead of her. Theia was off to the side and her beauty calmed Malkia's heart. She knew Theia would always lead her back home.

Focusing back on her abilities, her light was a tiny sun within, and her skin cast its own radiance. Glancing at the others, she was grateful they were preoccupied with the ship and not paying attention to her.

Suddenly, Balbo shifted his gaze toward her. "Ugh, the drugs have worn off already," he shouted, fumbling with his seatbelts.

Malkia surrounded herself with her light and slipped through her harness. She could feel her body healing faster, but her head was still pounding. Controlling her light as best she could, she floated over to the glass tank and turned to face her four abductors.

"I might not know what is happening, and I realize I was in the dark for years." Her eyes darted around the room. "And although I was deceived by people I cared about, I would never use a child to further my mission. You are all sick. I could kill you all, right now. Do you even have any idea how powerful I am?"

Dario stood closest to her, with his arms crossed over his chest, staring angrily at her with his gorgeous eyes. Kelsey had remained seated, piloting the aircraft, but had shifted her body and eyes to observe the scene. The mutt's soft growls were annoying, and Malkia threw him a hateful glare. Rory seemed to be the only one unconcerned by the return of her powers.

"We are not imbeciles, Malkia. You may feel you can win right now, but we always have a plan B." Dario stood straighter. "How do you plan to escape?"

As her eyes swept over him with icy contempt, she placed her hand on Misty's cage. "I will start by removing Misty out of her prison. You are all rotten creatures. If you wanted freedom from the Erisians, you could have asked. Did that not occur to you or were you so consumed by your mission that you forgot to be decent human beings?"

"You can't free Misty," Rory announced from the sidelines.

"Malkia, you would've never agreed to help us. The only thing you cared about was freeing your daughter. You would have never willingly fought for us," Dario clenched his jaw, as his voice echoed throughout the room. "Once you do what we ask, you will both be free to leave. Please don't force my hand here. I hate to see you in pain, but

I won't put you above my people."

"I am freeing Misty, *you piece of dirty slime*," Malkia cried at the man she had once loved. "I will *not* stand by while you use a child, scaring her in the process, all for the sake of your people. If you had just *asked*, I would have helped you."

Rory stepped in between Malkia and Dario, enunciating each word. "You. Cannot. Free. Misty."

Malkia ignored Rory, glaring over his shoulder into Dario's eyes.

"Malkia, I will only say this one more time," Rory's face screwed up in anger. "You will not, and you cannot free Misty."

Malkia shifted her stare toward Rory. "Watch me." She jumped to the top of the glass cage and brought her arm back, ready to punch through the top.

"You will kill her, if you do that," Rory's voice roared over Malkia's rage.

She stared back at this stranger and saw the truth written on his face. As she began to straighten up, a shot of electricity projected through the back of her shoulder, flaring out to all parts of her body. Her body went limp, and her light flickered out, as she fell face first onto Misty's glass cage.

SIX

Enyo's Welcome Party

"PLAN B WORKED," Malkia heard Dario say. His snicker was an ice pick to her heart.

Her eyes twitched open, and she stared over at the group. All of them, but Rory, had a smirk covering their faces as they watched her blood trickle down the glass.

"I told you she was too much trouble." Balbo moved closer to the cage, freezing contempt rising in his eyes.

"Move her off the cage, and clean up the mess," Rory ordered Balbo, shaking his head in frustration.

"Rory, you're absolutely no fun," Balbo chastised the serious, older man.

Rory's eyes narrowed as he muttered, "I don't find humor in someone messing with my daughter and the mission I was commissioned with." His purple eyes narrowed, and it was then Malkia noticed the resemblance.

"I thought you were taken back to Eris after the wars," Malkia whispered through the pain in her head. "Are you not on my parent's side of this war?"

Rory glanced up at Malkia. "Yes, I was returned to Eris after the wars, and yes, I was on your parent's side of the war. Problem is, they lied to me. My whole life was a lie. On top of that, they left my daughter and wife back on Esaki and they wouldn't let me come back." He stood in front of the cage, watching Balbo reach up and shift Malkia's body. "I spent years plotting my way off that forsaken moon. The Enyoans gladly took me in and sent me back to Esaki to help retrieve you and Misty."

"Why would you hurt her?" Malkia asked. She winced as the mutt pulled her off the top of the cage and carried her back to her seat.

His eyes rolled skyward, as he grumbled, "I wouldn't hurt my daughter. Yes, she might be scared, but that will end once she taps into all of her powers and ends the Enyo war. She has the telepathy, like you, but she has something you don't have." He moved around Misty's cage, examining the cords as he continued to explain his thoughts to Malkia. "Her ability, combined with your powers will create an unstoppable team. By concentrating her into this state and allowing you both to tap into each other's minds and focusing on her strengths, you will both be able to destroy the Eris and Artemis moons. I need to be free, and this is the only way. By freeing the Enyoans, we all win."

Malkia could feel her face scrunch in disgust. "You want us to destroy the moons? Some of those people have to be innocent in all of this, including my daughter."

"Collateral damage," Dario spoke up, smirking. He shifted his weight from one foot to the other, while cracking his knuckles.

"Dario, you are a sick bastard," Malkia hissed.

He winced but collected himself quickly. "I blame all those years of torture on Esaki, living under your watchful eye and pretending to be someone I wasn't." He stepped closer to her as he pinned her down with his icy scowl. "I blame your parent's for bringing my people into their war with the Artemis and causing our enslavement. I was forced to take on this mission because of the actions of your people."

"I had nothing to do with this war. They lied to me too," Malkia interjected. She did her best to not allow her heavy head to fall to the side of the headrest.

"You, my dear, are the reason your people thought they could take on the Artemisians in the first place. They thought they could rise up and take dominion over all the moons. Once you destroyed Artemis, they were next in line with the most power. This whole mad scheme started with your birth," Dario argued, hovering over her like a threatening storm.

It took everything Malkia had to keep her head placed on the headrest, so the most she could give Dario was a strained glare. She shifted her eyes back to Rory, who was checking on Misty's glass cage.

"What's Misty's mystery power?" Malkia asked. "Why is she struggling to tap into this power? And how do you know about it if she's never used it?"

"When she was a toddler she used it, right before the wars ended. I knew I was different, but I hadn't been released from my blocking spell," Rory admitted, moving to the other side of the cage as he spoke. "When she began to tap into these powers, we thought she was a witch. I wondered if I had witchcraft in my line of family, but I had not spoken to my parents in years and was too stubborn to break that silence. Little good it would have done, since I wasn't their biological son. Anyway, Misty was tiny as a toddler, but she was a feisty one. One day I angered her over taking away a toy. She stared at me with this intense look and—"

Dario purposely interrupted, as he continued to hover over her. "She can hear the rest of your story later. We need to lock her up downstairs. Enyo leaders are asking to speak with all of us, privately."

Rory appeared tired and irritated from the interruption. Malkia could see he wanted to talk. He wanted her to understand, but his desperate need for freedom was more important. He nodded and walked over to Kelsey. Balbo undid Malkia's restraints and threw her body over his shoulder.

"I'll be back. Don't start without me," he called out as he walked through the doorway and down the stairs.

Balbo breathed heavily as he made his way down the stairs and through the corridor to her room. He dropped her on the firm bed and sauntered out of the room. When the door slammed behind him, Malkia heard a click of a lock.

She was their prisoner and this time she wouldn't escape so easily.

Her body felt heavy as she willed herself to heal again and her brain was sluggish, preventing her from pushing through the fog. Between the poisons they kept injecting her with and the small device in her body, her powers were struggling to resurface. After several failed attempts, she let herself rest and allowed sleep to wash over her. Her mind needed the rest and went black before she could intervene.

The hum of the ship was the first thing Malkia noticed as her consciousness rose through the dark water of drugged sleep. The room was pitch black, as the light in the outside area had been extinguished. Malkia rolled onto her side and stared out at the room, waiting for her eyesight to adjust.

The pain from hitting her head on the wall and Balbo's blow to her stomach was acute, as she was no longer shielded by the numbness of drugs. She willed her powers to awaken, and her purple light flowed out of her body to surround her. The pain remained, but she already could feel her body healing. She let her light envelop her, spreading through every part of her body, willing it to heal and strengthen her. Malkia felt whole within a few minutes.

As she walked through the closed door and into the hallway, her light kept its barrier. Malkia glanced around at the kitchen area where Jasper's head had been stored. It was dark and musty, and she felt a sense of urgency. It was too dark and quiet.

Since I started this journey, what has been right? Malkia screamed inside her mind, furious with the cards she had been dealt.

She crept down the hallway and peered through the half-glassed door leading to the stairs. It was quiet as she moved cautiously and began to mount the stairs. The doorway at the top stood ajar, and Malkia could feel her heart sink as she regarded Misty's prison.

She was gone. The ship was on, but no one was at home.

What had transpired while I was unconscious?

Disoriented and wary, she walked around the room, opening every cupboard and door. When she reached the outside door, she could not figure out how to open it. She glanced at the windows and saw only the opacity of condensation. She didn't want to walk through the door to nothing. But what if they had landed?

This would be your best chance of escape, Malkia thought.

Just as she decided to risk exiting, she heard a clatter on the other side. The door began to slide open. Malkia hid herself on the far side of a cupboard, waiting for her captor to enter.

Dario sauntered by, heading toward the stairway. He paused when he reached the door and glanced around the room. His eyes travelled casually over her hiding place, but he showed no sign of seeing her. Opening the door, she heard him whistling as he walked down the stairs.

Malkia tasted bitter bile seeing his arrogance unmasked. *What did I ever see in him?* She thought in disgust.

She slid out of her hiding spot and peered through the doorway of the ship, examining the area where they had landed through the airlock. Cautiously, she moved through the small space and peeked outside. They were in some kind of docking building, where a few Enyo people worked on other flying machines. No one else could be seen from where Malkia was standing.

Masking her light, she stepped lightly down the gangway. She made her way around the ship's periphery, sliding through the first door she could find. A stairwell stretched above and below her. The way down seemed to be the route out, so she bolted down the stairs, stopping when she could go no farther. Sunlight danced through the small window, showing her the way out.

When she opened the door, voices rang out in alarm. Her vantage was lost. Running into the sunlight, she kept going until the building was no longer visible. Her run slowed to a walk as she surveyed her surroundings, searching for a hiding spot.

The buildings towered over her when she had first run from the ship, but as she got farther away the structures were squat, with little movement between them. A few humans lounged in doorways or peeked through window coverings, but no one spoke, and they appeared puzzled by her presence. The silence intensified her need to find shelter, before mute perplexity evolved into vocal suspicion.

As she walked through the quiet streets, she noticed the humans became even more sparse and there were far too many Artemis creatures roaming around. She knew of them but had always believed they stayed away from humans. Dario was serious when he said they were taking over his moon. The farther she moved away from Dario, the more creatures she ran into.

Many of them glared at her with their carnelian eyes, while others pointed. Their fingers resembled the talons her mother had warned her about. Their pointed stares sent chills down her spine, and she gathered that being a human was not the safest way to travel in these areas.

As soon as she could, Malkia ducked between two small buildings and ran down the empty alleyway. She needed to escape from the stares and find a safe hiding spot. The shadows of the buildings were moist with a recent rainfall, and she welcomed the slight breeze that cooled her skin from her frantic escape. She slowed her pace and glanced back behind her, to ensure no one was following.

The alleyway was deserted. Hiding in a recessed nook, she took some time to catch her breath. Her protective light had faltered. She wondered what drug they had given her to make it unpredictable, which worried her more than not having access to her powers.

Her powers still flowed inside of her, but they quivered unsteadily, on the verge of crashing. She felt naked without her protection, not knowing how she would safely pass through the Artemisians who dominated the streets beyond the alley. Earlier, her healing seemed to overcome the poison in her body. But now, as she willed her light to drive away the mounting sensation of the drug, the converse occurred. She became more powerless as the minutes passed.

Peering up at the strip of sky between the buildings, she gauged that the first sun was beginning its descent to the horizon. She glanced back down the alley, noticing a few creatures roaming past, but none looked in her direction. She proceeded down the alley, her eyes straining to catch movement in the cross street ahead. It remained clear as she crept forward.

She peeked around the corner at the end of the buildings and was taken aback by the massive pyramid dominating the skyline. She had seen one in her travels on Esaki and was surprised to find an identical one on Enyo.

Without thinking she stepped out of the shadows of the building and collided with an Artemis creature.

"*Filthy human,*" he roared. His large stature cowered above her. "How did you escape?" He didn't wait for her to speak, instead grasped her wrists with his talon-like fingers and hauled her down the street.

She struggled against his scaly body, but as powerless as she was, her struggles were in vain. The full weight of this realization was a boulder on her chest. "*Let go of me,*" Malkia cried in desperation, squirming against his grasp.

He tightened his iron grip and kept moving through the crowds of creatures. For the first time since she escaped Dario, she noticed other humans on leashes. Tattered clothing hung like rags from their dirty bodies. Their heads low and defeated, with scars overrunning their bodies. They were prisoners on their own moon.

What is going on here? Who do these creatures think they are?

Her captor yanked her inside the door of a rundown building and down a dark hallway. It smelled like rodent excrement and Malkia's stomach churned with nausea by the time they reached a room in the back. As the creature pushed her into the drafty room and walked in after her, she realized the smell was going to be the least of her problems.

He leered at her with contempt. "You'll be wishing you never strayed away from your owners, human. I will beat you senseless. When will you stupid humans ever learn who's in charge around here?"

He curled his fingers in a strange way, and Malkia didn't know what he was doing until it was too late. His fist came fast and hard and contacted her right cheek bone. She heard a crack before she collided with the wall behind her. Her head flung back and smacked the same spot it had when Balbo had struck her.

She groaned, tasting the metallic blood in her mouth. Her face was pulsing to her rapid heartbeat and her right eye was sealed shut. She begged for her light to protect her and cracked open her left eye, while attempting to scoot her body away from the creature.

Seconds later, the monster's foot make contact with her stomach, propelling her into the wall. His fist came down hard on her right shoulder, dislocating it with a sickening pop and a spasm of agony. Feebly, she raised her left hand in an attempt to ward herself. He rewarded her puny attempt to stop him by kicking her in the stomach again. Her backside hit the wall and it felt as if her lower spine cracked, but she forgot about that as he picked her up by her hair and threw her across the room into the other wall.

This time her left thigh cracked against the wall and pain screamed down her leg in sharp, blinding waves. Her leg bone shattered as she landed with a thud, forcing a shriek from her lips. He didn't give her moment to recover, before he picked her up again, throwing her again. The sensation of flight was the last thing she felt.

Malkia didn't remember when she succumbed to the blackness, but she did know her protective light hadn't been strong enough to stop the creature from fracturing her skull and breaking her body. In her last moments, she had wished for death as she felt her head once again crack against the wall and her body go limp with pain.

Her captor chuckled, as she lost consciousness, but not before she cried out inside her head to Misty. *Help!*

SEVEN
Selective Memory

MALKIA'S EYES FLUTTERED open to darkness. She felt cold and wet, and her head was pounding. She tried to lever herself into a sitting position, but bit back a scream as her upper left leg refused to hold her weight. She leaned on her right side and let her left eye adjust to the blackness around her. Her right eye was throbbing and almost completely swollen shut.

She remembered the beating, but she couldn't recall where she was or the reason this torture was inflicted upon her. Her memories were blurry and jumbled, as she tried to piece together who she was, why she was here, and what was going on.

Her memories showed her many faces, but the only one she recognized was Dario's. She knew she loved Dario and wanted to see him again.

"Am I still on Esaki? How did I get here?" Malkia murmured to the blackness, as more memories of her life came back to her in broken flashes.

There was no furniture in the room and only one small window, too high for her to reach. The door was closed, and she had a feeling it was locked. Either way, she knew she didn't want the monster back in the room with her; a thwarted escape attempt was sure to draw his attention. She needed to think about this.

Her head was throbbing in time with her pulse, and pain radiated all over her body. She was certain the wetness she felt was not water, but her own blood. Even weak and nauseated, she knew if she didn't find a way out of her prison, the creature would be back for more.

She willed herself to standing position and did her best to ignore the pain racing through her left leg. She was unable to place much weight on it and wondered if he had broken her leg bone. Her right arm had been yanked out of its socket and hung useless next to her side. Even if she made it through the door, she wouldn't be able to run.

She could feel a source of energy inside her as she limped toward the closed door. It seemed familiar, but she couldn't remember what it was. As she thought of her body in pain, the energy grew stronger and by the time she reached the door, her skin was incandescent.

"I can heal myself," Malkia whispered, recognizing her purple protective light.

She willed her body to heal itself as she leaned against the wall next to the door. Her body grew warm, and the pain subsided as her body mended the internal damage. She watched as her leg and arm readjusted themselves to their proper alignment, her light protecting her from the necessary pain of the repairing.

She was in awe of her own powers and delighted that she had found a way to escape this mess.

As she noticed the morning light creep through the window, she feared her captor would soon return. It was a miracle she could heal herself, but it was taking longer than she could allow.

No sooner than this thought occurred to her, she heard movement outside the door. She scampered to the far corner of the room and continued to let her body heal, as she focused on the creature she believed was about to come through the door.

There was the jiggling of some keys and Malkia watched as the doorknob turned and the Artemisian strolled into the room. He jumped in surprise as he checked the floor where he had left her and then quickly scanned the room, noticing her crouching in the corner.

"You little witch," he bellowed, his scaly skin turning as bright red as his eyes as he started toward her.

She leapt high into the air and flipped over his head, causing him to stumble toward the corner, grasping at empty space and caught off guard by her sudden movement. She ran through the door, grabbing a large knife from the table outside her door. Turning quickly, she faced her captor.

He stood in the middle of the room, eyeing her with fury. His chest heaved in and out before he hurdled his body in her direction. He misjudged her speed, as she ducked his blow and stabbed his lung with the knife. Yanking it out of his body, she twisted back in front of him, shoving the knife into his throat.

He gurgled in pain and shot her a surprised look. Releasing her, he flailed his arms, trying to find the knife.

"That's for the beating you gave me yesterday, *you rotten beast*," Malkia shrieked at the creature.

Bounding upward, she grabbed the sides of his head and tossed herself off to the side, hearing the crack of his giant neck bones as she landed on the other side of his body. He tumbled to the ground and hit with a bang.

Her strength had returned, and she felt her powers pulsing once again throughout her body. "Now if I can remember where I am, and how I arrived here," Malkia murmured out loud, brushing her hands together to rid them of any Artemisian residue.

She turned to face the outside door and strolled down the dark, damp hallway, wiping the sweat from her forehead with the back of her arm. The smell of the rodent leavings reminded of her of the day before but didn't bring back any useful memories. As she opened the door she came face to face with Dario.

"*Dario*," Malkia exclaimed. She threw her arms around his neck and kissed him hard.

His shoulders tensed with the embrace, but he quickly relaxed and kissed her back, pulling her body against his. They melted into one another just as someone cleared their throat behind them.

Malkia peered over Dario's shoulder at Rory. "Who are you?" Malkia asked. Her powers were ready to use if needed.

"Do you not remember me, Malkia? I'm Misty's father," Rory said quickly, noticing the light illuminating from her body.

"I'm sorry," Malkia frowned, shaking her head. "It seems I've forgotten the past few days or so. The monster inside, beat me awfully hard. For some reason my light didn't protect me, and I don't know why. My memories are jumbled, and I can't seem to grasp my last few days. Based on the way this place looks, would it be correct to assume we are no longer on Esaki?"

Dario nodded. "We left Esaki four days ago and arrived on Enyo yesterday, but you were captured by the Artemisians almost immediately." He shot Rory a strange look, as he led Malkia away from the building. "We have been searching high and low for you. Misty heard your cry for help and with the Enyo's technology we were able to use that to pinpoint your whereabouts. However, it isn't safe for humans to travel at night, so we came first light."

A confused look at settled over Malkia's expression. "Why did we come to Enyo? Shouldn't we be going to Eris?" she asked, as Dario helped her onto a two wheeled moving machine. "And what is this? Is it safe?"

"Malkia, do you trust me?" Dario eyed her intensely.

"Of course, I do. Everything feels off right now, but if there is anyone I trust, it's you," she replied, smiling back at Dario.

"We must free the Enyo people from the Artemisians. They are killing them off one by one. If they aren't dead, they are being beaten within an inch of their lives. You bore firsthand witness to that. Once we win this battle on Enyo, they've agreed to help us regain your daughter." Dario paused, running his hands over the two wheeled machine. "As for this, it's a motorcycle and it's perfectly safe. Just hold onto me and we'll be back to safety, soon."

Malkia smiled and nodded. Dario straddled the machine in front of her and she wrapped her arms around his waist. Rory was already out of sight, as Dario's machine roared to life.

The wind caught Malkia's long hair as they flew down the roadway toward a large building in the distance. She noticed the pyramid off to the side and faintly remembered running from someone when she had first seen it. It reminded her of the pyramid she had found on Esaki and her heart ached for her sister and friends back home.

She watched the small buildings and homes give way to more imposing structures. Her mind wanted to remember something, but she couldn't grasp what it was. The sky was saturated with the sun's rays and she enjoyed the warmth on her face. Knowing that she was safe with Dario was reassurance enough for her at the moment.

The motorcycle slowed as they neared a massive structure piercing the sky. She could see flying machines leaving top areas of the building, as they stopped at a gate and Dario had his eye scanned.

The gate folded backward, and Dario and Rory zoomed in and up a ramp that veered off to the right. Malkia was struck with a familiar feeling again but could still not pinpoint why it bothered her. She glanced around at the Enyo moon as they rounded their way up the side of building.

Malkia admired the rays of the first sun as it spread across the city below, the mellow light gilding all it touched. The colors of the vegetation struck her as odd, with their golden tint showing through with the reds, greens, and purples. It almost appeared unreal.

The pyramid could be seen, and Malkia noticed two more pyramids farther away, in a distinct formation. Her curiosity to be up close with the arrangement was overwhelming, as she strained her eyes for a better view.

The climb ended as Rory led them into what appeared as a machine deposit area. There were other motorcycles lined up against one wall and a door on the far end. The two men parked their machines and Malkia climbed off the back, allowing Dario the room to swing his leg over.

Dario grabbed her hand and they followed Rory to the door. It automatically opened as they neared it and Malkia gasped at the beautifully decorated room into which they entered. It had cushioned seats, with tables and plants scattered throughout the room. There were humans sitting in many of the chairs, talking amongst themselves or staring at flat objects in their hands. One person was talking to the flat object and Malkia laughed out loud, thinking how silly they looked.

Dario arched a sly brow, as she put her hand over her mouth to stifle her laugh. She followed the men through the room, entering a snug box of a room. When the doors closed, Malkia hit the door with her fist.

"What's going on?" Malkia snapped at Dario.

Dario clasped her hands. "It's called an elevator, love. Feel that? We are going up. Instead of walking, you just enjoy the ride."

The moving box, rocked and bumped as Malkia waited anxiously for the doors to open again. When they did, Malkia moved quickly into the hallway where she noticed several doors on each side.

"I will leave you two alone. I need to go clean up and check on Misty. Malkia, I'm glad you're safe and I look forward to working with you soon." Rory looked her in the eyes one last time, before he turned toward one of the doors.

Putting his hand on the door, Malkia watched as a light scanned his hand and then the door swung open. He disappeared inside and shut the door behind him.

"Our room is down toward the end," Dario pointed out, as he pulled her down the hall.

Malkia's mind was back on Esaki, gazing at Rory's closed door. "All this technology and the Enyo people aren't destroying each other.

They have monsters destroying them. Why?"

She shifted her gaze from the door to Dario. "Dario, do you know why?"

"Baby, I have only heard the bare minimum. We will learn more after we meet with their leaders. Do you think you could take a shower, sleep and be ready for a meeting by dinner time?"

Malkia glanced down at herself and for the first time noticed how filthy she was. She peered over at Dario and bit her lip as she smiled slyly. "I bet I could be rested and more. Would you like to shower as well?" She purred, as she eased Dario up against the wall. She raised up on her tiptoes, meeting his lips with hers and hungrily kissing him, begging for more.

Dario melted into her embrace and pulled her against his body, letting her know he was ready for her. He grabbed her hand and led her down the hallway toward their room. His hand held firm on the door as it scanned and then slid open.

Malkia nudged him inside the room, smiling wickedly as the door closed behind them.

EIGHT

Healing

MALKIA WAS RUNNING through the dark and damp cave corridors. She could hear her child crying, but wherever she ran she was met with empty chambers and dead ends. *Esta needed her. Why did her parents have her in a cave? Why did they keep moving her?*

Confusion set in, as she raced around the next corner and was back in the last chamber she had just left. The same chair was sitting in the middle of the room with the yellow bow lying on the ground next to it. Malkia made her way to the chair this time and picked up the familiar hair piece. The one she had put in Esta's hair the last time she had seen her on Esaki.

The tears came without warning. She sat on the chair and held her face in her hands as she wept for the loss of her daughter. *Why?* Why would her mother do this to her?

She knew her father only distinguished her as a weapon, but her mother had always been tender and loving toward her. Had it all been an act? How could two people be this malicious and cold to their own child?

Malkia looked up from her hands and jumped when she recognized her birth mother, standing in the entryway to the chamber.

"Malkia, come find me. Come find me on Eris," her mother's mouth didn't move, but the voice was hers. Haltia's frenzied expression shifted to fear, as she vanished into thin air.

"*Mom*," Malkia cried.

Malkia shot up in bed and glanced around at the strange room. Her cheeks were wet with tears and her heart was pounding ferociously inside her chest. The dream felt real, and Malkia yearned for her mother.

She could tell the suns were high in the sky, even though there was fabric covering the windows. Malkia swung her legs over the edge of the bed, adjusting to her bearings and sorting out the dream in her head.

The door eased open, and Malkia smiled when Dario strolled into the room.

He grinned back at her. "How did you sleep?"

"Pretty well, I think." She rubbed the sleep out of her eyes. "I had a dream about my mother and Esta. I'm a bit shaken up about it, but other than that I feel well rested."

"Good," Dario said, running his hands through her hair. "Would you like to eat, before we meet with the Enyo leaders?"

"Yes, please," Malkia sighed. "I'm starving."

He reached down, pulling her up into an embrace as he kissed her neck and nuzzled her cheek. "You're amazing, my sweet Malkia," he said, giving her a squeeze. "I'm so happy we were able to take a moment to connect and be close to each other."

Malkia leaned back and grinned, before planting a kiss on his lips. "I needed that." She kissed his shoulder and laid her head on his chest.

She could hear his heart beating, as she stared at the wall. A faint memory was sparked, one where her own heart was pulsating in her head, when she woke up in the flying ship.

Did I really throw up? Was that a dream? Her shoulders tensed and she worried Dario would notice the change in her embrace.

She slowly pulled away from him and walked to the door. As she glanced back, an intense sense of doubt built inside her as he stared at her with a deadpan expression on his face. As much as she wanted this to be real, his strange behavior and her flashes of memory were giving her a twisted churning in her stomach.

Dario quickly smiled back at her and followed her down the hallway to the kitchen. He pushed some buttons and spoke to a bright screen and moments later he was arranging different food on the counter.

How did he do that? The connection to him seemed to have subsided as her feelings of uneasiness grew.

Shaking her head, she strolled over to the window and peered out to the Enyo moon. The buildings towered above everything else, but off to the left she could see the villages with the pyramids overshadowing the dwellings.

"Dario?" She glanced back at him. "Do you know anything about the pyramids here on Enyo?"

His eyes closed for a moment, as he drew in a deep breath. He seemed agitated as he spoke, "I've heard some stories, just from what a few of the Enyo people have told me. The pyramid builders are a mystery, but the Enyo's factor them to be close to seven thousand years old. From what I've gathered, they are filled with tombs and the Enyoans forbid access because of their superstitions. They believe if one of the tombs is opened, the curse will destroy their civilization. That is the most I know about them. Why are you so curious?"

She turned back to the window, eyeing the pyramids. "Do you remember a few years ago when I went on that solo journey to the south?"

"Faintly. Was it the time we had thieves steal our water supply and you didn't make it back until we had nearly replenished it?"

Malkia remembered that year vividly. It had been one of the worst moments, but it was not the time she was talking about. "No. Not then. That was nearly five years ago. I'm talking about the time I left you in charge. Skye was off with a group to the north and Curtis's son was ill. You kept everyone safe, along with making sure Curtis's son got the proper care he needed to pull out of his illness. The year I began to see you as more than just my sidekick." She laughed, attempting to lighten up the conversation. She pulled out her chair to the table and sat down, shifting her gaze back up to Dario.

Dario smiled. "Yes, I remember. That was one of the good years."

"It *was* a good year. Remember, I wanted to ground myself and learn more efficient ways to track and hunt? I was gone for nearly a month."

"Yes, yes, I remember now. You came back and said you had experienced a life changing journey, but you never told anyone what happened." Dario gave her a sideways look, his interest piqued.

"It was a transforming experience. I found peace on that adventure, but part of that was from the pyramid I found." Malkia paused, taking a bite of her warm food. She slowly chewed her food, her eyes glossing over as she thought of the pyramid back on Esaki.

"And?" Dario asked. He had been eating, but set his fork down, waiting for her to continue.

Malkia picked up her glass and took a drink before continuing, "As I neared the ocean, I could see it up against the waves of the water. It was the only one, but it was large like the closest one to us right now. I searched for a way in, but never found the entryway. However, I had a moment." She closed her eyes for a breath, reopening them slowly. "I thought I was having a connection to God, but it seems after all that has transpired, and all I have learned, it was most likely something to do with parents. My question is, why did it happen the moment I touched a certain part of the pyramid?"

She paused again, taking a few more bites as Dario stared at her in silence. She watched his face crinkle into a glare, as she chewed her food.

"What part did you touch on the pyramid?" He asked, rubbing his right knuckles over the inside of his left hand.

"Hold on, and I will tell you. Just wanting to eat some of my food." She gulped down another quick drink. "I touched the outside of that pyramid for days, trying to find a way in, but when I outlined a symbol of a feather with my fingers, I was transported to another place. To this day, I have no idea where I went. I believed it was heaven. I thought I spoke to a heavenly being, but now—now I just don't know. But that pyramid has to be the key, and maybe these pyramids here have something similar."

Dario's eyebrows shot up in surprise. "What did these beings say to you?"

She shook her head, not sure if she could trust him with everything. "Their words are unimportant. Where I was transported is more significant. And how the pyramid connected me to them, is a crucial piece of the mystery. Would you take me, if the Enyo leaders gave us a safe passage to the pyramids?"

Dario stood up and began pacing the floor. "Malkia, from what I know it is impossible to approach the pyramids. Maybe, if you told the leaders of your experience, they would allow you close enough. The only way I see them accessing a way to the pyramids, is if you give up information to help free them of the Artemisians. Maybe the information the beings gave you would be key to their revolution."

His eyes crinkled with frustration, and a similar image of him flashed in Malkia's mind. She was peering over someone's shoulder at Dario and he wore the same expression. However, the memory bounced around in her thoughts, and she was unable to grasp a specific time period or if it was even a real moment.

"I can't remember their exact words," Malkia recalled, shrugging her shoulders. "But if they need to know what these beings told me, I don't mind sharing."

Dario didn't look at her as he bolted out of the room. Malkia gazed at the empty doorway, and desperately tried to revive the memory that was creating her uneasiness. She sat in silence, picking at her food. Her stomach was queasy from the constant changes in Dario's personality.

When Dario returned; his face was calm again. He strolled over to her with a smug smile. "Are you done eating? I thought we could take a stroll around while we wait for the meeting." He reached out his hand to help her up.

"Sure. That sounds like a great idea," Malkia replied. She hesitated before clutching his hand, still agitated by his behavior.

Walking around the building was easy, except when Dario urged her into the moving box again. No matter how many times they did it, she still was afraid it was a trap. The building was beautifully decorated. Each floor they visited, was designed for a certain use.

One of the levels they visited, was a school. There were classrooms filled with children sitting, fidgeting or playing. Watching the children, Malkia was reminded of Esta and Mataya.

"Dario, as soon as we finish helping the Enyo people, we have to find Mataya, and we must rescue Esta. I understand why I need to be here, but the longer we wait the more anxious I become. Promise me, we will leave as soon as I stop the Artemis creatures," she pleaded with such urgency that Dario stopped in his tracks and turned her toward him.

"I will do whatever it takes to find Mataya and save Esta. You have my word."

Malkia searched his eyes and desperately wanted to believe what he was saying was true. He appeared genuine, but her heart was warning her not to trust him. She nodded and forced a smile. As she turned away from him, she internally cried for her daughter and sister. There was something deceitful going on and she feared it would be too late to save them by the time she finished with the Enyo situation.

As they entered the elevator, on their way up to the highest level,

Malkia ignored Dario's teasing and quickly surrounded herself with her purple light.

Dario chuckled. "Are you still afraid of this little "moving box"? Even after all the times we've been in it?"

Malkia crinkled her brows. "This box is a disaster just waiting to happen."

Dario bent over in laughter. She scowled at him and turned to face the doors.

They soon slid open to a room blossoming with vegetation and exquisite furniture. Malkia was speechless as they made their way through the foyer, into a more formal room, arranged with elegant chairs and couches. Dario led her to a couch. As she reclined onto the cushion, he turned and walked from the room without another word.

There he goes again, she thought, rolling her eyes.

Moments later, the doors opened, and a large group of people slowly walked inside, swaggering their way toward her. Their dress was unusual and more formal than Malkia was used to. The women were dressed in a variation of gowns or long pants, but all their attire was form fitting and elegant, making Malkia feel out of place. The men wore long robes that varied in color, but underneath they all had black, long pants and a black shirt.

A tall man with a long, white beard approached her first. He held out his hand, smiling softly as he helped her to her feet.

"Malkia," his voice was soft and steady. "We have been anticipating this juncture. Thank you for making the decision to assist us. My name is Tarance. I am the companion to our leader and I'm here to speak on his behalf."

Malkia nodded, a wary smile surfacing on her lips as she shook his hand.

A frown creased his brow, as he continued, "We have reached a state of desperation. It's imperative we end this war with the Artemisians. This being one of the few areas of Enyo that hasn't been overtaken by those demons, we are positive it will only be a matter of time before their deimoses break through our defenses."

"Deimoses?" Malkia asked. She noticed Dario saunter back into the room.

"Have you not heard of the Artemis deimos?" He questioned, clenching his jaw. "My dear, we have much to speak about. Please take a seat, and we will proceed from the beginning."

Malkia sat back down on the couch, watching as the group of people each took a chair or couch around her. They all greeted her with a smile and it seemed they were excited by her presence. As she scanned the group, one woman with long, snowy hair, stood out. Her expression was unreadable as a blank canvas, staring at Malkia without a trace of the warmth or welcome displayed by the others. Malkia held the woman's gaze for a moment, before shifting her focus back to Tarance, who had sat on a chair facing her.

"When the Artemis demons arrived about ten years ago, we organized our defenses in haste." Tarance tapped his fingers on the arm of the chair. "They arrived in modest groups, so we concluded they were passing through and we could wait out their intrusion. The Enyo people who could afford sanctuary, paid for their spots in fortresses like this building. The barbarians couldn't penetrate the magic of the Thalians, although they have spent ages trying."

Tarance paused, taking a drink of water from the glass placed on the table next to him.

"The deimoses are devilish little beasts," he began again, shaking his head. "They are agile and minuscule, allowing them to fit in tight areas. As well, they have a mouth lined with blade-sharp teeth. Once they penetrate a building, it's overrun within moments. The unrelenting onslaught has been unstoppable. Our enemies allowed us no time to devise countermeasures, save the barrier of dark magic, for which we paid heavily." He breathed deeply, leaning slightly forward in his seat. "As well, the deimoses are nocturnal, but they can travel underground during the day. We have had to block every underground entrance and secure it with unspeakable magic. The rest of the building is secured from dusk to dawn. Our only saving grace, at this point, is their return to Eris to rage war on your people."

At the mention of her home moon, Malkia's body stiffened as she inhaled sharply. Her eyes flashed over to Dario, who was rocking back and forth on his heels, wearing a smirk on his face. His excited expression confused Malkia. He knew how worried she was about her daughter. Where had her Dario gone? It was as if something had invaded his body. He looked like Dario. He talked like Dario. He even acted like Dario most of the time, but he wasn't the same.

"Have the Artemis creatures invaded Eris, as they have Enyo?" Malkia asked urgently, focusing her attention back on Tarance. She rubbed her legs, anxious for the old man's response.

"No," he shook his head. "Their power and technology surpass ours. For many years they've held the demons at bay. However, if the Artemisians had known your identity and used you to their advantage, we would all be destroyed. You have the ability to bend magic, which means you could puncture our defenses, and those of your own people."

The room was silent, as Tarance stared at Malkia. She sat up straight, tilting her head to the side. "Bend magic? I'm still learning to use my powers. That isn't one I am familiar with."

"We will teach you," Tarance nodded, as his smile spread across his face. "Your childhood warlock is here with us. Asha created you. She shaped you into the powerhouse you are today, and she is also the one who blocked your memories and powers. She reached out to us several years ago, seeking refuge from your people. We have a surplus of information on you and your people."

Tarance waved his hand at the guards, standing by the double doors. They ushered in a silver haired woman. Tall and lean like Malkia, her hair glistened under the lights, falling elegantly below her waist. She walked with pride and care, holding Malkia's gaze as she proceeded toward her. Her purple eyes were warm and kind, as they had been when she was a child.

Sinking gracefully to her knees, she spoke, "My dear, sweet Malkia." Taking Malkia's hands in her own, she kissed them with tenderness. "I have dreamt of this day for many years. I have missed you."

Malkia, weeping unrestrainedly, threw her arms around Asha's neck, pressing her face into her fragrant skin. Asha held her tight, running her hands through her hair and murmuring smoothly.

"There, there dear child. I am here again," Asha whispered into her ear. "We will find a way to end this madness."

Asha pulled away and peered into Malkia's eyes. She nodded and smiled at the woman who had been by her side every day as a child.

Rising with a grace that belied her age, she sat down on the couch next to Malkia, cradling a protective arm around her. Tarance beamed with approval.

His smile faded, as he continued with his story. "The demons have been fixated on Eris for the past few years, but our people remain enslaved. They use our people for their war with Eris and have confiscated most of our land and resources. Our fortresses were never intended to be a permanent solution to this invasion." Closing his eyes momentarily, he paused, as he pressed his praying hands against his lips. As he opened his eyes, he stared intently at Malkia. "Now, we're in the midst of a crisis, in which we must choose to either surrender, or fight to the death. To relinquish our freedom would be a fate more dishonorable than death. The Artemis demons must be expunged from Enyo and forced to never return."

"I will do whatever is within my power to free your people, but I need to know what you have in mind," Malkia slid forward, sitting on the edge of the couch. "Do you have any allies? Do you have a plan in place that I can build upon? Are there any other fortresses, like this one still standing?"

The small woman sitting near Tarance stood up, smoothing down her long trousers. "Malkia, we have a way for you to use your powers and abolish these demons once and for all. We only ask that you keep an open mind." Her brows knitted into a frown, as her tone dropped an octave. "These creatures are not your comrades." She stepped forward, her fingers entwined with one another. "They have done nothing but wreak mayhem on one civilization after another and if we don't halt their advances, once and for all, they will extend their destruction. We do have a strategy to end their dominion, but we require your powers."

Malkia nodded, smoothing her lips with her fingertips, as she turned to Asha. The warlock bowed her head and gave her a warm smile.

"I will do it, with one condition," Malkia said, turning back to the petite woman. "You will agree to help me rescue my daughter, once I have freed your people."

Rising swiftly from his chair, Tarance approached Malkia with a grin. He took her hand, once more, and assisted her to stand.

"Agreed," he affirmed, shaking her hand with enthusiasm. "Errandor would be thrilled to hear of our exchange. It is a shame he is unable to be here. He is dying from a contagion injected into him by an Artemisian. He led the last battle against the creatures and returned in a ghastly predicament. His successor is Emelia." He pointed toward the small woman who had spoken earlier.

"Tarance, will you take me to Errandor? I may be able to heal him," Malkia shifted her focus to Emelia, noticing her narrowed eyes shift back to a monotonous expression, before anyone else detected.

Malkia paused, eyeing the small woman before saying, "Emelia, am I to assume you are the one who makes the tactical decisions, while Errandor is unconscious?"

Emelia nodded, her facial muscles tightening. "Yes, you're correct." Her eyes slightly narrowed again. "Being that our healers have been unable to reverse Errandor's dilemma, I doubt there is much you can do. However, we will go visit him first. We'll proceed to our drawing room, once you have executed your healing."

Dario spoke up from across the room, his voice echoing in her ears. "Malkia, please describe to the group your experience with the pyramid on Esaki." Malkia peered over at his unsmiling expression.

She stared at Dario, not sure of his intentions. Redirecting her gaze, she glanced around the room before telling her story. "I'm not sure of its significance. It was a few years back. I had gone on a soul journey and came across a pyramid, near one of Esaki's oceans. As I searched for a way in, I came across an etching of a feather. Now mind you, I had been touching this pyramid for days and had discovered nothing."

Malkia breathed in deep, looking down at the ground as she slowly exhaled. She closed her eyes, taking another deep breath before erecting her posture, and staring back out into the group.

"When I placed my hand on this feather, I was transported to another place. Or else I had a hallucination. Either way it was a transforming moment for me. There were luminous beings, who were nearly twice my height. They advised me on keeping my people united and that there would come a day where I would learn more about myself and have a decision to make that could change the whole way of life, on all the moons," Malkia disclosed, turning to face Tarance. "That was the essence of the whole conversation. I said nothing. Just stood there paralyzed to the ground. Next thing I knew, I was back at the pyramid standing near the ocean, except it was the middle of the night. I had lost over a half a day of my life, and it only felt like a few moments."

Tarance stood in silence for a moment, before turning back to Emelia. "We have something here, don't we?"

Emelia nodded, eyeballing Malkia. "Was this the only time you had this meeting with these beings?"

Malkia's brows bumped together into a scowl. "Yes," she hesitantly replied.

Tarance put his hand on Malkia's shoulder, giving her a reassuring pat. "This could be of importance, but for now I would love it if you could take a look at Errandor. If there's a chance to heal him from this poison, it would need to be done before we look further into your experience."

"Take me to him." Malkia peered into Tarance's eyes, trusting he wouldn't break his promise.

Tarance clutched her hand, leading her to the double doors. Asha, Emelia and Dario followed closely behind.

They slowly progressed toward Errandors quarters, courteously matching Tarance's stately pace. Malkia suspected he was over three hundred years old. His hand was wrinkled and soft and his face showed the age of wisdom, with the deeply lined forehead. She was an infant compared to him.

After following several different corridors, Tarance stopped in front of a wide door. He pressed his hand against it and Malkia watched as the blue lines ran down his hand, beeping quietly as it confirmed his identity. The door slid open, revealing the leader's chambers.

"Welcome home, Tarance," a woman's voice was heard overhead, as they entered the room.

"Thank you, Tia. It is good to be home," Tarance walked forward, allowing the group to enter.

Malkia glanced up at the ceiling and then scanned the room,

expecting to see the presence of a woman, but it was empty. She glanced back at Dario, clearly confused by the voice.

Asha touched Malkia's back. "It's a computer. It's programmed to know whom to address based on their hand scan."

Malkia shook her head. "I'm struggling with all of these new advances. Even the limited technology we had on Esaki, couldn't prepare me for what you have here."

She followed Tarance through the dimly lit room and into the hallway. As she entered the open door to a bedroom, she could see a man lying in an enclosed bed. Edging toward him, she placed her hand on the cold shell, biting her bottom lip as she contemplated what it was going to take to heal him. The man's eyes were closed, his skin gray with a hue of yellow, and wrinkles that matched the ones of his partner.

"Can we open this hatch? I will need to touch him," Malkia asked Tarance, keeping her eyes on the comatose man, while running her hands down the glass.

"Yes, yes. Let me have Tia prepare him. Give me a few moments."

Tarance walked across the room and touched the wall. In front of him, a screen glowed to life, and he began writing a message. Malkia took a step back as the shell slid open.

Placing her hands on Errandor's chest, she called upon her healing light, watching as it blazed down her arms and into the man's chest. The silence caressed her skin, as her energy flowed from her body and into his.

Time stood still, as her powers washed from her and her body weakened. She withdrew her hands but held the edge of the bed as a wave of vertigo consumed her. Asha curved her arm around her waist and helped her to a nearby chair.

"I don't know if I helped," Malkia mumbled, holding her head in her hands. "I thought it was working, but I have never used all my energy like that before. How long was I standing there?"

"My dear girl, you were in a trance. You stood there until the first sun disappeared over the horizon. It was the most amazing thing I've ever seen," Asha whispered, as she knelt down in front of Malkia's knees and clasped her hands within hers. "Your souls were one for quite a while. You gave him everything you could. If this doesn't work, then nothing will."

Malkia inhaled a sharp breath, her eyebrows raising. "The first sun has set? It felt like a few moments, not hours!"

"He's opening his eyes," Tarance exclaimed. He clapped his hands several times, smiling from ear to ear.

The group of people rushed over to Errandor's side, leaving Malkia to catch her breath. She watched as the aging man sat up on his bed and peered over at her.

"Malkia, you and I have much to speak about," Errandor hoarsely whispered, blinking owlishly.

NINE
And the Truth Will Set You Free

MALKIA ROSE SLOWLY and made her way to Errandor's bedside. He clasped her hand within his and kissed it with a sweetness she had only known from her birth mother. There was something oddly familiar about this man.

"Thank you for using your gift to bring me back to life," Errandor quavered, his hands trembling. "I feared I would be trapped in my mind until my death."

"Trapped?" Malkia asked, the muscles in her face tightening. "Were you aware the entire time you were lying there?"

He gave her a weak smile. "Yes, I was always conscious in my mind. I could hear the world around me. When I was able to open my eyes, I witnessed all that occurred in my view, but I couldn't speak, nor move my head. I was unable to even tell my brain to blink the right way. I was only capable of listening and seeing. My solitary confinement created a throbbing agony, fearing I was going to die without anyone ever realizing I remained mindful and alert. When I felt your hands and I heard your name, I knew I was finally being released from my prison." Errandor shook as he slowly rose in front of Malkia, holding onto Tarance as he steadied himself. He gazed at Malkia, as he smoothed out his wrinkled robes. "I met you so many years ago on your home moon of Eris, and even back then I knew you would be a powerful ally to have."

Malkia remembered that fateful morning when she had awakened to strangers in her house. The morning her parents had taken her and Palma on the flying ship and left them on Esaki. Errandor had been there, one of the strangers in her house.

"You were there," Malkia eyes widened slightly, as she connected the man before her with a memory grown dim. "I recognize you from my parent's meeting. I remember that terrible morning."

He bowed his head slightly, his weak smile dimming. "Your parents and I were great friends. We all desired what was best for this star system. The group of us were tasked to engineer the children and create the weapons we needed to destroy the Artemisians," Errandor confessed. He stepped toward Malkia, putting his hand on her cheek. "You were our gem. We were overjoyed to have created a weapon of such perfection. Do you remember all that you can do?"

Malkia's face flushed, as a bubble of rage formed inside her. She turned away from Errandor and glanced over at Dario and Asha. Dario's face wore a blank expression, but Asha was pale, her body shaking from the conversation. Tarance's smile suffused his face, as he watched the love of his life moving and speaking again.

The realization that neither her life, nor the life of her daughter, had ever meant anything to these people spread numbly through her body, followed by waves of bitter rage. She was a means to an end. Their weapon to destroy the Artemis creatures. Who she was now, meant nothing to any of them.

A gentle hand touched her arm, bringing her out of the harrowing vision. To her surprise, Errandor was peering at her with concern.

"Is this not something you already knew? Did you not know what your role was in this war?" Errandor's forehead puckered, his smile all but gone from his face.

"Yes, I know," Malkia snapped. She backed away from him before continuing. "What would you have me do?" She glanced around the room, eyeing each person as if they had the answer. Dario's unrelenting stare forced her to shift quickly to Emelia, who was smirking back at her. "Should I go to Artemis and leave no stone unturned? Am I simply the means of execution for you, a weapon with which to wreak vengeance on those who enslave you? Why stop there?" She threw her hands in the air. "Should I travel to Eris to slaughter the ones who have attempted to conquer it, so they will never return to Enyo again?" Malkia paused, straightening her posture, and glaring at the silent group. "I'm not sure what your expectations are, but since it's evident that I'm nothing more than a tool for you and my parent's, let me be clear. I am here to stop the war against your people. Nothing else. When I've completed this battle, my only desire is to rescue my daughter."

Errandor reclined back onto his bed, his body shaking from weakness. Despite his frailty, he was gazing at Malkia, as if she was a goddess. "My dear Malkia, the only thing I want you to do is liberate my people. Yes, you will need to go to their moon. I believe destroying Artemis is the only way to end this permanently. I will support you in rescuing your daughter. All I ask is that you free my people."

Malkia took a deep breath, reigning in her storm. "I apologize for the outburst." She glanced at Errandor, and then shifted her focus to

Tarance. "My frustrations aren't with you. I ache to see my daughter again and every day I waste, is one more day I lose with her. Please forgive my charade."

Tarance nodded and smiled. Errandor had slid back onto his side and his eyes had closed, but he nodded and smiled as well.

"Good, good," Emelia interjected. "Let's leave Errandor to receive some proper nutrition and rest. You and I will take over from here." The petite woman pivoted on her heel, leaving the room in a rush.

Malkia quickly followed behind her, without looking back at the two men. Asha walked next to her, keeping her thoughts to herself as they remained in the presence of Dario and Emelia. Malkia knew she would need to find some time to speak with Asha in private. She knew more about her childhood and parents than anyone else did. When the time presented itself, she would pick her brain for information.

When they arrived at the drawing room, Malkia could see why they called it such. It was crowded with tables, just like in the flying ship. Several people stood around random tables, talking, and drawing with their fingertips.

"This is where we strategize," Emelia interrupted Malkia's thoughts, tapping her fingers on the table in front of her. "We have been laying out plans for years and aside from a few, most of our ideas have failed. Until recently." Emelia leaned forward on her palms, using the table to hold her weight. "We have developed a cloaking device that will enable us to advance on the Artemis moon undetected. However, in order to take the demons by surprise and annihilate their entire civilization, we will require an enormous amount of energy. This is where your role has come into play." She paused, focusing on Dario before peering back at Malkia. "And that is why Misty will have to accompany us."

Malkia's eyebrows rose quickly, her forehead puckering. "*Misty is not coming with me into war*. She's a child."

"What about our children?" Emelia eyed Malkia with icy contempt. "What about all the people those barbarians have slaughtered, all in the name of power and greed? Why do we have to sit around and watch them destroy us? At this point, you and Misty are all we have."

"Misty has already agreed to help," Dario interjected, breaking his long silence.

Malkia swiveled around to see him. "You're comfortable with this?" She glared, balling her hands into fists.

Dario's body stiffened at the remark. "We have no choice, Malkia. You've witnessed how destructive these creatures can be. What would you do if they penetrated the barrier, protecting this building and they maimed and killed all the children? Would you allow Misty to help you then?"

"I wouldn't need her help for that." She whispered, shaking her head and shifting her feet.

"But you will need her help in destroying their home moon," Dario shot back. "Their ravenous lust for power drives them relentlessly. Once they take over Eris, who's to say they won't go to Esaki. They want you. If they discover that was where you lived in concealment, it will be their next target."

Malkia stared at Dario, wondering whether or not to trust this man. She wanted to. He had given her no reason to distrust him, but she had a nagging suspicion he wasn't who he portrayed himself to be. He wasn't the same man she had fallen in love with back on Esaki.

"If Misty is willing to help, it seems I have no say in what happens here," Malkia grumbled, forking her hand through her hair. "I understand the desire to destroy these creatures. Let's move forward with the planning, so we can begin the voyage to their moon."

The night wore on as Malkia observed Emelia and others reviewing their idea to safely travel to Artemis. Travel alone would require two days. Once they arrived, they would need to remain undetected. Their cloaking mechanism was unstable, and they were unsure how reliable it would be. They needed Malkia to keep the ship secure, if the system malfunctioned.

"Once we destroy the whole moon, we will return to Enyo, exterminating every Artemis demon, along with their deimoses. They will be powerless without support from their home moon," Emelia explained. The screen lit up in red dots wherever an Artemisian was detected. Emelia pointed to each one as she spoke.

Malkia nodded in agreement. Seeing the Enyo moon overrun with the demons and knowing the destruction and bloodshed the Artemisians had inflicted on innocent people, made this genocide a necessary evil. As much as Malkia wished she could end the war with little or no bloodshed, she was finally convinced there was no alternative.

It is us or them. Malkia thought. Her head was pounding from all the information packed into her mind.

"Can any of you explain Misty's role in all of this?" Malkia asked, rubbing her fingers over her temples.

"Did Dario not explain this to you?" Emelia questioned. She looked over at Dario.

"No, I haven't had a moment to give her the details," Dario snapped at Emelia. His eyelids were heavy and his voice hoarse. "I was hoping for the chance, after we finished here. If I don't end up sleeping first."

"Please make time for it," Emelia ordered. She turned back to Malkia. "We need to depart before tomorrow night. Please be up to date at that time. Make sure you procure enough food and sleep, and then come back to the drawing room and educate yourself."

Malkia nodded as she watched Emelia walk away. Without a word, Dario clutched Malkia's arm, leading her out of room. Asha strolled a few feet behind, all of them silent from the long day.

There is something not right about this whole situation. Malkia thought to herself. *Dario has been cold and distant, while Asha seems to be hiding something. I cannot remember how we got to Enyo. I agreed to come but the more I hear, the less certain I am of everyone's true intentions. Why would I leave Tantiana and Parowan? Why would I not be in communication with Jasper? Why would I not know if Mataya is safe?*

As they approached their quarters, Asha took her leave of them, promising to meet in the morning. Their room was dark when they entered and Malkia felt exhausted from the long meeting, the healing of Errandor, and the discussions in the drawing room. Her eyelids were heavy and her head continued to pound.

"Dario, I'm exhausted," Malkia yawned, as she rubbed her eyes. "I will see you—"

He interrupted her, as he slid his arms around her waist and drew her body into his, kissing her neck and chin. His hands ran up and down her spine pulling her tighter, as he met his lips to hers. His tongue searched her mouth, growing hungry and more aggressive.

Malkia felt the urge to love him again and she met his hunger. She slid her hands under his shirt, and he groaned as she touched his skin. Her worry and stress disappeared as they entwined their bodies together and settled onto the floor next to the couch. Malkia lost all sense of fear as she gazed into Dario's eyes, and once again detected the man she had fallen in love with.

TEN

Misty's Imprisonment

MALKIA AWAKENED EARLY the next morning. They had moved their love making to the bed and had fallen asleep entangled in each other's exhausted limbs. When Malkia looked over at Dario, her heart swelled with an intense love and wondered why she continued to doubt her trust in him. Her mind was still warning her of danger, but her heart wanted to pretend she lived in a dream world. She slid her legs out from underneath Dario's knees and slipped off the bed, heading for the shower.

She sighed with bliss as the steamy water cascaded over her body. As she scrubbed her hair and every inch of her body, she realized this was one of the luxuries she had missed after the wars. The baths under the waterfall couldn't be compared to the hot, clean water pouring on her now.

She stood under the water until it turned cold, thinking of her parents on Eris and her daughter being under their control. She still didn't understand why they hadn't tried harder to retrieve her. The excuse of leading her people didn't seem like a situation that would concern them. Their story had more holes than her old undergarments, which made her more determined to discover their secrets.

She dressed in a skirt and a clean white shirt, brushing her hair until it shone. Her nimble fingers dressed her hair into a long braid, hanging loosely down her back. Tiptoeing into the kitchen, she stared at the mystery before her. She had never seen a kitchen as complex as what was before her now. Deciding she wasn't hungry enough, she curled up on the couch, resting her head on the pillow while staring out the wall of windows. The tops of the pyramid stood out above the unsubstantial buildings. Her desire to be near them hadn't diminished. In fact, it had only heightened since the day before.

"You woke up early," Dario spoke from the kitchen.

Malkia sat up on the couch and glanced over at him. "I'm anxious to finish this battle. It weighed on my mind most of the night," she admitted, playing with the end of her hair, as it hung over her right shoulder. She tilted her head toward the kitchen, smiling sheepishly, "I don't know how to work their kitchens, so no breakfast. I'm hoping you have some kind of clue about their gadgets."

"I do. Come over here, and I'll show you." Dario waved his hand, signaling for her to stand next to him.

Malkia rose from the couch and made her way over to Dario. He spent the next several moments explaining different buttons for beverages and then showed her a screen where she could request what she wanted. The computer would cook it, delivering it to a slot in the wall. Malkia caught on fairly quick but allowed Dario to continue his explanations.

"What would you like to eat?" He asked, strumming his fingers against the wall, staring at her intently.

Malkia stood next to the screen and pushed the appropriate buttons for breakfast, then spoke just as Dario had shown her. "Three eggs, yolk uncooked, two rolls and four slices of meat." She glanced over at Dario, smirking, "I'm hungry."

He winked, pointing to the slot in the wall. The food was already there, steaming.

"I could become used to this." She grabbed the plate and took it to the table.

While they ate in silence, she stared out the window, keeping her eyes on the pyramids and letting her mind wander back to the day she found the one on Esaki. She had never told anyone about her experience and now that the story was out in the open, she shivered imagining what the leaders might be thinking. The Enyo people seemed kind, but that nagging feeling in her gut would *not* disappear.

After breakfast was over, the two of them left their nook and headed to the drawing room. Asha and Emelia were there when they entered and motioned for Malkia to join them.

"Malkia, I spoke to Misty's father last night. She is ready to use her powers alongside yours. Did Dario go over the details of her ability and why it's so important both of you work together?" Emelia stared at her, arching a crafty brow.

"Actually, no," Malkia replied, folding her arms over her chest. "We were distracted by other issues. I would love to hear the details of Misty's power and its importance to this battle."

"Technically, she won't be in the battle. Only you will be amid the conflict," Emelia retorted, her eyes flashing with anger toward Dario. "Her powers can be filtered through your mind, once you're both connected. Together the annihilation of the Artemis demons will be uncomplicated. If possible, we will need you to burn the moon, ensuring all life is consumed when we leave. That's the first order of business. Once that's complete, we can focus on the demons here on Enyo."

"Alright," Malkia slowly breathed, her brows knitting into a frown.

"Misty's power is what will give you the ability to destroy the Artemisians stronghold with such ease." Emelia paused, eyeing Malkia.

"Stop repeating yourself," Malkia demanded, gritting her teeth and leaning forward against the table in frustration, eyeing the older woman. "Why the mystery and suspense surrounding her ability?"

"There is no mystery," Dario interrupted. "We are only concerned with what your reaction will be, once you observe our means to channel her power." He curled his arm around Malkia's shoulders and drew her in, as if he was protecting her.

Malkia pulled away from him, glaring at the group as she hissed, "What won't I like? Quit it with the games. Give it to me straight or I'll find someone who will."

"Malkia, in order to give her power, the strength it will need, Misty must be confined." Dario stepped toward her again. "At first glance, it doesn't appear humane, but she *is* safe."

Malkia put her arm out, to halt his advances. "Confined in what sense?" she asked, tapping her foot against the floor, as she peered at the small group in front of her.

"Misty is ready to go and has already boarded the ship," Emelia replied. "When you board, you'll see she is well taken care of."

"Let's go now," Malkia's shoulders stiffened, as she entwined her fingers. "I'm through with the secrets. I understand this is your moon and your people, but you have requested my help. All I expect is transparency. I haven't seen Misty, or her father, since I arrived at this building, and the mere mystery around her safety makes me question your motives. Either you take me to her and reveal all your plans or I will rethink my terms with Errandor."

"Fine," Emelia huffed, clicking her tongue. "We will do it your way. One thing you need to understand when you see her—you cannot remove her. It will kill her. That being said, don't allow your emotions to run your decisions."

Emelia led the way to the ship. Malkia glanced over at Dario and noticed how aloof he had become again. His signals confused and unsettled her. The more she noticed it, the more she felt there was something he wasn't telling her.

Asha reached for Malkia's hand during the walk. Malkia smiled over at her but felt suspicious of everyone with whom she'd interacted with during the past two days. As much as she wanted the comfort of Asha, she couldn't bring herself to lower her walls.

The flying ship was gigantic. Malkia paused in the entry, admiring the massive piece of machinery.

"We are going in that?" she asked Dario.

"We sure are." Dario was smiling again, putting his hand on her shoulder. "She's a beauty, isn't she?"

"Yes, she is," Malkia whispered.

Malkia lagged behind the others as they made their way to the ship. She was anxious to see Misty, but nervous about what she would find.

In the distance, she could see two figures approaching them and was relieved to see Rory's face. She had been wondering where he had gone. Recognition swept over Malkia as she saw the tall, white-haired woman from her initial meeting, sauntering behind him. Her demeanor remained cold, glancing over at Malkia with icy contempt.

Rory hugged Malkia and shook Dario's hand. When the woman joined them, she embraced Dario and kissed his cheek. Then, leaning closer she whispered into his ear. Malkia noticed her fine network of wrinkles and reckoned she had to be over two hundred years old. However, even given such an advanced age the woman's familiar behavior with Dario, made Malkia feel uneasy.

She turned her attention back to Rory, who had been speaking to Emelia.

"Misty is prepared to depart. I require a few items from my room, but when I return, we will be prepared to leave. What is the timetable for departure?" Rory asked. He glanced over at Malkia and gave her a sheepish smile.

"We need to move out before the suns have set, so you have time. I will escort Malkia to see Misty and explain her role. Once we're all comfortable with the arrangements, we will pack our belongings, have our evening meal, and return to the ship. Don't be late," Emelia ordered, placing her hands on her hip as she skimmed over the group.

Going their separate ways, Emelia led the group to the ship and through the bay doors. They trudged along various hallways and up the elevator, where Malkia gritted her teeth and closed her eyes to drown out the view of the four walls surrounding her. Feeling the motion end, she opened her eyes and watched as the doors opened. As much as she wanted out of the moving coffin, she wasn't sure she was prepared to see Misty.

"Malkia, are you coming?" Asha asked. She held out her hand, signaling Malkia to grab hold.

"Is there something wrong?" Dario noticed Malkia's glazed eyes.

Malkia shifted her focus to Dario, balling her hands into fists and then relaxing again. "I'm fine. I'm just preparing myself for what I'm about to see."

She grazed past Asha and Dario, jogging to catch up to Emelia. The tiny woman had briskly cantered forward, not wasting time convincing her to follow.

Emelia stopped in front of a closed door. She held her hand up to the scanner and it slid open moments later. What was behind the door was not what Malkia expected, but it seemed oddly familiar. Bug-eyed, she gawked at the glass cage with Misty's unconscious body floating in the clear liquid. Her long, ebony hair spread out around her pale face.

"What is this?" Malkia asked, her expression melting into horror.

She glanced at Emelia and then over at Dario. He wore an expression that she recognized, but more from a dream then real life. Glaring at her, his eyes burned with hatred.

Where has my Dario gone? Her thoughts shaking, feeling her fury slide through her.

"This is the only way to intensify her ability and allow her to tap into your mind, creating the power we need to eradicate the Artemisians," Emelia interrupted her thoughts, patting the glass cage lightly. "I know it appears harrowing and that's why we have hesitated to reveal her. She is safe. Her father has ensured she remains secure. We want you to feel satisfied in our capability to keep her out of harm's way."

Malkia peered around the room. The faint buzz from the machines was familiar, but she couldn't put her finger on why. She grimaced at the black cords connected to the machines behind the cage, as they snaked through the liquid and leeched into the back of Misty's body and skull.

"I'm remaining calm, if that is why you are all watching me like hawks," she assured, frustration crinkling her eyes. "I don't approve, but since her father is involved, I will follow your lead. When will I be allowed to communicate with her?"

"She's been kept in a subdued state for the past day, until we had the machines connected properly," Emelia deposited her hands on her hips. "Now that we are leaving, her father is reviving her."

Malkia sighed, her eyes rolling skyward. "Looks like I need to pack my things." She turned on her heel and began the long walk back to her room.

ELEVEN
Ready for War

DINNER PASSED QUICKLY and Malkia was eager to return to the flying ship. She snuck off, wanting some time to herself. Strolling through the corridors and up random stairs, she familiarized herself with the layout of each floor and unlocked room.

She was having flashbacks of the small flying ship that brought her to Enyo. As much as she wanted to believe it was a dream, she had a sneaking suspicion she was being played and Jasper had paid with his life. Several images stirred in her mind: Misty in her glass cage, the mutt striking her, and Kelsey sitting next to the controls. To think they could all be conspiring against her, made her stomach churn.

What else have I forgotten? She was deep in thought when she felt the gentle hand on her back. She jumped and whipped her head around to see who was there. "It's you, Asha," she breathed out.

"You disappeared from dinner, and no one knew where you had gone." Asha's brows furrowed with concern. "But I had a feeling you came here."

"I don't trust them," Malkia admitted, biting her lip. "I don't trust anyone. Not even you. My whole life has been one lie after another and this war with the Artemisians seems like another ploy to force me into being my parent's weapon."

"My dear," Asha pulled her hair in front of her shoulder, raking her hand through the ends. "The Artemis creatures are foul and spiteful and the combat with them is genuine. You saw how easily they can inflict pain on a human being. You witnessed their scorn for humanity. This war isn't a lie. However, I don't trust the Enyoans either. Then again, I don't trust much of anyone right now." She clutched the arms of a chair, as she reclined near Malkia.

"What is really going on here, Asha?" Malkia asked. "I'm having strange flashes in my mind. One, with Misty in that glass cage. And after seeing her there—" Malkia's voice trailed off. She glanced around making sure they were alone. "After seeing her there, I'm beginning to wonder if my other memories are real as well. The mutt, Kelsey and Dario all working together to entrap me. Jasper dead. Being drugged and having a device put in my body." Her eyes narrowed as she reached back, touching the back of her shoulder.

The object was no longer bulging, but she could feel its smooth exterior. "I didn't want to believe it," Malkia continued, rubbing the object with her fingers. "I didn't want to believe Dario would deceive me, but his behavior is erratic and alarming."

"Malkia, I can't tell you if those memories are factual," Asha's hushed voice shook. "But I'm confident your suspicions are accurate. The Enyoans need you to end this war. You have been on their radar for a long time and they used me to help find you. I can tell you this." She leaned forward in her chair, resting her elbows against her knees for support. "Trust your instincts and memories. Don't allow Dario to place doubt in your mind. You're far more intelligent and your powers outmatch anyone on this moon. Do *not* allow him to manipulate your memories. Finish this war but do it with conditions. Once we return from Artemis, free the people here, but do it after you and Misty are safely away from Emelia. I have my own suspicions, one of them being, the Enyo leaders will confine you once the war has concluded."

Malkia suspected that as well. The hunger in Errandor's eyes and knowing he participated in the creation of the gifted children, sent chills down her spine. He wanted her for himself. Then there was the freezing contempt in Emelia's eyes. For reason's unknown to Malkia, the woman despised her.

Moments later Dario sauntered into the room, a gleam of deviltry in his eyes. Emelia paraded in behind him, grimacing at Malkia and ignoring Asha. Malkia rose from her seat, following Emelia over to the controls.

"When will I be able to communicate with Misty, so we can create a plan?" Malkia asked, entwining her fingers, and rubbing her thumbs together.

"Soon," Emelia sighed in exasperation. "We will be departing shortly. I suggest you find a seat, until we are safely pass the Artemisian ships."

Emelia strolled away from Malkia, making it very clear that her instincts were accurate. Turning toward the door, she left the room, wanting to be near Misty. When she entered the room, Rory was already there fidgeting around with some gears and speaking quietly to a petite, black haired woman. She glimpsed at Malkia, shook her head and walked out the door.

"Did I interrupt something important?" Malkia asked.

"Not really," Rory replied, avoiding her gaze. "Do you need something?"

"I was told to find a seat and figured this was the best place for me. I want to communicate with Misty as soon as she's ready, so we are aware of what it will take to combine our powers." She bit her bottom lip, easing herself into one of the seats and fastening her safety straps. "It's a bit perplexing the Enyo leaders don't want us to test our collective powers before we arrive to Artemis."

"It will work," Rory mumbled. "You have to stop doubting yourself."

Malkia sat quietly, thinking of his words. *Why am I doubting myself? I know my capabilities. I'm fast, strong and have the ability to keep them out or not allow them to escape. Why am I allowing them to take control? This whole scenario doesn't make sense. When did I give up my voice?*

I don't think you have. Misty's thoughts quietly interrupted her own. *Malkia, my memories are blurred. What has been going on?*

Do you know where you are? Did they tell you what their plan was? Did they tell you what they did to you? Malkia replied.

Yes… Misty responded slowly. Her thoughts were silent for a moment. *They told me what I could do and why it was important for me to be in this cage of liquid. I can't feel anything, and I'm not scared any more. But I don't trust them. They had you locked up and now you are here with me. I don't understand.*

I don't either, Malkia thought, as she sighed aloud.

Rory glanced over at Malkia and then turned back to a screen in his hand. Staring at the gadget, a smile flitted across his face, as if he had discovered a new secret.

Misty, explain to me how your powers and mine will destroy the Artemis creatures. Since I arrived, I haven't received a clear answer and now we are about to leave for

Artemis. I have no idea what to expect. She paused, as she leaned forward on her knees, covering her eyes with her hands. *Did they tell you?*

Yes. I can show you. On a small scale that is. Will you brighten your light?

Your father will see me do it. Malkia uncovered her eyes and glanced at Rory. *Are you okay with that?*

I don't think any of it matters, at this point. Misty replied. *They all have their own agendas. We need to end this bloody war and disappear. I don't think it will end with the Artemis creatures.*

I agree. Malkia responded. *Here I go.*

Malkia felt her light build inside. It burst outside her body and enclosed her in a safety net.

Misty, I have my light surrounding me. Now what?

Just watch. Misty replied.

In an instant Malkia's light intensified, widened and strengthened. The energy pulsated around Malkia, electrifying the air and creating waves of static.

Misty! What are you doing? This is amazing! Malkia grinned, flashing her eyes around the room.

I can intensify any ability. My own power of mind reading is intensified. I can read other people's minds, not just yours. Misty paused and Malkia glanced at Rory's joyful face. *I didn't understand it until one of the wolf-men explained it to me back on Esaki. He wanted me to read Damon's mind. He taught me to focus and use my heightened mind reading to penetrate Damon's mind.*

Wait a minute... Malkia interrupted, sitting up straight as her light faded. *Were you in alliance with Dario and the mutts this whole time?*

No. No. Please believe me. Misty pleaded. *I didn't know how to tell anyone about my different power. I was afraid it would scare everyone off. It's one thing to be able to be able to converse telepathically with another. It is entirely different to read someone's mind who is unaware I'm intruding. You and I know when someone has pushed through, but most don't have that ability. I wanted to be free of those monsters and after I was, I stopped using my powers. Except with you.* Her thoughts were more urgent. Rory frowned, as he took his seat, taking his eyes off his gadget while putting on his restraints. *It takes effort to push through other's barriers, so it was easier not to intrude. I'm with you on this. You and me. But Malkia I only knew of the mind reading. I didn't know I could intensify other's abilities.*

Malkia sat in silence for a few moments, scrutinizing Rory as he began tapping on his hand-held screen again. The ship jolted and Malkia felt the movement of its departure, as she was forced back into her chair.

You and I, Malkia responded to Misty. *I must know I can depend on you. I know it's important to end this quickly and I'm now aware that with our powers combined, we will be capable of eradicating these creatures.* Malkia rubbed her chin, peering up at the ceiling. *Just promise, you won't leave me.*

I promise Malkia. I promise I'll see us both through. And in the spirit of promises, will you please make sure the Enyoans follow through on their end.

Yes, of course I will. Malkia replied, closing her eyes.

Malkia, I'm losing myself in here. Misty's hushed thoughts disclosed her sorrow. *It's always dark. When I do sleep, my dreams are horrifying, and I can't escape the images when I wake. I can't go on like this.*

We will leave this place together. Malkia thought, her eyes scouring over Rory with bitter contempt. He avoided her stare, keeping his eyes on his gadget. *You won't be in that cage forever.*

Thank you, Malkia. Thank you for always being there for me.

I will always be here for you. Malkia closed her eyes again, disgusted by

Rory's face.

I love you, Malkia. Misty replied.

I love you too, sweet girl.

TWELVE

The Moon of Artemis

DURING THE VOYAGE to Artemis, Malkia and Misty experimented with their combined powers. She only left Misty's room to take care of her immediate needs but returned quickly. It was her way to avoid Dario and Emelia, while learning more about Misty's abilities.

However, Dario interrupted as often as he could. Malkia's suspicions grew, as he continuously hovered over her work with Misty, scrutinizing all her mistakes with a straight-faced expression. The only time he touched her, was to force her to leave the room when Emelia requested her presence. He was becoming more of her guard, than her lover.

Asha stayed close but didn't interfere with their work. Malkia knew she would have to find time to speak with her childhood warlock but was distracted by her nerves and the impending destruction ahead of her. Not to mention, Dario's insisted presence at the most inopportune times.

When they reached Artemis, Malkia stood in between Emelia and Dario, and for the first time noticed the similarities in the pair. He had Emelia's eyes.

How did I miss that? She quickly blocked Misty from her thoughts. *No wonder I am constantly fooled by everyone I know. I can't even recognize members of the same family. First Kelsey and now Emelia.* At this point she had the odd sense they were using Misty to read her thoughts, and project them to the screen Rory was gawking at most of the trip.

She knew she was in the arms of one enemy, while battling another. The only reason she stayed was her knowledge of Esaki's lack of resources to protect themselves against the Artemisians. The moon's civilization would be annihilated by those creatures. She had to remain, in order to protect them.

She watched the Artemis moon grow closer. They had cloaked their ship and were able to slip by the three warrior ships waiting in high orbit. Emelia's orders were to burn the moon, then return for the ships.

Dario reached for her hand. She was scared not to take it, so she gave it a squeeze and smiled up at him. His slow and sexy grin was familiar to her, and she breathed deeply, desiring his gentle touch.

"This whole nightmare is nearly over," Dario exclaimed, rocking back on his heels. "I cannot wait to be free of these demons."

Too happy, Malkia thought, shattering her craving for his love. *He isn't from Esaki. He's from Enyo.*

The memories were washing over her like a flood. She remembered being drugged on Esaki and waking up nauseated on the flying ship. The bug in her shoulder had been excruciating, and she worried they would again use it on her. Once she finished their struggle with the Artemisians, she was going to find someone to remove the object and then disappear.

"It's time to begin your work," Emelia commanded, her eyes raking over Malkia with harsh revulsion. "We will fly you as close as safely possible, then you and Misty will need to take over. Destroy everyone and don't hesitate. Remember we *are* at war. Don't allow your emotions to control the situation. Whatever you see down there, do *not* stop until the job is done." Emelia turned on her heel, moving toward the hallway. "Please prepare to board onto the landing ship."

"Yes, ma'am," Malkia replied. She trailed behind the woman as they left the room, turning to glance at Asha before the door closed.

"Why is Asha not joining us?" Malkia twisted to look at Emelia. "I could use the support of a warlock."

"You won't need her help," Emelia chided, as she continued to march down the corridor.

"Does it hurt to have the back up?" Dario returned to Malkia's side.

Emelia paused and glanced back at Malkia and Dario. "No, it won't hurt. Tell her to accompany us."

Dario rushed back to the control room, peeking inside. "Asha, we need you to join us on the smaller ship."

He clutched Malkia's hand again and kissed it. "Do you feel better now?"

"Yes, thank you." She smiled up at him but grimaced inside. He was treating her like a child. She wondered if it was his way to make her feel inferior and keep her under his control.

Once they had all boarded the ship, they were ordered to take their seats. Malkia sat beside Asha. She reached over and grabbed Asha's hand.

"When this is over, I would like to hear your story," Malkia whispered, while keeping an eye on the ship crew. "Why you created me. Where you came from and how you knew my parents. And most of all, I want to hear about my mother."

Asha nodded. "I will tell you the whole story."

Malkia faced the bridge and watched as the pilot eased the ship out of the dock and into the silence of space. As the pilot turned the ship toward Enyo, she caught a glimpse of Theia, stirring her desire to protect Esaki and her daughter.

The ride through the moon's atmosphere was shaky and Dario informed her the surface air was denser than Esaki's or Enyo's. "When you enter their air, remember this. It may be more difficult to breath. Your light will be the only thing between you and their atmosphere."

Malkia nodded. *Are you ready for this?* She asked Misty.

Ready as I ever will be. Misty replied. *Let's finish this.*

As they approached the first city, Malkia entered the air lock hatch and waited for the door to separate her from the others. Dario's face lit up like a small boy, as the door came to a close. She realized he was actually confident in her ability to destroy these creatures.

You're doing this for Esaki, Malkia reminded herself.

As the air lock door began to open, Malkia encircled herself with her protective light and floated over the threshold. Moving toward the large city, she balled up her energy, feeling its powers in her hands.

I'm ready, Misty.

Malkia watched in amazement as her energy force flashed through her body, hurtling quickly toward the city below. The light intensified as Misty stretched and enhanced its flame, hitting the buildings like a seismic wave. The explosion burst in every direction, ceasing each structure as it radiated over the surface of the moon.

The screams and howls could be heard from the sky, as she observed the Artemisians running from the destruction and massacre, Misty and she were creating. Her heart was cold, remembering the Artemis monster who had tried to kill her.

She could feel the hot air collide with her protective light as the explosions stretched all around her. Focusing on the towns and cities surrounding the first one, Malkia directed her force at each one. Misty continued to strengthen each burst of fire, spreading it like wildfire to every inch of land.

They had no idea we were coming. Malkia thought, looking around for any retaliation. *They weren't prepared for an attack.*

Malkia lowered herself down into the fire and destruction and watched from the protection of her light as the structures crumbled around her. Without warning a small beast leapt out of a burning building and bolted her way. Its large mouth exposed massive fangs that oozed with saliva, while its scaly skin stood with jagged edges. She moved high into the air, avoiding its teeth and watched as it lurched, attempting to ensnare her feet. It snarled and exhaled a horrifying growl. Even the ritters on Esaki were not this quick, nor did they have the fangs this animal possessed.

I would hate to meet this creature in the dark woods, Malkia thought. *This must be one of the deimos animals, Errandor spoke about.*

The flames moved quickly toward the creature and Malkia stared into its large, yellow eyes as it was consumed by the fire. The shrieks of agony escaping its mouth, as the flames devoured the flesh. As it squealed in pain once more, before succumbing to death, Malkia shook her head and flew back into the sky.

I'm moving to the next area. Malkia thought, knowing they were viewing her thoughts.

She flew to the neighboring city, continuing to shower the moon with her energy and watched as Misty helped her destroy the fiends.

It's too easy. Malkia thought. There was still no reprisal.

The Artemisians scrambled to escape the flames, but the fire was everywhere. It consumed the vegetation, the structures and every living thing that was in its path. It had taken on a life of its own as Misty urged the blaze to build and burn, progressing at Malkia's speed.

As they rounded the small moon Malkia noticed a small fleet of Artemisian ships heading toward her.

The monsters fighting ships are moving in. Are you ready to focus on each one of them? There are about a dozen coming my way.

I'll follow your lead, Malkia. Misty replied.

As the ships approached, their weapons collided with her light exploding into a green glow around her. She could feel her powers weaken, and needed what was left to hold her protective light in place. Searching deep within her she was able to build enough energy and aimed it at one of the ships. As it shot out of her, Misty grabbed hold, enhancing its strength destroying three ships all at once. As they exploded in mid-air, their debris rammed violently with two more ships, sending all five plummeting to the ground.

Thank you! Malkia breathed in her mind.

The ships crashed into the burning moon and created more explosions, which Misty pressed forward. Malkia directed what was left of her energy at two more fighter ships, the rush of their explosion twisting toward another Artemisian vessel. The craft spun out of control and burst into flames. They were down to six fighter ships and Malkia felt her powers dwindle and her light flicker.

I can't continue, Malkia thought. *My powers are depleted. I need to recharge, or my light will no longer hold.*

The uncloaked Enyo ship appeared over the horizon and as they closed in on her position, she watched as they vaporized two more Artemisian ships. The Enyo vessel took a few blows from the other four ships, but their shields held steady.

Malkia closed her eyes, pulling energy from the deepest part of herself. With her arms outstretched in front of her, her palms facing the suns, the light surged out of her hands. Misty used this energy force to strike the last four ships, creating such an intense explosion that when the ships thundered to the ground, the backfire knocked Malkia backwards.

Misty's mind grasped onto the flames, pushing it along the ground as Malkia surveyed the devastation. She was no longer needed. Settling onto the ground ahead of the fire, she watched as it advanced on the last area of the moon. The Artemisians were no longer running from the fire. They huddled in fear, glancing up with tears in their eyes and for the first time Malkia observed something different.

These creatures had human eyes. They peered over at her and then back at the inferno, as it progressed toward them. It was in that moment, Malkia realized these weren't the same monsters she had met on Enyo. They were part human.

Wait! Malkia screamed in her mind.

It was too late. The blaze and heat consumed the village, seizing every creature in its path.

Malkia flew back into the sky, frantically looking for any area of the moon that was untouched by the destruction. The fire exploded and engulfed every inch of the moon. As she searched for survivors, the heat sucked at her weakened light, forcing her to retreat back into the sky.

Why had she not seen this in the beginning? Were they all part human? Was it her imagination deceiving her? She had agreed to annihilate the demons who were intent on destroying humankind. She didn't sign up for the destruction of anyone else.

There were no more screams or howls. The only sound on the moon was the explosions of the fire as it continued to eat away at its charred remains.

Malkia flew high into the atmosphere and waited for the ship to catch up with her. She watched the moon burn and felt a regret in her heart. *What have I done?*

We did it Malkia! We destroyed the monsters, Misty thought.

They did not look like monsters. Malkia replied. Her body stooped low, as a flood of emotion raced through her body. The image of their burning body's would be forever etched in her mind.

Misty could see what she was remembering.

Are you sure they were part human?

Malkia could feel the tears burning her face as she replied. *Yes, Misty. They had human eyes. The monsters have the slanted serpent eyes that cover most of their upper face.*

The ship drew close to Malkia and the air lock door opened to let her in. She glided into the hatch and waited for the door to close.

"What are you not telling me?" Malkia demanded when she entered the control room a few moments later.

"We don't know what you're talking about, Malkia," Emelia barked, clenching her jaw. "What you saw was another breed of demons, but they were all the same… demons."

"I don't believe you," Malkia screamed at the hateful woman, quickly closing the gap between them. "They were afraid to die. They were *not* like the creatures I identified on Enyo, nor were they the monsters I was told about as a child." Malkia's face was inches from Emelia's. Her tone quieted, as she hissed, "You planned it this way. You wanted their moon destroyed so there would be nowhere for the real monsters to escape to. Now the innocent ones are dead, while the barbarians remain breathing. Why is it so difficult for you to be honest with me?"

"Malkia, I don't know what you glimpsed down there, but there are no friendly Artemisians," Dario said. His hushed voice had become calm and soothing. Malkia wanted to punch him in the face.

"You weren't ready to face this war," Emelia snorted, interrupting Dario's placid voice. She snickered loudly, running her hands down the side of her uniform. "You were nearly killed because of your lack of power. I don't believe you are the warrior we have been searching for."

Malkia glared at Emelia before turning around and rushing out of the room, down the corridor to an empty sleeping room.

Malkia? Misty whispered.

I want to be alone, Misty. Malkia reclined onto the bed, tucking her hands under the cool pillow. *I just destroyed a whole moon with the sweep of my hand, and I have no proof of who they really were. Those creatures weren't the same as* the ones on Enyo and I fear there were more of them, than there were of the monsters. I don't know how I will ever live with all that blood on my hands. Please leave me alone.

I helped, Misty replied. I made it happen faster. If I had slowed it down you could've found out. I'm just as much at fault here as you are.

Except you're stuck in a glass cage, with no sight except what I see. The death of these creatures is on my shoulders. Malkia closed her eyes, seeing flashes of the burning Artemisians.

We have to finish it, Misty replied. We don't know if those part human creatures were spread over the moon. We don't even know if they were peaceful creatures. We can only rely on what they have done to Enyo and Eris, and what they could do to Esaki.

I'm not sure what I am going to do right now, Misty. For now I want some time to myself. Please. Give me a few moments to rest and figure out what I should do next.

Okay, Malkia. Misty was silent for a moment before continuing. I'm sorry, Malkia. I wish I had known. I wish I had stopped.

I know you do. This isn't your fault.

The silence echoed through her mind as Misty depart. Malkia turned onto her back, opening her eyes to stare at the gray ceiling above her. Her guilt consumed her mind, not knowing how to correct her mistake. As she dozed off, she was still unsure of her next move, but when she woke from her short nap, she had a clearer head and a better understanding of why she was fighting this war.

THIRTEEN
Ice Cold Heart

SHE LEFT HER bed, finding Dario in the control room waiting for her. He shot her an irritated look when she entered, even though she had only been missing for a half of an hour. Without speaking he gripped her arm, viciously yanking her out of the small ship.

"Knock it off," Malkia demanded, pulling her arm free from his grasp.

Dario's eyes narrowed, as he barged ahead without another glance.

This is becoming too uncomfortable. Malkia thought, picking up her pace to match his.

They finished their walk in silence, entering the control room in the main ship a few minutes later. Asha greeted her with a warm embrace.

"How are you feeling?" Asha asked. She was clearly the only one concerned.

"I needed to clear my head. I'm fine now." She peered over at Dario and Emelia. "Just desired a moment of peace to remember what is at stake," Malkia said the last words loud enough for Emelia to hear. She needed her to believe she was on board with the plan. "Where are the Artemisian ships?" Malkia asked, inspecting the dark space outside the control room window.

"According to the crew left on this ship, three vessels departed after the moon began to burn," Dario responded. His facial muscles tightened, breathing heavily. "Two additional ships have been circling the moon and waiting to catch us. They don't have the cloaking technology. That being one of the tools they've been seeking to steal from Errandor, since they discovered our development, and the reason the Enyo people have concentrated their defenses on the building where we are staying." His tall and erect posture edged closer, hovering menacingly over Malkia.

"We need to eradicate their ships, then search for the ones that escaped," Malkia requested, sliding away from Dario and leaning back against the wall post.

Crossing his arms over his chest, Dario sneered at Malkia's retreat.

"And how would you like to accomplish that feat?" Emelia questioned, as she stepped past Dario and shadowed Malkia. "Do you really think you are up for the task?"

Malkia's eyes flickered, staring at the petite woman. "Now that I have recharged my powers, I can finish off those two ships," she declared. Focusing on Asha, she quieted her tone, "I wish I knew what Errandor meant when he said I could bend magic. Maybe that would enable me to conclude this without Misty's help."

Asha frowned, her forehead puckering. "I can teach you, but it isn't something you can learn in few minutes."

Malkia nodded, glancing at Emelia again. She straightened back up as she announced, "I have to leave the ship again, but my protective light will provide me with the oxygen I need. Stay close and Misty and

I will finish it quickly."

"Whenever you are ready," Emelia responded, with an expressionless countenance. This is who taught Dario to be callous and manipulative.

"I'm ready now. Is Misty ready?"

Yes, I am. Misty's thoughts were quiet, but she was there.

Alright, miss. Let's end this.

The Enyoan ship eased away from her, as she bolted from the outer door and directed her body toward the two Artemisian crafts. Moving closer, she allowed her powers to build inside her body, but before she had the chance to angle toward her target, she was struck with a strong energy force. The Artemisians had already seen her.

She felt her light weaken almost instantly, her breath coming in short, as she realized she wasn't prepared to take a direct blow. She glanced up at the ships, just when the next hit fragmented her light. She inhaled a deep breath, as her energy exploded around her, and she began to float into the darkness, her body growing frigid and frost forming around her lips and eyes.

What have I gotten myself into?

She could feel asphyxia setting in, as the remainder of her oxygen was sucked from her lungs. As the frost spread across her face, and her body became numb, she used the remaining remnants of her powers and enrobed herself in her protective light, shutting out the deadly vacuum. Her body became incapacitated from the lack of oxygen and within seconds the blackness enveloped her eyes.

Awaking from her unconscious state, she could feel the cold, hard surface below her. She forced her eyes open, blinking at the bright lights above her. Surveying the small room, it was apparent she wasn't in the Enyoan flying ship. This had to be an Artemisian vessel, with its horrendous odor and larger entryway.

Her fears were confirmed when the door to her prison opened and an obese Artemis creature shuffled in. He was followed by two, brawny Artemisians.

She eased herself to her elbows, eyeing the weapons they were carrying.

The lead creature spoke to her in a strange dialect and Malkia crinkled her eyes in disgust. "I don't speak your dirty language."

Without warning, he punched her in the jaw and knocked her into the wall behind her. One of the guards brought up their weapon and smashed it into the side of her body.

"Are we speaking the same language now?" The fat creature barked.

Malkia moaned as she attempted to sit up again. "Loud and clear."

The Artemisian leered at Malkia, his icy hatred sweeping over his face. "Now, filthy human. Your people have destroyed my moon and for that, you will perish. As well, your people will succumb to the same fiery flames, along with any other humans I come in contact with." He stepped forward, leaning in close to her face, his rancid breath blowing in her face. "How were you able to create such a quick destruction of my home? Who are you and what moon did you travel from?

Malkia stared intently back at his eyes. "I'm not telling you."

Her body tightened, knowing there would be another blow, but she didn't see it coming. The other guard struck her in the chest, and she felt her ribs crack from the collision. As she took her next breath, she cried out in agony, just as the subsequent blow came down on her head and her eyes lost their focus. As they readjusted, she saw the staff come down on her side impacting one of her cracked ribs.

Screaming out in pain, she glared at the two guards and the plump Artemisian, a sneer covering his face as he flicked lint off his uniform. "You must be that warrior princess, your Erisian parents have been searching for. I believe Esaki is where they hid you for so long. Maybe we will begin our extermination on your home moon." He chuckled loudly, his whole-body quaking, as he held his stomach and tilted his face toward the ceiling.

Her powers were already healing her body, and her fury erupted violently. "I will wipe those smiles from your face."

She encircled herself with her light and bounded off the hard platform. The three creature's eyes widened, surprised from her swift undertaking and glowing light. She glowered at them, as her body blazed like the sun.

"*I don't think so,*" she shouted, straightening her posture, as she glared at the creatures before her. "I won't allow you to injure me or my people ever again. Your supremacy ends now."

Her powers were increasing in strength, and she sensed the hot flush of her skin advancing down to her toes and she laughed, watching the dread race over the monsters faces. They scampered for the door, scrambling over each other as they tried to escape.

Malkia clutched onto the slowest Artemisians arm, halting his withdrawal, and forcing him to turn toward her. As the other two raced down the corridor, she twisted the demons grasp on his weapon, easing it into her own control. She danced around the side of him, pressing his weapon into the small of his back.

"How about we join the remainder of your crew?" She nudged him forward, a smile dangling on the edges of her lips.

Following the demon down the corridor, he grunted as she urged him onward. The third time he stalled, Malkia struck him with her energy force, holding the weapon to her side. "Your technology is useless to me."

He groaned, rubbing the side of his head in pain, but he forged on, leading her to the control room. As they approached, Malkia reached out with her light and wrapped her energy around the Artemisians torso, squeezing the life from his body. After she dropped the shell to the floor, she turned to face the door and drifted through the metal particles. A smile swept over her face when the creature's jaws dropped in disbelief.

Their weapons fired on her, scattering across her light. "You cannot touch me!" Malkia howled. She moved into the midst of the demons, holding her hands at hip length, palms upward.

Misty, are you there?

Malkia heard her sigh. *I am. I have accompanied you the entire time.*

It's time. Let's vaporize this vessel from the inside.

Are you sure? Misty was hesitating. *What if your light isn't strong enough to protect you?*

I'll survive. Are you ready?

Yes, she replied.

Malkia glared at the dreadful monsters surrounding her. They continued to fire their weapons, striking her protective light, but failing to penetrate it, sending the large creatures into a feverish frenzy. The hysteria in the room grew deafening, as Malkia watched them tumble over one another, fleeing in desperation.

"You can all go to hell," Malkia whispered.

Her powers detonated from her like a bomb. As if in slow motion, she watched as the demons' bodies shredded from the explosion, spiraling them through the room, while the ships interior divided in every direction, fragments crumbling into the quiet of space. Closing her eyes, she waited, holding her protective light around her body.

Moments later, Misty whispered in her mind. *Are you okay?*

I am, Malkia replied. *Is the ship gone?*

I don't know. You have to open your eyes.

Malkia slowly widened her eyes, glancing around the once chaotic area. The ship was no longer there, and the monsters were obliterated. She smiled at the smoky darkness around her, breathing in deep, as she gazed at Theia and the burning moon of Artemis.

FOURTEEN
A Warlock's Confession

THE SECOND VESSEL was eliminated by Malkia and Misty, moments after the first one disintegrated. Malkia returned to the Enyoan craft, and they had begun their journey back to Enyo. She watched the charred moon disappear into the blackness and was no longer regretful for the slaughter. *More than likely all those creatures were monsters,* she thought, allowing Misty to hear her.

Misty was quiet, but after a moment replied. *I agree.*

The trip back to Enyo was a quiet one. Malkia avoided everyone on the ship by finding a secluded room, far away from the bridge. She blocked her mind, keeping to herself while she thought of ways to free herself and Misty, once this fighting was complete.

Her thoughts became dreams, dozing off from the solitude, and when she woke, Asha was sitting on the bed staring at the opposite wall.

Malkia cleared her throat, turning over onto her side. "How did you find me?"

Asha smiled, before twisting toward Malkia, "I created you. I think I can find you."

"That's funny. You left me on Esaki." Malkia frowned. "You

didn't seem to want to find me at that point."

"That's not fair, Malkia." Asha entwined her fingers together and settled them on her lap. "Leaving you on Esaki was never the plan, however, keeping you in the dark was always for your own protection. Not only from the Artemisians, but from your father. I would hope by now, you would realize, nothing is what it seems."

"So, you say," Malkia muttered. She sat up and rubbed her eyes. "Are we close to Enyo?"

"We will be there soon. I wanted to talk to you about your questions. We won't have much time when we arrive, and I want you to know what happened."

"I'm listening." Malkia propped herself against the wall with her blanket and pillow and focused on Asha.

"Why you were you created... so many reasons. It was your mother's idea. She was pregnant when the Artemisians first attacked Eris. Your father and mother were influential citizens of our moon, and their hometown was one of the first destroyed." She leaned up against the metal bed frame, before continuing. "They had escaped with Palma in your mother's womb. I met your parents shortly after they settled into their new home. She was only half-way through her pregnancy and was distraught she would be unable to protect her child. Because of their fears, the community united with an idea to enhance the abilities of their unborn children. At first—" She paused, glancing up at the ceiling and sighing. "At first, it was only to assist the little ones' abilities to protect themselves and hopefully survive the invasion. However, one mother desired more power for her children. She wanted them to be capable of slaying the Artemisians, if necessary. It was then we began experimenting with some darker magic." Asha stopped, glimpsing over at Malkia.

"Whatever you say won't change much," Malkia reassured, seeing the anguish in Asha's eyes. "Unless you intentionally did something to hurt me or my daughter, nothing you can say will change how I feel about you." She reached over and touched Asha's leg. "I might be angry, and I don't fully trust you, but I do love you."

Asha closed her eyes, resting one of her hands on top of Malkia's. "You might reconsider after you hear the full story."

"I might," Malkia agreed, nodding her head. "But I want answers, and your story holds information about my existence."

Asha inhaled deeply, before continuing, "Your parents and I became fast friends, especially your mother and me. I worked on Palma, creating liquid concoctions to directly inject into your mother's womb. We wanted Palma to be the best. We desired her to be unstoppable."

"She wasn't unstoppable," Malkia stated, her brows knitted into a frown.

Asha shook her head. "No, she wasn't. When she was born, there was only a microscopic impression that she had acquired powers. That wasn't what we had hoped for. I had expected to feel her strong light, but instead I perceived weakness." She cleared her throat, as she glanced around the room, "I need some water."

"There's a kitchen area around the corner from here. Will you bring me a glass of water as well?" Malkia asked, giving Asha a sheepish smile.

"Yes, I will. I'll be back in a few moments."

Asha left and Malkia stared into space, thinking of her sister. *Palma was going to be the powerful one.* She thought, keeping Misty blocked. *I wonder why the magic did not magnetize.*

Moments later, Asha walked back into the room with two glasses of water. She set them down on the table next to the bed and quietly shut the door. "I don't think anyone else knows where you are, but this is going to infuriate Dario and Emelia."

"I don't care," Malkia snapped. She quickly regretted her tone. "Sorry, I'm not intending to jump down your throat, but I'm tired of being deceived. I'm irritated by Dario's outrageous ploy. I remember his scheme to force me to Enyo, and I know he's one of them." She paused, taking a large drink of water. She set the glass between her thighs and wiped her mouth with the back of her hand, before continuing, "It's completely apparent Emelia is his mother, and I'm almost certain they both want me dead or imprisoned, after I save Enyo. I don't give a rat's ass what they want from me. Once I'm done destroying the Artemisians, I will vanish from their lives."

Asha cocked her head to the side, looking at Malkia from a sideways angle. "Why don't you destroy them while you're at it?" She asked.

Malkia eyes flashed. "Do you mean destroy the Enyo people or just Dario and Emelia?"

"You have the ability to destroy them all. You have tasted the exhilaration of death. Why don't you just finish them all off and do the same with the Erisians?"

"You're foolish, Asha," Malkia scolded. "Why would you say such a thing? The exhilaration of death? There was nothing exhilarating about what I just did."

Asha smiled again. "Just checking."

Malkia glared at her. "Don't play games with me."

"I'm not. Are you ready to hear the rest of the story?"

"Yes," Malkia downed the entire glass of water, settling back against the wall.

"Your mother was devastated. She and I had become very close, and it was heartbreaking, witnessing her turmoil. She wanted a warrior child. She desired a child she knew would be safe, even if she was no longer alive," Asha admitted. "She adored Palma and she nurtured her, praying her abilities would surface. It was only months later, she discovered she was pregnant with you." Asha paused again and glanced at Malkia, who was now staring at the opposite wall.

"I'm listening," Malkia reassured her, but kept her eyes directed at the wall.

"She was only a few weeks along when I sensed your heartbeat. It was a moment of elation, because it is unheard of to develop a heartbeat that early. We already knew you were going to amazing." Asha put her hand on Malkia's leg, watching her face. "Your mother was overjoyed, but your father... your father wasn't pleased. He was angry at your mother for being so reckless. It was difficult enough protecting one small child, but two—" She paused, her eyes wearing a badge of regret and sadness. "He didn't want any part of it. He wanted to terminate the pregnancy."

Malkia drew in her breath slowly, knowing his hatred had always been there, even when she was only a tadpole. Her heart ached, and she didn't have the means to barricade the pain.

Asha gave Malkia's leg a gentle squeeze. "Your mother refused. She and I retired to a private residence of mine and began the spells immediately. You were created with magic in you. Not only with what remained from Palma, but the magic I diffused into you even before you had the chance to form. We could feel your power before you were even born and your light protected you, even in your mother's womb. Her stomach would glow, and we would laugh." Asha smiled wide, as she spoke about Malkia's birth mother. "We knew you were going to be magnificent. No one had created what we had. No one knew the magic I performed, to make you into the beauty you are today."

Malkia turned to look at Asha. "What did my father say when he found out what you had done?"

"He was furious, at first. I worried he would kill Haltia. When he found out she hadn't terminated the pregnancy, he lost it. He struck your mother in the face, but you were already strong."

Malkia's eyes widened. "He did what?" She hissed.

Asha nodded. "But you were already protecting yourself and your mother, as well. You encircled her with your light and would not allow your father near her. I've never seen resentment, like on that day. He wanted to kill her and exterminate you in the process. I was afraid, but I finally intervened and insisted they spend some time apart. He told me that was excellent advice. Without telling anyone, he left that day and took Palma with him."

"Why would you let him do that?" Malkia gasped. "You're a warlock! You could have stopped him. You could have kept Palma out of his grasp."

"Yes, I could have, but things were different back in those days. If a warlock went against anyone of high authority, they were executed, without exception." Asha peered down at her hands. "It's still rough on Eris for warlocks, but we are no longer slaves to your people."

"You were a slave?" Malkia was surprised.

"Magic has always been a frightening subject for the uninitiated. No matter where you travel, they fear it. As slaves to people, we were forced to wear collars, of our own incantations, around our necks. Our own magic, revoked all our powers." Asha sighed, her eyes closing for a moment. "I was young when the collars came to be considered inhumane, and we were freed from them, but I remember them well. Even after they were removed, we were treated as the enemy. It wasn't until I was older that I was allowed to live in the same town as other humans."

Malkia clasped onto Asha's hand and held it in between both of hers. "That sounds awful," her voice shook with emotion. "To be persecuted because of something you were born with or for being someone different. I could *not* imagine being a child in those circumstances."

Asha's eyes glazed over, nodding her head, while staring at the wall across from her. "It was dreadful, and difficult to reside on Eris when I was young. If anyone discovered I was a warlock, they labeled me and kept me isolated. It wasn' until I met your mother, that I finally felt as if I belonged somewhere... with someone."

Malkia's eyes crinkled in confusion.

"Yes, your mother and I are lovers," Asha responded to Malkia's unspoken question.

"What? How?" Malkia stammered, her eyes darting over Asha's

face. "Does my father know?"

"He knows, now." Asha pulled Malkia's hand toward her, kissing it and then smiling. "He suspected for many years, but I think he was so fixated on Palma, and the Artemis problem, that he chose to ignore it. He required my assistance and he needed Haltia to provide you the nurturing he could not. He bestowed all his fatherly love onto Palma. He knew it was wrong to hate you, and I honestly believe he wanted to love you. But something snapped when you protected your mother while you were in womb. He refused to forget." She paused, closing her eyes. "Or forgive."

"I wasn't even born," Malkia sputtered. "What *is* wrong with him? He blamed a fetus for his problems? I only wanted him to love me. I knew he adored Palma, but he never treated me the same. Never. All because I shielded my mother from his blow." She shook her head, looking down at her hands. "I will never understand." Malkia brought her knees up, cradling her head in her hands to hide her tears. That insufferable man had ripped the best from her again. He was a hateful tyrant. "Please continue," she mumbled with her head still in her hands, the tears burning her eyes.

"Are you sure?" Asha placed her hand on Malkia's back. "We can finish later, if you want."

"I'm sure. I need to know all of it."

After a few moments of silence, Asha spoke quietly. "After your father disappeared with Palma, my affair with your mother began. We were already close, and with your father's lack of affection, it didn't take much prompting to seek comfort in each other's arms. She needed to know she was loved, and I was already in love with her. Your father was gone until after you were born, which made it easy for us to grow even closer. I was there when you were born, and I adored you from the moment I laid eyes on you." Asha paused again. Malkia could feel her eyes on her and turned to meet them. "You were my daughter. I had created the magic inside of you and for that I think your father despised both of us. His Palma was never going to be as strong or as powerful because her body rejected most of the magic. Your father blamed me for that."

"In all honesty, you're no better than he," Malkia snapped, pulling away from Asha, as her anger surfaced again. "You abandoned me on Esaki, as well, and you didn't stand up to him when he treated me like dirt. I never remember you being an enemy to him. All of you acted as if nothing was wrong. I knew he didn't love me as much as Palma, but if there was any animosity between the two of you, I never witnessed it."

"We mended ways when he returned," Asha responded, straightening up from the wall. "He needed you. I needed your mother and you. Your mother wanted her whole family together, while remaining close to me. I'm not saying it was an easy task, but we made it work. We only had each other, and we all knew that."

Malkia shook her head, knowing her erratic outbursts were not helping the situation. *I need to stop taking my hurt out on Asha.*

Asha continued to talk, despite Malkia's glazed expression. "After he returned, he wanted me to focus on Palma. As I said, he wanted to love you, and I think a part of him succeeded. However, I also believe he spent that time away finding ways around your protective light and searching for a way to make Palma stronger. I had friends who warned me of what he was doing, but he never did discover a way to rectify either situation. I believe he felt meager around you, even when you were an infant. You were very protective of your mother, and he knew it. She kept you close and made sure he maintained his distance." She glanced over at Malkia, as she crossed her legs in front of her and leaned against the wall again. "Palma never improved, but when she was three, she began telling your father what you were thinking. We knew you were both telepathic at that time, but that was the only ability she ever possessed."

"He wanted to know how to discover a way around my protective light?" Malkia asked. "Why? So, he could control me?"

"Your guess is as good as mine." Asha leaned forward, clasping Malkia's hand. "I don't think he wants you dead, so control could be his motive. He wants you to wipe out the Artemis demons, which you have, in large part. However, they remain in orbit of Eris and occupy parts of the moon as well. Because of this, I fear for your mother's safety."

"I fear for my daughter's safety," Malkia clinched her jaw. "Those animals stole her from me and then put her in harm's way. I could have guarded her from the Artemisians, but my parents had to show everyone how powerful they were, and in the process separated Esta from her mother."

Asha sighed. "That was not supposed to happen. I'm paying for that failure. I had to escape Eris, because your father was going to make me pay with my life. If you wanted to witness some animosity, you should have been around for that moment."

Malkia peered over at Asha. "I'm sure it wasn't easy. I'm sorry I'm so mean right now. I feel this anger inside of me directed at my father, and even at my mother. It was her idea to hide me on Esaki in the first place. And then she thought it would be acceptable when she retrieved my daughter, but not me?" She shook her head. "I don't understand and my heart aches for the lost time."

"You have every right to be angry, Malkia. I deserted you, too." Asha twisted on the bed, sitting on her knees as she faced Malkia. "We thought this was the best plan to protect you. No one ever traveled to Esaki, being that it is the farthest moon from Artemis, so it seemed like the safest hiding place. When we received Esta and not you, your mother and I were both heartbroken." Asha leaned forward, clasping Malkia's hands within hers, staring intently in her eyes. "We knew you were hurting inside, and we knew you would hate us for taking away your daughter. Please know that we attempted to contact you, but we were always watched. We could not chance the Artemisians finding out where you were hidden and destroying Esaki before we had the chance to protect it. You have seen what they can do. We may have made mistakes, but we aren't barbaric, not even your father."

"I believe you," Malkia whispered. Her thoughts had returned to Mataya and all her friends back on Esaki. Asha was right. The Artemisians would have destroyed Esaki, and all her people.

Her thoughts were interrupted by Misty. *Are you there, Malkia?*

Yes, I'm here, she replied quickly.

We're going to be landing soon. My father just told me Dario is searching for you, and he's furious. You might want to come out of hiding and prepare to land on Enyo.

Tell them I'm on my way, Malkia responded.

She glanced at Asha as she stood up. "They're looking for us.

We're landing soon, and Dario is upset from his lack of control over me. It's time to go face the fire." Slipping her hand into Asha's as they left their hideout, she murmured, "I want to hear more, later."

"I'll plan on it," Asha responded, with a warm smile.

FIFTEEN
Bonding

DARIO STOOD JUST inside the door to the control room, tapping his foot, his nostrils flaring. "Where have you been?" He barked at Malkia.

Her body jerked slightly from his harsh tone. "Really?" She asked. "That's how you want to speak to me, after everything I just accomplished for the Enyoans?" She paused, waiting for an answer, but only heard his heavy breathing. "None of your business," Malkia snapped. "You do *not* own me, so stop acting like it."

Dario muttered something under his breath, and she ignored him. Turning away from him, she took a seat in the control room. Asha followed suit, and they silently watched as they made their descent to the safety of Errandor's building.

Malkia tapped her fingers on the armrest and closed her eyes, as she waited impatiently for the ship to finish its descent and dock. Her desire for this war to be complete, intensified, as she imagined finally arriving to Eris.

When she felt the ship come to a halt, her eyes flew open, and she floated through her safety straps, using her purple light. She resumed holding hands with Asha and left the ship without another word to

Dario or Emelia.

She leaned her head toward Asha. "Can I stay in your room?" she asked.

"Of course, you can, but do you think that's the best move?"

Malkia sighed. "I can't stand him. He lied to me." She paused, glancing around to make sure they were alone. "Even if I disregarded the drugging, and the deceit, how can I ignore his desire to control my every move? I'm disgusted by his face right now. I truly believe once this war is over, he won't allow me to leave."

Asha inhaled deeply, squeezing Malkia's hand. "Play their game for just a while longer. We need to purge the Artemisians orbiting Enyo, along with those occupying Enyoans lands. They're vile creatures, and we cannot allow them to follow us to Eris or Esaki." Asha abruptly halted, turning to face Malkia. "Insist they let you begin this tomorrow. You need to rest. Go back to your room, after you meet with Errandor, and tomorrow, we will commence this new battle."

Malkia shot her a sideways look. "Only one more night," she insisted.

Asha nodded, as they began walking, silently strolling toward the meeting room. When they arrived, Malkia lounged into a chair near the door and waited. Asha followed suit, staring at the door. It was a comfortable silence and Malkia felt a connection to Asha. They were each wrapped in their own thoughts, and the peace helped her anxiety dissipate.

Not long after, they heard whispers in the hallway. Moments later, the double doors to the meeting room swung open and Errandor, along with Tarance and their servants, strolled into the room. Errandor's smile quickly spread across his face, seeing the two women waiting, and his eyes danced with joy as he rushed to greet them.

"Malkia," he gushed, clasping her hand, and kissing it. "You did it! You halted the invasion. The end of this war is near, and I couldn't be prouder of the warrior you have become."

Malkia's nosed crinkled. "Speaking of—" she began.

Dario and Emelia sauntered into the room. Her voice trailed off as she noticed the irritation in Dario's eyes.

"Why did you not wait for me?" Dario growled at Malkia.

She stared at him, her jaw dropping. *Way to announce your true self.*

"Be quiet, Dario," Errandor grumbled, glancing over his shoulder. "Malkia and I were just enjoying a friendly conversation, and your interruption ruined it. If you can't be unobtrusive, then vacate the room."

Malkia was growing fonder of Errandor by the minute.

Dario gritted his teeth, glaring at Malkia, before plopping down in a chair on the far end of the room. Emelia remained standing, her lips set into a grim line as she eyed Errandor and Malkia with disapproval.

"Now where were we?" Errandor asked, looking flustered.

"The end of the war is near," Malkia reminded him patiently, smoothing her smile with her fingers.

"Yes, yes!" His eyes shot up to meet hers, his smile returning. "I'm so pleased by your expeditious actions. You eliminated those demons before they knew what was upon them. It won't be long before our entire moon is unbound from their grasp."

"About that—" Malkia began again. She glanced over at Asha, who smiled with encouragement.

"What is it dear?" Errandor asked.

"Tomorrow," Malkia hesitated for a moment, twiddling her thumbs, her hands clasped against her torso. "Tomorrow, I want to begin."

Dario snickered. Emelia's eyes widened, and Errandor looked delighted.

Tarance reached forward, placing his hand on her arm. "Do you not require more rest?" He asked.

"No," Malkia replied. "I want this war to be over. I need those demons to suffer for the pain they have caused me, and of course, for the offenses they have rendered upon the Enyoans."

Errandor's smile grew, and Tarance laughed out loud.

"I cannot believe this nightmare will finally be at an end," Errandor sighed.

He curled his arms around Tarance, and she could hear him weeping. *He's not such a horrible man.* Malkia glanced at Asha again, waiting for the awkward moment to pass.

Separating himself from Tarance, Errandor dried his eyes with the sleeve of his robe. The two men moved forward, hugging Malkia.

"Thank you for choosing to liberate us. Thank you for taking the journey to Enyo," Errandor paused, then whispered into her ear. "Dario is not the man you believe he is, so be warned. I can protect you once this war is over." He leaned back and gazed knowingly into Malkia's eyes.

She nodded, giving him the response he desired. *I won't be sticking around long enough to require protection*, Malkia thought. She blocked Misty from her mind once again, knowing they would still be monitoring her thoughts. *They're all going to need protection from me if they even attempt to control me.*

She smiled at Errandor and Tarance. "I must eat, and then call it a night. I'll meet everyone in the drawing room after breakfast in the morning. I have an idea to end the Artemisians lives, without harming the Enyoans."

"We are eager to hear your knowledge," Errandor said. "Go eat and have a good night's rest. We will speak in the morning."

The two men turned and left the room, followed by their servants and a tight-lipped Emelia. Dario sauntered toward Malkia, managing a straight-faced countenance. He clamped his fingers into the tender flesh of her arm, dragging her from the room.

Malkia dug her heels into the ground, yanking her arm back. "What are you doing?" She hissed.

"Taking you back to our room." He reached toward her, grabbing at her arm again.

Malkia took another step back, her eyes burning with hatred. "Excuse me?" She retorted. "I don't need you to *take* me anywhere. I'm not sure if you noticed, but I'm capable of caring for myself. You can *take* your uncaring ego, back to your room, and leave me alone."

Dario's face turned a dark shade of red, eyeing her with his hands balled into fists. "Listen here, you ungrateful twit. I kept you alive. I made sure you arrived in one piece and saved you from that demon."

"I saved myself," Malkia shouted, interrupting Dario. "Stop acting like the hero. You're nothing but a liar, a manipulator, and a waste of my time."

Dario snickered. "Do you know we were able to read every single one of your thoughts while Misty was connected to her machine? Don't you realize you were *never* calling the shots?" He stepped toward her, leering as he hovered over her. "I brought you here, and now you are mine to do with as I please. Once the rest of Enyo is free of those demons, you will be my pet."

Malkia glared at Dario, her hatred for him flooding her body. Her heart pounded rapidly inside her chest as she thought about ripping his head neatly from his body. She took a few steps back, avoiding his advance. "Dario, you may think you have won, and you may be deluded enough to believe I'm yours, but I assure you, I can, and I will make you pay for this."

With that, Malkia pivoted on her heel, and strode from the room before Dario could stop her. She didn't know where she was going, but a destination was unimportant as long as it was away from the most spineless and despicable man on this moon.

She wandered aimlessly, enjoying the quiet. As she passed a large window, she paused, leaning her forehead against the glass, savoring the beauty of the outside world. Theia hung in the night sky, brightening the ground below. Although Malkia knew there were monsters roaming the terrain, they were invisible in the still of twilight, giving her a sense of victory and peace.

Hearing her stomach grumble, calling for nourishment, she closed her eyes and breathed in deep, taking a step back. Swiveling toward the mess hall, she smiled when she caught the aroma of food. After a few more turns and corridors, she plodded into the large, communal eating room.

Malkia peered around, noticing Asha sitting at a table by herself, picking at her food. She walked over to her only friend and sat down next to her with a smile.

Asha glanced up and smiled back when she saw who it was. "I was worried. You departed so quickly, and Dario looked like he was going to detonate. I had no idea what he would do if he found you."

Malkia rested her cheek on her forearm, looking over at Asha. "Did he leave?"

"No. I hexed him." Asha shook her head, her tired eyes glossing over. "He'll probably try to murder me when the hex wears off, but I thought he would go after you and do something awful."

"You hexed him." Malkia giggled, sitting up straight. "What do you mean you hexed him? Is he frozen in place? Did you turn him into a toad? What did you do?"

Asha laughed. "Not a toad! I scattered him, which is better than being a toad. Why did I not think of that?"

"You scattered him?" Malkia eyes widened.

Asha played with her food, as she explained, "It's difficult to describe, and it isn't a spell I do often because it takes a great deal out of me, but I essentially scattered his energy and every cell in his body. It's almost as if he is made of fractured glass. Slowly, he will pull himself back together, although, it could take him most of the night."

Malkia burst out laughing, tears running down her face as she laid her head on Asha's shoulder. Asha grinned wide, as she patted the top of Malkia's head.

"I had no idea you could do such a thing," Malkia sputtered, after calming her laugh down. "I'm actually looking forward to seeing his face tomorrow!"

"He will be furious."

"Who cares?" Malkia smiled widely in the aftermath of her amusement, wiping the tears from her face. "I need food. Save my chair." She winked at Asha, as she stood up.

The women enjoyed their food and each other's company throughout the rest of the evening, only leaving when the lights began to dim, the workers ushering out the remaining crowd. Taking the long route back to Asha's room, Malkia pointed at the smudge on the large window, from where her forehead had rested. Their laughter was contagious, as others smiled warmly at their display of joy.

After arriving at Asha's room, they added extra security codes to the door, ensuring Dario didn't intrude during the night. Malkia bounced on the couch with a grin, grabbing her pillow and curling her arms around the silky material as she laid her head down.

Asha walked by, and kissed Malkia's brow. "I'm thrilled to have you back in my life." She pulled the blanket up to Malkia's chin.

"And I as well," Malkia yawned. Her eyes closed, and she was out before Asha left the room.

It seemed only moments had passed by, when Malkia was torn from her sleep by tremors and a glaring light from the windows.

SIXTEEN

Catastrophe

MALKIA LEAPT OFF the couch, stumbling over the chair as she shielded her eyes from the bright light. The rumbling of the walls caused a glass vase to fly by her. Her gaze flashed around the room, searching for shelter, but resorting to surrounding herself with her protective light, as a light stand came tumbling toward her.

Asha staggered into the room, her brows raised and her eyes wide. "What's happening?" She shouted.

"I don't know," Malkia called back, over the deafening rumble. "We need to leave."

Malkia grabbed Asha's arm and flew to the door. They disabled the security and locks and stumbled into the corridor. Other residents were crowding into the hallway, and the miasma of panic was apparent.

"We need to go to the drawing room," Malkia frantically whispered to Asha, flashing her eyes over the crowd. "This must be a reprisal from the Artemisians."

"I'm right behind you," Asha said.

Malkia levitated and flew down the corridor, dodging the Enyoans. Reaching the staircase, she peered back at Asha and saw her stumbling through the crowd. Asha waved her on. Whisking down the stairs,

Malkia found the correct floor for the drawing room on the first guess. She flew down the corridors and stormed into the drawing room. Emelia was the only one there.

"What took you so long?" Emelia yelled, her icy contempt scouring over Malkia.

Malkia rushed forward, scanning the room. "What *is* happening?" She asked, ignoring Emelia's question.

Emelia switched on an overhead light, leaning over its table, which was filled with digital maps. "The Artemisian ships you missed are using their full force against us. I haven't been able to identify the source or type of their weapons, but this barrage is going to destroy our defenses."

"Where is Misty?" Malkia moved in closer, sneaking a peek at the graph in front of Emelia.

Emelia brows knitted into a frown, as she glanced over at Malkia. "She was moved to a safer place on the lower floors."

"What is your problem, you old bat?" Malkia snapped. "I'm here to support you. Why are you against everything I say and do? I need to know Misty is close so we can make a united attack."

"She was drugged, so she could sleep," Emelia confessed. She closed her eyes, supporting her head in her hands, while resting her elbows on the table. "Her father is trying to wake her as we speak, but until he succeeds, we're on our own."

Malkia groaned. She flew to the arched window at the far end of the room and searched the skies for the Artemis ships. The light blinded her, and she blinked rapidly as she spun away from the window.

"I need to stop the shaking," Malkia shouted to Emelia, who had stayed at the other end of the room.

Dario burst into the room, just as she finished her sentence. He glared at Malkia, his nostrils flaring and his face crimson with fury. She stared back at him, her lips pursed.

"What's going on?" Dario bellowed at Emelia.

Emelia rushed to his side. "Calm down, Dario," she pleaded.

"I won't calm down," Dario screamed, stepping away from his mother. "I want to explode right now."

A giggle escaped Malkia's lips. She was enjoying the irony of his words. Dario returned to glare at Malkia, lumbering in her direction. "I think there has been quite enough exploding for one night, don't you agree." She laughed harder at Dario's abhorrent expression.

His speed ability kicked in and he thundered toward her. Malkia leapt out of his way, floating to the ceiling as he smashed into the window behind her.

Unfortunately, the windows were protected by something stronger than Dario. The glassed bowed outwards, etched with fractures, but it did not shatter the way Malkia hoped it would. She smiled as she envisioned, his twisted corpse lying motionless on the turf below the windows. She was growing more cynical, with no desire to stop.

Dario groaned as he rose from the floor. He searched for Malkia, spotting her in a new position, on the opposite end of the room.

"I hate you," he muttered.

"I'm sorry, what was that?" Malkia mocked him, cupping her hand to her ear. "You'll need to speak up when I'm so far above you."

"You little bitch," Dario yelled, his eyes narrowing to crinkled slits. "I hate you."

"Well, look at that, Dario still possesses some kind of emotion," Malkia smiled. She clapped loudly.

"Stop it," Emelia screamed, darting her eyes between the two. "Both of you. Dario stop performing like a child and pull yourself together. Malkia, I may not like you and I do detest you for how you are treating Dario, but we have a common enemy. Both of you stop behaving like children and let's please end this war."

Malkia lowered herself to the floor, landing with her light around her. "Wake up Misty and then I can finish this," she responded. "I will do it my way, and will kill both you and your son, if you interfere."

Malkia bolted from the room, before either one could object. After moving through several empty corridors and stairwells, she found an empty meeting room with a couch. She sat down, cradling her head in her hands.

"Why can't I just go home?" She cried out. "Why did my parents block me from channeling them? And Jasper has perished by Dario's hand, so I can't channel him." Malkia stopped talking and sat up straight. "Damon!" The name burst from her lips.

He was there in front of her moments after she spoke his name, standing in Jasper's castle, and talking to Koleton when he noticed her. "Malkia!" Damon exclaimed, advancing toward her in one swift move. "Where are you?"

"Oh my god, Damon!" Malkia cried. She reached out to touch his face but clasped only empty air. "I thought I would never see home again. I'm on Enyo. Dario kidnapped me and brought me here to fight a war against the Artemisians."

"Why would Dario kidnap you?" Damon questioned, shaking his

head in confusion. "That makes no sense. I thought he was on your side." His eyes grew wide, exclaiming, "Is he the one who stabbed me?"

Koleton was doubly confused, as he looked for Malkia, but didn't see her. "Damon, have you lost your mind?" He asked.

"No, no!" Damon snapped, glancing over at Koleton and then back at Malkia. "Malkia is channeling me. I can see her because we both have Erisian blood. Malkia, what happened?"

"I believe he's the one who assaulted you," Malkia responded, biting her lip. "I don't have time to go into details right now. I need you to find a way to Enyo. Have Jacob speak to the pixies, they have to know a way. We are being attacked and I have to focus on ending this strike." She paced back and forth, glancing up at Damon while she spoke. "Once I'm done, I will channel you again. Find a way soon. The Enyo people will kill me, before they allow me to leave this place."

"I'll talk to Jacob. Be safe, please." He held out his fist, squeezing it three times.

Malkia smiled, remembering the code she had taught him only weeks before, as the vision faded. Despite all that transpired back on Esaki, Damon would always hold a tender place in her heart.

She shook her head and stood up. *Why had I not thought of channeling Damon before now?*

She retraced her path at a run but avoided the drawing room. She built up her powers around her as she climbed to the top of the building, her speed increasing as she hurtled herself forward.

"This madness ends tonight," she muttered to herself. She flew through the top of the building and set her eyes on the ship above her.

"Say good-bye, you arrogant pieces of shit," Malkia screamed at the vessel.

Malkia stood on the top of the building, watching the suns climb above the horizon. An ocean of sorrow welled up within her, as she watched the moon burn below her. She had gone too far, and she hadn't needed Misty to accomplish it.

The Enyoans in the building had survived her explosion, thanks to their Thalian magic. However, the two ships, along with the Enyo people and the Artemisians outside the building, had met her fire and wrath. One ship had escaped, and Malkia had been tempted to leave with it, as a stowaway. She was certain they were heading to Eris.

Malkia waited for Dario or Emelia to find her, hoping they would kill her quickly. The powers that Asha had bestowed upon her, were a gift she had shattered, as all those innocent people perished in her flames. She didn't deserve to survive another day.

"Malkia?" Asha's voice was barely a whisper.

"Go away," Malkia responded.

"What happened?"

"I said, *go away*," Malkia screamed. She turned to face the one person who cared about her on this moon.

"I'm not leaving." Asha edged forward. "You need to talk this through. Tell me what happened."

Tears spilled down her cheeks as Malkia thought back to the moment she'd stood atop the building, gazing at the underbelly of the first ship. "I'm confused by the chain of events, because the explosions spiraled so quickly," she whispered. "After seeing their ship, I flew through the base of it, stopping in the middle. I allowed my powers to erupt, watching as remnants flew across the sky. One of the larger fragments collided into one of the other vessels and it exploded from one area to another until it plummeted to the ground below." Malkia paused, raking both hands through her hair and closing her eyes. "After that it was chaos. The ground was engulfed in flames and people were shrieking. I hesitated to help them and found myself staring at the pandemonium below me." She looked at Asha, shaking her head, and biting her bottom lip. "My body became frigid from the screaming, freezing in place, as I listened to the most horrifying wails I have ever heard."

Malkia's sobs came, as inexorable as the tide, and Asha rushed to put her arms around her. Malkia clung to her tight, feeling a sharp ache twist through her stomach and chest, as the scene of the inferno and the sounds of the screams played through her mind.

"What have I become?" Malkia cried.

"Your mother and I bear the responsibility for this," Asha whispered, rubbing Malkia's back. "We were the ones who wanted you to be unstoppable and destroy the Artemisians. We did this to you, not being cognizant of the impact this would have on you. I am so sorry, my sweet Malkia," Asha's voice quavered as she said the last sentence.

"I still had a choice," Malkia sobbed. She stood and backed away from Asha. "I could have stopped the war, found another way. Instead, I watched them burn, and did nothing. I am a monstrosity just like the Artemisians you wanted incinerated." Her gaze darted over the burning land. "I have developed into the demon."

Sinking to the ground, she curled upon herself, her sobs muffled by her hands, as she rocked her body mindlessly. The wails of those she had slaughtered rang in her skull, endless and maddening. A rage enveloped her heart and mind, as she lifted her face and screamed at the sky, hating herself for feeling the warmth of the sun on her cheeks. She screamed again, before hiding herself back within her hands.

Asha curved her arm around Malkia, again. "I'm here and I won't leave you. Allow the agony to move through you, so you can fully experience the pain you inflicted on those innocents." She slid her fingers down Malkia's hair, her hushed voice cascading through the air. "This war was forced upon you, but your part in the Enyoans demise cannot be ignored. Feel the anguish, and then together we will face the flames."

Malkia cried and rocked, gripping Asha tightly. "I want my mom," she whispered. Her voice shook as she remembered her Esaki mother's love and adoration. The pain intensified, when her thoughts shifted to her Eris mother, yearning for her embrace. "I need my mom."

"We will find her," Asha promised. "We will leave this moon and save your mother and your daughter. This isn't the end, my child. These people didn't die in vain. We will finish this war for good, and we will be reunited with our family."

Malkia peered at Asha. "Thank you for being here." Her hands trembled, as she reached up to wipe her tears.

The suns were rising higher, and Malkia could feel their heat on her back. She raised herself off the ground and surveyed the dimming chaos. The fires remained burning, but this wasn't the only region of

Enyo. She needed to free the rest of the moon from the Artemis grip. Then, she could leave.

Turning to face Asha, she asked, "Will you help me finish this war?"

"I will be with you every step of the way," Asha replied. She grabbed Malkia's hand. "We are in this together and we will end it united."

SEVENTEEN
Making Amends

"ERRANDOR, I AM only here out of respect for you," Malkia divulged. She stared at the Enyo leader, sitting on the edge of the chair with her arms folded on the table in front of her. "What happened outside could have been prevented. I was unaware of the extent of my powers, and I didn't know the destruction of the Artemisian ships would create such havoc." Her eyes closed for a moment, taking a deep breath before continuing. "For that, I apologize, and I grieve for the suffering of your people. I want you to know, I'm eager to finish this. I'll free the rest of your moon." She paused again, searching Errandor's serious expression. "I require Asha's company. She has the ability to reign in my powers, if they reach an uncontrollable point. As well, I desire Misty's release from her enclosure. She deserves to be a child again. There's no need for her to experience any more destruction, when I can do this on my own. I have finally discovered what you mean by bending magic."

Errandor sat quietly, staring at Malkia. He made no move to object, neither did he seem to approve. Malkia waited, but as she rose from her chair, he spoke.

"What assurances do I have that you will finish this? How do I know you will not run before the Artemisians are completely destroyed?" He questioned, his forehead creasing. "If I let Misty go, then what will stop you from leaving?"

"I have sacrificed my soul for you," Malkia eyes widened. She placed her hands down on the table and leaned toward him. "Please do *not* question my motives after all I have done. I understand you believe you can protect me from Dario and Emelia, but I'm not the one who will need security from them. I believe they colluded with the Artemisians to breech your defenses, just enough to incite hysteria and undermine faith in your defenses. For this, I have confidence in their intention to collapse you from power."

Errandor didn'r appear shocked when he heard Malkia's accusations. Silently, he exchanged glances with Tarance, who nodded in agreement.

"Malkia," Errandor straightened his posture, shifting to the edge of his seat. "I'm sure you are correct. I realize there has been too many coincidences where Emelia is concerned, and her children are no better. Both Dario and Kelsey have plotted to sabotage my leadership on more than one occasion. There actions may be seen as a bid for power on behalf of their mom and mamu. Perhaps I needn't say that the repercussions of such a coup would be dire, at best." He stroked his beard, staring at Malkia intently before continuing. "Yes, I will have Rory remove his daughter from her glass cell. I'll allow you to finish this war the way you see fit, and once it is complete, you are permitted to leave the moon. Please just end this insanity. We would like to have our home back."

"Who is Dario's mamu?" Malkia questioned.

Errandor hesitated before speaking, his eyes dropping to his lap. "You might have seen her, a beautiful woman, tall like Dario, graced with snow white hair and brilliant, dark eyes. Emelia is the late wife to her son, and performs Ginny's bidding without reluctance. However, while Ginny craves power, she prefers seclusion. This is where Emelia's bombastic personality serves her interest. Unified, their influence is devastating, and the wills that wield it are twisted. Both of Ginny's grandchildren are of a similar cast, perverted in their lust for power."

Malkia eased back down into her chair. "Did you know they came to Esaki years ago to infiltrate my town and gain my trust?"

"I knew they were gone," Errandor's muscles in his face tightened, "But, I didn't know they were on Esaki. I knew they would go there eventually, but their only task was to find you, help you remember who you were, and then convince you to save Enyo. That was all. The planning was up to Emelia, and at the time, I had full confidence in that woman. She was my ally and my friend."

"Power changes people," Malkia whispered.

"It does." Tarance responded first, setting his hand on Errandor's shoulder.

Malkia shook her head, flashing a worried look at Asha. "One more person for me to watch," she responded. "To return to our discussion, once I know Misty has been released from confinement, I will complete the assault on the Artemisians. But her safety and comfort precede any other concern."

"I will inform them immediately," Errandor replied. He pushed a button on his chair and a few moments later a guard walked into the room. "Please summon Rory."

"Yes, sir," the guard responded.

As they waited for Rory to arrive, Malkia reached for Asha's hand, finding comfort in her touch. She stared out of the nearby window, half listening to Tarance and Errandor whisper amongst themselves. The fires had cooled, no longer consuming the ruins of the settlement surrounding their stronghold. While the citadel itself had been buffered against the destruction, she could see that the town at its base had borne the brunt of her assault on the flying ships. Malkia stared at the charred and fragmented land before her, suffused with remorse for her carelessness.

She could see the pyramids in the distance and noticed that their periphery was unscathed. She wondered if they had been protected, as well, and resolved to find out, even if she must do it alone. The Enyoans seemed determined to prevent her from investigating the structures.

There was a soft knock at the door, and Rory entered without waiting for a response. "You asked to see me?" He asked. His confused eyes grazed over Malkia, before resting on Errandor.

"It's time to release your daughter. Go ahead and begin the process, and have Malkia join you as soon as she's alert," Errandor responded, nodding his head in approval.

"Are you positive?" Rory asked, stepping toward the table. "I want our agreement to be complete. I want what I have earned, and a safe passage away from Enyo."

"You have it," Errandor confirmed, nodding his head. "Malkia will finish the assault with support from Asha. The forms will be brought to you, along with the code to your ship. Once the process has been finalized, and your daughter is alert, you will both be free to depart." He waved his hand, indicating for Rory to leave.

Rory's smile spread over his face, as he hurried toward the door. Turning to Malkia, he exclaimed, "Thank you!" He reached over, gently touching her arm. "I know this hasn't been easy and I know you don't owe me anything but thank you for making this happen."

"I didn't do it for you, this was all for Misty. She doesn't deserve to suffer in the darkness and fight wars that she didn't start. She's a child, so allow her to be one." Malkia closed her eyes and breathed in deep. "All I ask is this. Take her far away from this foolishness and allow her the chance to grow up without the scars of death behind her eyes."

Rory nodded vigorously, smiling at Errandor before racing out of the room.

"There you have it," Errandor said. "You can prepare for the next battle. When Misty is able to leave, I will have my guards send for you, so you can speak to her yourself."

"Thank you, Errandor." Malkia rose from her chair and pulled Asha up next to her. "Once this is over, I suggest you rid yourself of Emelia and her family."

"I'm already working on that," Errandor agreed, standing alongside Tarance. "When you return to Eris, please let your parents know what has happened and that I send them my best."

"I will," Malkia replied, turning as she spoke. She left the room in a rush, with Asha following behind her, using her warlock powers to keep pace with Malkia.

"Asha, we have to conduct this differently," Malkia advised, her long-legged strides moving her swiftly through the corridors. "It will take longer, but it will keep the innocent Enyoans out of harm's way. We will have to go city by city, ridding each place of the Artemisians before moving onto the next target. There won't be any easy way to do it with my powers. If you have any hidden resources that will speed up the process, without jeopardizing the Enyoans, now would be a great time to use them." Malkia glanced over at Asha, who nodded in response.

"I might have a few ideas," Asha replied. "Are we leaving now?"

"Don't you want to?" Malkia asked, as she slowed down to a walk.

Asha nodded. "I do, but I need to go back to my room to retrieve some items. There is a spell that might be able to help us separate the people from the demons. I would have to be close to each city, but once I cast the spell on the immediate area, it will draw all the creatures to one place. Then, when you release your energy, you can bend and mold the magic appropriately. We would just need to figure out a suitable space once we arrive at each city."

Coming to an abrupt halt, Malkia pivoted to face the warlock. "Asha?" She whispered.

"What is it, dear?" Asha asked, stepping closer.

Malkia placed her hands over her eyes and cheeks, shaking her head. "Are we doing the right thing? Wiping out a whole civilization, even their young? Can they not be reformed or taught differently?" She sagged against the wall behind her, breathing in deep. "I'm struggling between protecting Esaki and Eris from these vultures and killing off a whole civilization, all because I want to protect mine. Are there not better means to accomplish peace?"

Asha inhaled deeply and paused for a moment before responding. "I can understand how you feel, and acknowledge the conflict, but I don't have an answer free from prejudice." Asha reached forward and clasped Malkia's hands. "I have seen what these demons can do on a much larger scale, the death and destruction they have brought down on innocent people. You believe the war that took place on Esaki was the doing of your people, but you're wrong. The atrocities were the actions of the Artemisians. They suspected that was where the special children of Eris were secreted, despite our avoidance of that moon. But instead of investigating, they attacked the Esakians without warning, and without bothering to determine the cost of their actions."

Asha sighed, her eyes hot with tears, as she quickly wiped them away. She stepped backwards, allowing her backside to rest against the opposite wall. Malkia glanced down the corridor, checking for stalkers, returning her attention to Asha after she was assured they remained alone.

Asha stared intently at Malkia, as she spoke in a hushed tone, "We didn't have a chance to stop them. You're worried they will return to Esaki, and you should be. Now that they know they didn't destroy you, they will return, annihilating any life that remains on your beloved moon. Asking me those questions stings my heart, not because I worry about the Artemisians, but because I have seen their utter lack of remorse. They are greedy and hateful, and they will stop at nothing to destroy us. For that, I won't hesitate to strike first."

Malkia brows furrowed. "I thought it was my parents who started the war on Esaki."

"No, it wasn't," Asha shook her head. "Although many believed it was. Your parents and the other leaders of Eris did their best to bring all of you home before you were killed. Not all the children we hid, have the powers you possess. Of the four of you who were left behind, you were the only one who received injuries from bomb shrapnel. While you bear the scars of that experience, your regenerative powers restored you, even in unconsciousness. Because of your powers, you and your sister survived."

Inhaling another deep breath, Asha stood up straight, reaching for Malkia's hand. Gripping her fingers, they progressed toward Asha's room.

"While it remained a mystery as to how you had achieved it, your mother insisted that you remain hidden after that," Asha continued. "She watched you, and wept with longing to have you home safely, but once the portals closed, all contact was lost. We had sacrificed our technology to save so many. The drain on our resources rendered the damage irreversible. She forfeited her wish to have her daughter near her, because she felt those on Esaki needed you more desperately than she." Asha gave Malkia a sideways glance, softly squeezing her hand. "I won't defend her decision, but once she made it, she wouldn't allow anyone to retrieve you. Your father despised her for some time, but they worked through it. I do know one thing, in a fragile moment she confessed to me that her main objective was to keep you away from your father. She insisted you were better off where you were and would not explain. She just contended it was for the best, even though I could see it was breaking her heart."

"It doesn't make sense for her to abandon me," Malkia muttered, twirling the end of her hair with her free hand. "If she loved me, wouldn't she want me with her? And all those people who perished on Esaki. They were killed because of us, *because* of *our* people. The innocent were blindsided by the devastation, as my parents watched the calamitous events take place. And what about the technology that our people brought to Esaki. If they wanted us to remain hidden, why draw attention by delivering us the knowledge?"

They had reached Asha's room and she paused to open the door. Turning back around, she looked at Malkia. "It wasn't the Eris people who brought the technology to Esaki," Asha whispered.

She walked through the doorway and Malkia followed behind, feeling confused and frustrated. The lights flashed on and she felt a prick in her neck. As if in a dream, she watched Kelsey jab Asha with a needle. The room spun wildly, her sight dimming to darkness as she lost consciousness.

EIGHTEEN

Rotten

MALKIA SHIVERED AS she stirred awake and felt the chilly air surrounding her. She was disoriented, and as she opened her eyes, she could see the world was upside down. The sky was dark and when she leaned her head back, she could see the icy water below her, hitting the reef not far from where she was hanging. The splashing and spraying of the ocean reminded her of her childhood on Eris, but the fist of fear that clenched her heart was something far different.

She writhed, attempting to see more, but her restraints prevented her from moving. Her hands and arms were bound tightly against her body and her legs had something cold and hard wrapped around them, immobilizing her completely.

The cold air, washed over her bare legs, chills rippling down her unprotected skin. Her skirt pooled around her hips, and she wished she had worn her long pants. Being upended had caused her blood to collect in her upper extremities, and her head pounded with it. More blood oozed down her back, leaving a sticky trail, from where the rough bindings had cut into her flesh.

Her focus shifted from the outward world, concentrating on her energy. She could feel her light, but it had been subdued again thanks to whatever toxic substance Dario had delivered into her body.

I need to find out what this is and why it restrains my powers. I'll never escape if he can pacify me, every time I let my guard down, Malkia thought, frustration sweeping through her mind.

She fixated on healing her body and forcing the poison out of her system, but before she could make progress, she jolted upwards. After a few moments she was enclosed in a glass cage, peering at Dario and Kelsey on the other side.

"Well, lookie here, sleeping beauty has finally come back to the living," Dario taunted, his grin stretching across his face, as he pressed his hand against the wall of the cage.

Kelsey's nose crinkled, her mouth puckering with disgust. "Grow up, Dario," Kelsey snapped back. "Get this over with, so I can go home."

"You're always so serious," Dario joked. He gave her a little nudge. "Loosen up. Enjoy the moment. We've won."

Kelsey cracked a smile but returned to glaring when she spoke. "Malkia, dear," she said. "You've been a difficult guest, and I'm growing weary of the games. We aren't asking much. Finish this, our way, then we will allow you to have your freedom."

"If your brother keeps injecting me with this poison, I won't be able to finish anything." Malkia glared back at her old friend.

"That's just a precaution," Kelsey replied. "We want you very clear on our conditions, and what is at stake if you choose to escape."

Kelsey shifted to the side and pointed to the far side of the room behind her. Rory was bound and gagged, with Misty unconscious on the table next to him. His eyes were wide with fear, and Malkia cringed knowing Dario had hurt Misty again.

Malkia's eyes narrowed in disgust. "Where is Asha? I need her to help finish this. Especially if Misty is unconscious."

"We have her," Dario smirked, breathing heavily on the glass and doodling in the condensation. "Once our conditions are laid out to you, and you have agreed to complete the tasks, we will let you both go."

"What are your conditions?" Malkia asked, wriggling her arms against her restraints.

Dario gazed thoughtfully at Malkia, as she squirmed. "Are you going to play nice?" He asked.

She relaxed her arms, frustration crinkling her eyes. "You've given me no choice. What are your conditions?"

"You go on this mission and eliminate what remains of the Artemisians. Wipe every single one of their filthy lives off this moon." Dario stood up straight with his arms crossed over his chest. "When you are done, you're to return to Errandor and advise him on your victory. When the time is right you are to end his life, along with Tarance, and any of his guards and followers. Once we have seen Errandor's lifeless body, we will allow Rory and Misty to leave, unharmed."

"Alright," Malkia replied.

Dario sneered, as he leaned in close to the cage, his breath again fogging up the glass. "That's it? No arguments? No amendments?" He taunted again. "Sucks to be on the other end, doesn't it?"

"I agreed to your terms." Malkia managed a stony expression. "Free Asha and loosen my bindings, so I can finish this mess."

"Not so fast," Dario said. "Remember that little bug we buried in your shoulder, some time ago? Do you recall the pain I was able to inflict upon you? Well, just so there are no more surprises on either end, I repaired it after the damage the Artemisian inflicted upon it and placed it deeper inside you. Not only can I control your every movement, but I will be able to hear everything you say. Don't think twice about double crossing me again. Destroy the Artemis demons and kill Errandor. Simple."

"Fine," Malkia snapped. "Let me go!"

Dario stepped back, rubbing a hand over his dark stubble. "When the drug has dispensed out of your system and you can conjure up your little light, you are more than welcome to free yourself," he pointed out. "We will open up the door below you and you can leave through there. The glass is protected by a spell, so it would be unwise to try any other way except down. Asha will be waiting on the shore for you."

Dario threw her another wicked smile before walking away from her glass cage. Kelsey sat on a chair nearby, scowling at Malkia.

"What?" Malkia barked.

"I don't understand you." Kelsey leaned forward, resting her elbows on her knees. "Why did you not escape after you destroyed the Artemis ships? Why did you remain when no one cares about you on this moon? You risked your life on Esaki for your people, and then you come here and do the same for strangers. To me, that is senselessness. Why would you stay when you could have escaped?"

"Are you serious?" Malkia replied, rolling her eyes.

Kelsey rested her chin in her palm, looking thoughtful. "Yes. I am."

"You're that coldhearted that you would ignore others who are in need?" Malkia shook her head.

Kelsey shifted her weight, as she sat up straight. "I didn't say that. I came to Esaki, didn't I?" Her eyes crinkled to narrow slits. "I surrendered six years of my life, to draw you out of hiding and bring you to Enyo, in order to liberate my people. I'm the hero, and soon I will be worshipped like a saint."

"Expending six years of your life to overthrow the leaders of Enyo, does *not* make you a hero," Malkia jeered, her eyes flashing. "There was no sacrifice on your end, at least not any which extols sainthood, especially when you would permit your people's demise. You are nothing, but a coward, and your only motive in this whole ploy is to gain supremacy."

"You have no idea what my motives are," Kelsey snarled, rising from her chair. "Nothing is what it seems. You would be wise to remember that."

Malkia wanted to rip Kelsey's pretty little head off, watching her smirk as she tossed her hair over her shoulder and strolled away.

Glancing around at the parts of the ship she could see, Malkia noticed three guards standing close to Rory and Misty and three farther down the corridor near them. She couldn't see behind her, but she imagined she was surrounded. However, the drug was wearing thin, and her inward fire was being lit.

Without notice, the door below her opened and the chilly air blew across her face. She shivered, as she slid out of her chains, glancing over at Rory before flying out of the cage and heading for the shore.

Asha was sitting in the sand, gazing at Theia when Malkia finally found her. She landed nearby and settled next to her.

"How do we keep allowing these problems into our lives?" Malkia asked.

"The same thought has been perplexing me since I sat down." Asha cradled her arm around Malkia's shoulders. "That man is a piece of work. What did you ever see in him?"

Malkia leaned against Asha's shoulder, watching the ebb and flow of the ocean water. "At this point, I'm beginning to wonder that myself. He was a valiant man on Esaki. I thought I knew him well." She shook her head, bringing her knees in closer to her chilly body. "They maneuvered their way into my circle of trust, and I never questioned them, they were that skilled in deceit. Dario arrived first, as a solo traveler. He told us he had left his city down south, after the wars ended and had been on his own ever since. He was searching for a place to start fresh and forget the past. Jumping right in, he assisted with the development of our town and never hesitated to help. He was always there. Now I see that. He knew how to gain my trust."

"It isn't your fault," Asha reassured. "They're both experienced manipulators. They were taught by that evil filth of a mother and a conniving mamu."

Malkia growled. "Kelsey was my friend. We weren't close, but I thought we knew each other." She shivered, wrapping her arms around her knees, and enclosing them both in her warm light. "She came waltzing into my little town with a group of people about a year after Dario. I had no reason to doubt their story and when she decided to stay, even though her group wanted to move on, I was happy to call her family. Their personalities were so dissimilar, that I would have never guessed they were from the same blood." She shook her head in frustration. "How will I ever trust my instincts, if they fooled me so well?"

"Listen," Asha said, "they knew what they were doing. They had planned this and had been trained to deceive you. I'm sure when you first met them, there was doubt."

"Sure, there was," Malkia paused, "but, apparently, not enough."

"Let's not dwell on what you could have done." Asha stood, reaching down to help Malkia up. "We need to move on with our plan. Dario retrieved the items I required from my room, along with a bag of clothes, so we are prepared for our new adventure."

"Finally, he does something useful," Malkia laughed, pulling on a pair of long pants, and shoving her chilled arms inside her jacket.

"I'm sure he had his hidden agenda behind it," Asha joked. "The man does nothing, unless it serves his interests."

Gathering up all her items, Malkia linked arms with Asha. "Agreed. Let's go end this sovereignty of the demons, so we can leave this ungodly moon."

NINETEEN
Releasing Them from Their Shackles

"ARE YOU READY?" Malkia stood at the edge of the cliff, admiring the golden hues of the vegetation.

"Give me another moment." Asha's forehead puckered in concentration. "Once I cast the spell, the demons will migrate quickly to the meeting point. Your window of opportunity will be brief, so you will need to act as quickly as you can. Are you sure you understand how to bend magic? Do you want to go over it one more time?" Asha questioned.

"No, I'm not sure, but we can't stand around twiddling our thumbs." Malkia glanced over at the warlock. "If I fail at bending magic, then I will resort to slaughtering them all, as I did on Artemis."

Asha nodded and then closed her eyes, whispering an eccentric dialect over the ingredients she had mixed on a piece of parchment. Malkia's blood was part of the mix, purported to assist her when she unleashed her energy upon the demons. She'd be able to twist and mold her powers the way Misty had, but on a smaller scale.

Asha opened her eyes. "Your turn."

Malkia jumped into the air, making her way to the area Asha had summoned the creatures. She could see them merging collectively, in confusion, peering around at each other. Her powers launched out of her body and shot out at the large group of Artemisians. As her energy collided with them, she used her mind to push through the crowd, ripping apart each creature as it swirled around them.

There were hundreds of Artemisians in the group and as her powers shredded through their bodies and their lives ended, Malkia felt each of their souls move through her. She didn't feel any remorse for ending their lives.

The deimoses gathered with the demons, and although it helped that they were in a trance, Malkia's energy struggled to wrap around their bodies. Expending double the energy, she was finally able to end each beast's life.

This is going to take ages, Malkia sighed in her mind.

She pressed forward, terminating each life, as they fell prey to her light. As the final beast took its last breath, she swallowed hard, and eased down onto the dirt, placing her hand on the energy of the moon. The connection filled her with vitality, and slowly she began to feel restored.

Glancing back up, she could see the people of the small city move cautiously toward her.

"What's happening?" An emaciated woman asked.

Malkia stepped away from the crowd, seeing their anger toward her. "I'm destroying the demons."

"Why?" An older man yelled through the crowd. "They will retaliate."

Malkia shook her head, her shifting eyes missing nothing. "I won't let them."

"How are you going to stop them?" Another man questioned.

"You are the first city we have liberated. As we progress through each town, we will place a spell on the perimeter, which will barricade the Artemisians from entering."

A frail young woman touched Malkia's arm. "They will just come back, once the magic has been removed," she whispered.

Malkia breathed in deep, standing up straight. "There's a chance I will miss some, however you now can defend yourselves. Once I finish, there won't be enough Artemisians to gain control of your lands and people." She scanned the scared woman's eyes. "You may not believe me, and you may feel there is no chance, but I am determined to end this invasion." Turning to the growing crowd, she shouted, "Stay in your homes and city, and when it is finished you will know."

"How will we know?" The same woman spoke louder.

"That's not up to me. I'm here only to exterminate these demons. How you discover the outcome and rebuild your lives, is entirely up to the leaders of this moon." Malkia enveloped herself with her light and began to rise above the Enyo people.

"Don't leave us," a child cried from the crowd.

She moved toward the child, landing softly in front of her. Kneeling, she peered into the child's eyes. "I have many other cities to visit. Go home with your family and stay in your city. It will be over soon."

Before she received any additional questions, Malkia flew into the air and out of the crowd's reach. Shaking her head, she settled down next to Asha.

"This is going to take us a year if we don't move faster." Malkia sighed heavily, resting on a nearby boulder. "Those deimos beasts are nearly impossible to destroy, and they're draining my energy too quickly."

Asha nodded. "Let's move onto the next area. I have set the protection spell on this city." She gathered up her items, shoving them into her bag. "If we require a more concentrated spell to speed up this process, then I will need to collect a few more items."

The day flew by, but they only managed to release three cities before the suns set. Malkia was drained, despite the energy she drew from the moon. They ended their day hiding away in the last city they freed, finding an empty home that they cloaked with magic, allowing them to sleep in peace.

Malkia watched as the people swarmed the dead Artemisians. Some were weeping, not because they were happy, but because they were devastated by the deaths of their masters. She watched in amazement as the Enyoans threw rocks and objects at her, screaming for her death. She was saving these people, and they wanted nothing more than to see her dead.

She turned away and flew back to where Asha was hiding.

"These people are crazy," she grumbled. "Each city and town are the same. They want me dead and their awful demon owners to be alive. I can understand they have been brainwashed, but it is blowing my mind how little they are grateful. They're either afraid the monsters are going to come back and kill them, or they want me dead for killing their beloved demons," Malkia groaned with exhaustion, and she realized she was expending more energy than she could generate.

"They've been enslaved for years," Asha said. "Some of them can't remember life without the Artemisians around. Many have come to accept their fate and are petrified to think of life any other way. These people have been trained, and they've been told they can't live without their owners. It's extreme brainwashing, and to think of life any other way is frightening."

Malkia sighed. "We have been at this for eight days. I'm exhausted. I don't expect them to be overjoyed, but a little bit of gratitude would help my mood."

Asha rummaged through her ingredients. "We are running low on supplies. I know these extra ingredients have increased our speed, but I don't know if they will last. Is there any other way we can accelerate the process?"

"I'm fresh out of ideas," Malkia shook her head. "Let's finish the last city for the day and then find some food and a place to sleep. I desperately need a day off from this. Do you think Dario would mind if we took a day to relax and replenish our supplies?"

"We can always just do it and see what happens."

Malkia reached back and ran her hand over the slight bump on the back of her left shoulder. "Supposedly he can hear everything we say. If he has a problem, I'm guessing I will feel it soon."

"Stupid man," Asha mumbled under her breath.

Malkia pulled a piece of parchment from Asha's pile and wrote with a charred stick.

I need three things to happen before we head back to Errandor. First, we need to find a way to remove this device from my back. Second, I have to channel Damon. Third, we must stop at the pyramids and see if I can find the same symbol of the feather on it. If we do, I'm hoping I can communicate with the same beings I saw back on Esaki.

Asha read the parchment and nodded. "Agreed on all three," she mouthed.

Malkia sat against a large rock. She laid her head in her hands, thinking of her daughter and her sister, Mataya. Her sister's whereabouts remained unknown, and she couldn't channel Damon because Dario was listening to everything she said. No matter which way she looked at it, she was stuck until she finished what she had promised to do.

"I'm ready to go, Malkia," Asha said.

Malkia raised her head. "Ready to continue our murdering spree?"

Asha's body stiffened from the remark. "Malkia, please."

"What do you want me to say," Malkia crushed the parchment with her fist. "Let's go have some fun? Let's dance the night away? I'm drained and my only focus is retrieving my daughter and finding my sister. My heart aches for two men, who never loved me. My mother abandoned me. The parents who raised me, lied to me. What should I say?

"Self-pity does *not* suit you." Asha's lips set in a grim line. "I'm tired too. We can't fall apart, now, not when we have come so far. Do you really think you can look at your daughter and sister, knowing you left these people to rot with the demons? Do you think it would be wise to leave now when the Artemisians know you're still alive?"

Malkia shot up from her spot beside the rock. "They know I'm alive!"

"Yes, that's what I just said."

"The Artemisians who escaped back at Errandor's building, they know I'm still alive." Malkia inhaled sharply, placing her hand on her forehead while pacing the ground. "They're aware I was hidden on Esaki. What if they journeyed there, destroying what little life my moon has left? My people are doomed. They will perish, if the demons decide to invade. I need to know they are safe."

"How will you possibly make that happen?" Asha grabbed Malkia's arm, forcing her to stop. "Dario doesn't care about the people on Esaki."

"He'd better care." Malkia leaned her head back and shouted at the sky. "Dario, I'm channeling Damon now. Give me the chance to warn them."

Malkia focused on Damon.

Nothing happened.

Maybe I'm too worn out, Malkia thought.

She concentrated on seeing Damon and wished to be with him.

She could feel something stir around her and then seconds later, Damon stood not far from her.

"Malkia, finally!" Damon exclaimed, moving away from a group of people.

"Damon, how are you? Is everyone safe?"

"Yes, we're fine." He edged closer, his brows bumping together in a scowl. "I've been waiting for days to hear from you. What happened?"

Malkia breathed a sigh of relief, her muscles slightly relaxing. "It's bad here and a very long story. Dario is forcing me to finish their war before I can leave. He has put a device in me that…"

She felt the surge of electricity shoot through her body before she dropped the channel of Damon. Shaking violently, she tumbled forward into the vegetation in front of her and was powerless to arrest the fall.

"Malkia," Asha's voice was far away, as if she was in a tunnel. "Malkia, can you hear me? Come back to me. Say something. Please, please God, bring her back. Please don't take her from me again. Malkia. Malkia. Come back to me. Please!"

Malkia could feel the pain coursing through her body. Dario must have amplified the pain sensors, just for a moment like this. Her heart was beating in her head again and she felt blood on her face. Blackness enveloped her, although her eyes seemed open.

The laughing came out of nowhere, and she realized she was the source. She didn't even think it was funny. *Why am I laughing?*

"Malkia, you're scaring me?" She could hear Asha's voice above her own laughing. "What's going on?"

Why can't I stop laughing? This isn't funny! Her eyes began to focus and she could see Asha's concerned face above her. Malkia's head was propped in Asha's lap.

"I. Must. Be. Going. Insane." Malkia panted in between her fits of laughter.

The pain engulfed her, but the laughing seemed to soothe it. Malkia calmed herself and frowned up at Asha. "I can't win, can I?"

"Yes, you can. Don't give up." Asha ran her hand over Malkia's hair, comforting her. "Take a deep breath and release the pain. You're better than Dario—than all of this."

Malkia sniffed, taking a deep breath. "Asha, we need to just end this. He's won. I will finish this war, kill Errandor and his followers, and then we can leave. I can't fight him anymore. I can't do this anymore. Dario has won."

Malkia allowed her body to heal itself, while rising slowly. She glanced around, before standing. "Let's go find a place to rest and tomorrow we plow through the cities. No more protecting every human. It's time to complete it once and for all, no matter who is in our way."

TWENTY
Broken

"MALKIA," ASHA SCREAMED from the top of the tall hill. "You have to pull back!"

Malkia stood amid the flames, her light surrounding her and watched as her powers grew and strengthened. She pushed and twisted the energy and fire, driving it through the area. She had warned the humans to leave, but most of them had remained.

The Artemisians and the few deimoses in this city had gathered as usual, but the humans came running for them. They had heard what was occurring around their moon and they were desperately trying to save their masters.

What is the point? Malkia thought in exasperation. *Why am I freeing these people when they want these monsters enslaving them?*

She could hear Asha yelling at her but didn't care what she was saying. As she allowed her energy to take shape, bursting through the flames, a smile dangled on the edges of her lips. This was what she was destined to do, what she had been created to accomplish.

The humans howled as a wall of fire blocked them from their masters. The ones in the front receiving burns and charred skin, while the others behind pushed their friends and families into the flames.

Why don't they listen?

She sighed as she pulled the fire back and eased in between the humans and the destruction. "Stop," she shouted over the chaos. Her voice had never been that loud before, but her mind was growing stronger by the minute, and she could feel the power of the moons and Theia coursing through her body.

Most of the people froze, causing many to stumble backwards. They stared, dumbfounded at the glowing woman.

"You are *free!*" She brightened her light, yelling over the mountain of people. "Leave now and go discover a life, absent of slavery. Stop trying to protect them. I have slaughtered all the Artemisians here on Enyo, so end this foolishness and pull yourselves together. This will be the last time I ask. The next time, I will allow the fires to consume you all." She pushed forward, permitting her light to build and drive the people away from the inferno.

The humans stepped back, fear in their eyes. Some began to run away, while others kept their eyes on her, slowly receding back. Before long, the humans were all gone and she was left with the howling of the deimoses, still fighting to stay alive.

What is it with those beasts?

She turned her attention back to the wall of fire and strode through the devastation, to find the wailing deimos. As she approached the scorched bodies of the creatures, the heat from a living body radiated behind her.

She dropped to the ground before she realized what was hovering over her. The creature was biting at her energy, attempting to break through her protective light. Shooting her powers out of her body, they collided with the beast, knocking it off to the side. She quickly soared upwards and stared at the deimos, breathing hard from the attack.

"Why are you not dead?" She shrieked.

The deimos howled into the smoky air. It leapt again, missing Malkia as she shot to the side, but quickly whipped around, snapping at her legs.

Malkia growled, flying higher above the mayhem. "You little brute. You're misjudging this human."

Seizing the beast with her powers, she used what was left of the magic in the air, twisting her energy to snap the beast's neck. She watched in amazement as the creature resisted, fighting her light on every turn.

"What are you?" Malkia whispered.

She drew her energy inwards, allowing the beast to settle back on the ground. Strolling up to its face, she peered into its hazel eyes. Those eyes were so familiar. They weren't the bright yellow, like all the other deimoses she encountered.

"You aren't the same as the others, are you?"

The beast sat back and nodded its head ever so slightly.

"What are you?" She stepped closer, reaching out to touch the animal. "Who are you?"

The deimos quickly turned away and ran through the wall of fire. Malkia pulled the flames down and settled it out, the charred remains of the demons and beasts lying still and lifeless. She observed the beast as it ran for the hill where Asha was perched.

Malkia rose into the air and flew after it. She knew Asha could protect herself, but she wasn't taking any chances. When she reached Asha, they both watched as the deimos bounded up the hill and stopped at Asha's feet. It bent its head and whimpered.

"Do you know this beast?" Malkia asked Asha.

"I don't think so, but it looks different from the other deimoses. Where did it come from?"

"It was in the fire." Malkia crossed her arms over her chest, moving closer to Asha. "I could hear it whining and stirring in the flames, so I entered to terminate its life. But it wasn't burning and no matter what I did, nothing would hurt it. Are you sure you have never seen her before?"

"Is it a she?" Asha twisted to look at Malkia.

"I think so," Malkia replied. "I sense the presence of a female and those eyes seem so familiar." Malkia bent down, as the deimos raised her head and stared back at Malkia. She searched her memory for this beast.

"Did we have deimoses on Eris?" Malkia asked. She stood back up, looking at Asha for answers.

"Never before the Artemisians invaded," Asha whispered, examining the beast from a safe distance. "Their loyalty has always been with the demons. I have never had one so close to me before, but I swear this one is not the same as the others. The scales appear softer. The fangs are not as gruesome. You can see the beast, but there is something more."

The deimos whined and pawed at Malkia's feet. Its eyes searched Malkia's face and she felt the urge to hug the beast. "She's scared, but I can sense strength and dignity in this animal. She seems to be trying to convey something."

The beast nodded her head again and growled loudly.

The hum of Dario's ship warned Malkia of its approach and she whipped around to face it. The air lock was open, and Dario stood on the edge with a weapon. Seeing what he was pointing at, she hurdled upwards to stop him, but was too late. The deimos whimpered as the three darts implanted into its scales and flesh. It turned to run, but only made it a few strides before stumbling over and passing out.

Malkia jumped into the air lock door and slammed her fist into Dario's nose. "Why are you such a horrible human being?"

Dario chuckled, wiping the blood from his nose. He pointed the firearm at Malkia's chest, as a grin swept over his face. "You touch me again, I will execute that beast, and make you a witness as I rip it to shreds. We are landing. Summon your witch, and we will gather your beast. Now that you have completed your undertaking, we can return to Errandor and enjoy your victory feast." He laughed again, nudging Malkia off the edge of the ship.

She watched as the ship moved away, landing in a nearby field. Turning back to Asha and the beast, her fury began to form, once again. She scrutinized her surroundings, as Asha gathered her items, shaking her head.

"What am I going to do with you?" Asha muttered.

"What do you mean?" Malkia settled back onto the ground and began gathering her own possessions.

Asha stood up straight, eyeing Malkia. "You lost it down there in the city. You lost it on Dario. You have let humans die in this war, even though that could've been avoided. You're changing and Dario is enjoying the way he has been able to mold you to his liking."

"That isn't fair. Every day we have been on this destructive

Enyo's Warrior

journey, I have died a little more inside. I may be changing, but I'm not shifting into anything that would please Dario."

Asha shook her head, not believing what Malkia was saying.

"Isn't this what you wanted?" Malkia stepped forward, her face crimson with fury. "Weren't you the one who articulated why we couldn't go back to Eris without finishing this war? I did what everyone wanted." She threw her hands in the air, fighting back the fountain of tears threatening to flood her eyes. "No matter how challenging it was, I didn't stop until it was completed. You stand there in judgment, when what I desired from you, was to eliminate all the agony I just witnessed. I needed you to be my strength, the rock that holds me up after the annihilation was accomplished. I never needed you arbitrating me, when this is what you engineered me to do!" She paused, placing her hand over her mouth and chin. "This is what you created me to *be*." Her last words quivered on her lips, and she glanced away as the tears rolled down her cheeks.

Asha closed her eyes, raking her hand through her hair. "This war has ruined us both."

"Well, isn't that tender," Dario boasted just below them on the hill. "You two are reminiscing on all the mess you made of my moon. How sweet is that?"

Malkia turned away from Dario and peered at the deimos lying up the rocky hillside. Asha came closer and entwined her hand with Malkia's. "Let's return to Errandor and put the rest of this nightmare behind us."

Malkia nodded and walked slowly toward the ship. Looking over her shoulder she watched as Dario's soldiers wrapped the deimos up

192

with ropes and chains. Moments later the deimos lifted off the ground and floated down the hillside, guided by the soldiers.

The flight back to Errandor was uneventful. Malkia kept her thoughts to herself and ignored Dario's never-ending pokes and jibes. Asha was silent as well but stayed next to her the entire trip.

As they began to unload, Malkia saw the soldiers moving the deimos. The beast was beginning to stir, as they shifted its cage onto a wheeled cart. The beast whined as she woke, and Malkia flew quickly to the side of her cage.

"I'm here, whoever you are. I won't let these monsters hurt you."

Dario laughed from behind her. "The beast has you wrapped around its paw. How in the moon did it accomplish that?"

Malkia ignored the hateful man and reached into the cage to touch the deimos's nose. "Ignore him. Someone peed in his drink today."

The electric current tore through her body, causing the convulsion to come in waves as she slumped against the cage. Her eyes stung from the electricity that slid from her, into the metal cage, making the beast yelp in pain. Malkia could hear it growl and snap as the cage moved away, allowing her unresponsive body to slam onto the hard ground. Her head bounced like a rock, cringing from the blow as she watched the beast being taken away.

The deimos shifted its weight toward Malkia and stared into her eyes. Those hazel eyes. They were so familiar.

Malkia's heart stopped for just a moment.

TWENTY-ONE
The Deimos

MALKIA PLEADED WITH her body to respond. She could see feet and legs walking past her, but no one stopped to see if she was alive or even to move her out of the way. Without the use of her muscles, she could feel the trickle of her saliva and tears puddling around the side of her face.

"You imprudent girl," Asha whispered, kneeling next to her and holding Malkia's head in her lap. Gingerly, she wiped the tears and spit off her face. "Why can't you just wait until there is a better time to strike? Why do you insist on being bullheaded?"

Malkia tried to laugh, but it came out as a snort. Slurring her words, she said, "You created me, why don't you tell me."

Asha shook her head. "You can't help it, can you?"

Malkia's laugh turned to tears. "I knew I had a connection with that beast. I knew there was something about her that was so familiar. Dario must have suspected it as well, or else he would have slaughtered the animal. And now... now I know why."

"What are you talking about?" Asha questioned.

"The deimos. She isn't really a deimos."

"Wait," Asha interjected. "Don't say another word. First, let's return to my quarters and clean up your face."

Malkia nodded, knowing Dario was listening. If he didn't already know who the deimos was, he would figure it out before she had a chance to save her.

Asha helped Malkia stand and propped her up, as they began to walk. Malkia's body was already healing, but she could feel those awful drums again in her head. She was destined to move from one nightmare to another.

The crowds had thinned and the deimos was gone. Malkia searched for Dario, but couldn't find him or anyone else she recognized, as they eased down the ships ramp. The walk to Asha's room took more time than Malkia would have liked. Her body continued to heal, but without the direct connection to the moon, she was unable to draw from its energy. She was back to healing at her normal speed.

They bolted the door and Asha placed a protection spell around her room.

"Let's remove that bug," Asha said. "He can't hear us while the protection barrier is strong, but he will make the connection soon enough and might careen you down another electric spin, if it's not removed immediately."

Asha pressed her hand on Malkia's shoulder, just over the device. Her strange language spilled from her lips, causing Malkia's skin around the device to boil with heat. Feeling it move inside of her, she peered down and could see small tentacles swirling inside her chest.

Her pulse quickened, as she slammed her eyes shut. *Oh, my Theia. What did he put inside me?*

The tentacles could be felt down into her fingers and toes and

Malkia slowly opened her eyes, watching with dread, as they fought to stay entwined with her body. He had implanted a living device in her and it wanted to stay, a parasite that had every intention of dominating her body, little by little.

That monster. She cursed loudly in her mind as hot tears festered, threatening to spill over. *I'll strangle him with my bare hands.*

Asha spoke louder and faster, forcing the device to tighten its grip, even more. Malkia could feel a discomfort in her stomach and winced when she saw her insides bulging in uncomfortable areas.

"Asha, what's it doing to me?" She grabbed her lower torso and closed her eyes again, forcing the tears to tumble down her cheeks.

Asha remained in her trance, speaking fast and furious. The words slipped out of her mouth and Malkia could hear the urgency in her voice.

After a few more moments, Asha quieted down and stopped chanting altogether. She raised her hand off Malkia's shoulder. Malkia opened her eyes, the pain quickly subsided as Asha slammed her hand back down on the device and at the same time, uttered a few loud words. Malkia felt the tentacles squirm through her body and slide rapidly toward her shoulder. It seemed like an eternity, but seconds later Asha held the device in her hand, shaking from exhaustion.

"Now that was a nasty little contraption," Asha muttered. She braced herself against the wall, dropping the device and stomping hard on the top of it.

Malkia felt the back of her shoulder where the device had been. There was blood oozing out of the hole, but her body was already healing itself. She bounced off the couch and tucked her arm around

Asha's waist. "It's my turn to be your support."

"Thanks," Asha breathed deeply, clasping onto Malkia's shoulder. "That was more exhausting, than I had anticipated. Dario is going to be furious, but then again, that makes it worth every ounce of energy."

The device squirmed and Malkia took her booted foot and smashed it to pieces. Then she propped Asha up against her body and helped her into her room.

"Rest for a while," Malkia ordered, assisting Asha onto the bed. "I'm going to lie down on the couch and allow my body to recuperate as well. When we wake, it will be time to devise a plan to rescue Rory and Misty, along with the deimos."

Asha yawned as she settled back into her bed. "Who is the deimos?"

"Those eyes," Malkia muttered, staring off into space. "Those eyes are a dead giveaway. Dario will figure it out soon, if he hasn't already."

She glanced down at Asha, whose eyes had shut and was snoring quietly.

"We can figure it out when you wake," Malkia whispered. She turned around and left the room, shutting the door behind her.

Malkia stared up at the ceiling, seeing those hazel eyes in her mind. *How could this be? Is it really who I think it is?*

The quiet was deafening, as she thought back to Esaki. Bella had seen the vision of Mataya and Justin. She had witnessed the dark figure, strike Justin over the head and Mataya had disappeared. The idea of her family descending from witches had appeared farfetched, but now the possibilities were becoming endless.

"Nothing is what it seems," Malkia whispered out loud, remembering the words Kelsey had carefully said. *What does Dario know? Why was he so eager to capture that deimos? And why did he threaten to kill it?*

"I have to go find the deimos," she said to the ceiling. "I have to discover what is really happening. Dario knows something, and if she is entrapped inside the deimos body, I have to rescue her."

"What are you mumbling over there?" Asha's quiet voice interrupted Malkia's thoughts.

Malkia sat up and glanced over at her friend. "I can't sit her much longer. That deimos is going to be Dario's final revenge against me. I don't know how it happened, but I'm certain that beast is my Esaki sister."

Asha seemed taken back but recovered quickly. "I've heard of people turning into animals for various reasons, but why would your sister be a deimos? Why would she be here? It doesn't seem likely."

"You never knew her," Malkia retorted. "I know it seems outlandish, but *you* don't know those eyes. So familiar. She was attempting to communicate, and she wanted me to see her eyes, so I could recognize her. Why didn't she burn in the flames? Why could I not snap her neck? Why was Dario so interested in capturing her? There are too many questions and I intend on finding the answers." She pulled her legs up on the couch, crossing them in front of her.

Asha settled in a chair near Malkia, her brows bumping together in a frown.

Malkia searched Asha's face, placing her elbows on her knees and setting her chin in her hands. "Kelsey said, 'Nothing is what it seems.' What does she mean by that? Why has nothing become easier? I completed the battle on Enyo. It's over. So, why do I feel like the war is just beginning? Why do I feel like I am farther away from rescuing my daughter? There is a mountain of thoughts racing through my mind right now, and Mataya being in that deimos body isn't as impossible as I would have believed a year ago, or even a month ago. My life has completely flipped. At this point, anything is possible."

Asha had closed her eyes, staring intently at the floor.

"Asha, do you know what's happening?"

The intercom sounded as Asha observed Malkia, tears brimming on the edge of her eyelids. She quickly rose, rushing to answer the call, at the other end of the room.

"Who is it?" Asha asked.

"Errandor desires to speak with Malkia," Tarance requested. "Is she present?"

"I am," Malkia replied. "Can Errandor wait? I have loose ends to tie up, before I meet with him?"

"Malkia, it isn't wise to keep Errandor waiting, when he requests your presence," Tarance sounded irritated. "I suggest you finish what you need to do and make yourself available quickly."

"Tarance, do you believe I'm indebted to you?" Malkia asked, rubbing her throbbing temples. "I just spent multiple days destroying those dreadful creatures, watching them burn, hearing them scream, feeling them leave. I'm entitled to a day of rest."

There was silence on the other end.

"Tarance?" Malkia's pulse quickened.

"Malkia, there is more happening," Tarance whispered through the intercom. "They have something. Someone. You won't be able to say no to them. I have to end this conversation, but I suggest you arrive soon to visit with Errandor. This is *not* over."

The connection ended and Asha stared silently at the wall.

"What have you not told me?" Malkia demanded.

Asha didn't budge.

"Don't ignore me," Malkia's voice grew loud. "What am I missing? Please don't shut me out now. Who do they have? Is it Mataya? Is that deimos really Mataya?"

Asha turned to face her. "I don't think it is. I think you are close, but the deimos is not Mataya," her voice shook with emotion.

"Stop it!" Malkia screamed. "What's going on? Spit it out."

"Please don't yell at me," Asha cried, fear and pain sweeping over her eyes. "I don't know for sure. I don't know if it is who I believe it to be. If I tell you my suspicions and it doesn't turn out to be true, I will have hurt you all over again. Please don't force me reveal what I suspect." Asha's tears toppled over her eyelids, and down her cheeks as she peered at Malkia.

Malkia could feel her body shaking, as if the moon was crumbling beneath her. The whole universe felt like it was ripping apart.

"Go to the pyramids, and find your feather," Asha pleaded. "Don't go see Errandor or Dario. I can't give you the answers you are looking for, but maybe they can."

"No!" Malkia cried, standing with her arms outstretched, her face hot from frustration. "You know something. Please don't make me go find Dario and rip him apart. Please, please tell me what is going on."

"I can't," Asha shook her head, taking a step back. "If it is true, what I believe, then you will rip Dario apart anyway. I'm not sure you will be able to contain your fury."

Malkia could feel her temperature rising. She turned away from Asha and before she walked out of the room, she surrounded herself with her light. The hallway was dark and quiet as Malkia raced down to the moving box. She pushed the button for the floor she knew has an outside entrance, facing the pyramids. The doors closed, and Malkia held her breath, until they opened a few moments later.

She flew through the rooms, ignoring the people she passed, controlling the urge to find Dario instead. The outside doorway was barred shut, but she flew through it with her light protecting her. She stopped on the other side, leaning over the stair railing and scrutinized the ground below her.

The stairs led down to an open grass area. The flowers inside the walls, were blooming and the trees were dancing with the wind. She peered past the broken buildings and charred homes and could see the tips of the pyramids. This time she didn't waste the time of running through the streets. The land had been scorched and the people were dead. There was no one down there to stop her from seeing the pyramids, and she didn't require concealment any longer. She flew, feeling the wind in her hair and the warmth of the suns.

When she reached the first pyramid, she could see it had been untouched by her fires. The rocks were jagged but aligned perfectly to form the giant triangle. She walked along the base, running her hand on each stone, examining the pictures and writings.

It took her the rest of the suns lights to finish the base. There were no symbols of feathers and now it was too dark to keep searching. Brightening her light, she attempted to search more, but settled back into the vegetation with frustration, unable to properly view the symbols. She would have to start again in the morning.

Dario was waiting for her when she arrived back to Errandor's building. "Where have you been?"

"Out and about. Away from you," Malkia snapped.

"Let me see your shoulder." He reached for her arm as she strolled by him.

"No." She twisted her body out of his reach and flew away.

"Don't you want to find your precious beast?" He yelled from behind her.

Malkia halted abruptly in her tracks and pivoted on her heel. Dario ambled toward her, his head cocked slightly to the side, and a grin dangled on the corners of his lips. "Isn't that right? You want to find that beast? There is something about that filthy deimos, that has you twisted into a knot. I can help unravel it for you."

He was close, too close. He put his hand on the small of her back and pulled her even closer. His warm breath on her face gave her the chills, as she thought of punching in the nose again.

"We could go back to the room and make everything better again," he breathed into her ear.

"Alright," she whispered.

He smiled down at her and clasped her hand before leading her back to the moving box. She grinned at him in the elevator and rubbed her other hand down his arm.

NIKI LIVINGSTON

"I knew we could always make this work. I can keep you safe. Once we finish off Errandor, you and I will acquire a significant role on this moon. I'll always take care of you."

Malkia gave him a wicked smile. "You always do take great care of me."

When they entered the room, Dario edged Malkia up against the wall, his hand roaming over her body while his mouth hungrily tasted her lips. Moments later, they eased their way into the bedroom. Malkia pushed him onto the warm bed where she climbed on top of his body. He groaned as she removed his black shirt, kissing his pecs and abs, moving slowly down his torso.

Reaching her hand up to his chest, she pressed hard just above his heart. She could feel her powers coursing through her hand as she sat up straight, holding him on the bed.

"Did you really believe I would allow for our unification, after all that has transpired? Are you that delusional?" Malkia questioned. Her facial muscles tensed, as her eyes burned with hatred.

His eyes widened, arching his neck in pain. "Malkia, stop! That hurts. What are you doing to me?"

"I'm stopping you from hurting me, ever again," she hissed, her energy growing in power, as her sparks slithered down her arms. "I'm preventing you from hurting anyone I love, *ever again*. It won't take long for the fire to burn inside your body. It will be over soon."

"Please Malkia. This isn't you. Please don't kill me," Dario pleaded, the fear rising in his eyes.

A frown spread over her face. "Are you serious? I'm exactly who you wanted me to be. I'm performing exactly the way everyone has intended me to act. You can't take it back now. You don't poke at the ritter, and not expect her to rip your head off."

Dario's body was heating up quickly and she could feel his heart racing. She hesitated long enough to feel the guilt, pulling back and enclosing him in her light. Her lips repeated Asha's dialect, although it was foreign, it came naturally. She could feel the magic enveloping her mind, and for the first time, performed the power of bending magic with no one's assistance. Her light around Dario thickened and strengthened, as it coursed through his body and held him in a vegetative state. His eyes had closed, and his body had cooled, but his heart remained beating in his chest and his lungs continued to breath.

"You stay here, big boy," Malkia patted the top of her barricade. Her smile had spread to her eyes, delighted by how powerful she had become. "I'll finish you off, after I know everyone I love is safe."

TWENTY-TWO
Misty's Freedom

MALKIA FOUND RORY and Misty before she ran into anyone else. She had searched three floors of the building, unable to find the deimos. Frustrated, she stormed into a small room that had been partially hidden behind some shelving.

"Malkia!" Misty cried. "How did you find us? They hexed this room, and I was unable to break through to you."

"The old-fashioned way," Malkia swooped over and embraced her little friend. "You have no idea how good it is to see you two alive. Let's leave now. Rory, do you still possess the paperwork that allows you onto your ship?"

"It's in my room," he replied, rising from his seated position. "We didn't have a chance to do much of anything, before Dario and that dog of his grabbed us."

Malkia sighed. "I forgot about that mutt. He's going to be looking for Dario. We need to act fast. Let's retrieve your items first, and then move onto the ship. I need to have you two departed, before I finish this conflict."

Rory and Misty were already moving through the door with Malkia. They raced through the quiet corridors and up the stairs, pausing at every corner in anticipation of Kelsey or the mutt.

As they stood outside Rory's door, Malkia encircled their quarters with her light, checking for any intruders. Easing their way into the room, she cloaked their presence, ensuring no one would discover their whereabouts. The more she used her ability to bend magic, the more skillful she became. Her powers pulsated within her, as she watched the other two gather up their meager possessions.

The race began when they were nearly to the ship. Malkia could feel the presence of others, and she knew they were advancing upon them. *Misty.* She thought. *Can you use your mind to find who is close to us?*

Yes, I think so.

They rounded the next corner, into the ships' hangar. Rory handed his paperwork to the red-headed woman, manning the entryway to the ships. She scanned a section with her handheld computer and Malkia saw the light turn green.

"This states, only two permitted to board the ship. Misty and Rory are listed as the occupants. Will you present your IDs, please?

Rory handed the lady his and Misty's picture IDs and waited while she scanned those as well.

The red-haired lady returned their IDs and signaled for them to walk through the gate. "Your ship is prepared on dock thirty-four. Here are your ship instructions, along with your schedule to depart. We will radio five minutes to departure time."

The woman turned to Malkia. "You're allowed to accompany them to their ship, but you aren't cleared to board. Please scan your ID when you arrive to the entryway to the ship, and the workers will give you instructions to the exit."

Malkia nodded, and Rory gathered all his paperwork and IDs. They began the long walk to dock thirty-four, putting them in full view of everyone in the docking area.

Malkia walked cautiously, her eyes scrutinizing the area. In her mind, she could see Misty searching for others, but now that they entered the docks, there were many workers roaming the walkways. The area was beginning to bustle with life, and the noise was growing, as they moved closer to the ship.

Misty gasped and Malkia could see Kelsey's mind. They were watching them from above and planning to swoop in before they reached the ship.

Misty, stay connected to her. I'm going to move us out of their view and then we can see what they do.

Okay. Misty thought.

Malkia used Misty's images in her mind to maneuver them toward a row of larger ships that placed Kelsey at an odd curvature and blocked them from her view. Once they were hidden from Kelsey's eyes, Malkia encircled all of them with her light, and using the same magic she had performed in their room, cloaked the three of them. She believed it would work, but as a new magic handler, she was unsure.

"Let's walk slowly now," Malkia whispered. "I have us enclosed, I hope. We will see once we are out in the open."

The trio began their walk again, keeping it slow and watching all their surroundings. Malkia watched Misty's thoughts, as she kept herself in Kelsey's mind. Kelsey had shifted, trying to obtain a better view of their whereabouts, allowing Malkia to discover their position.

"They are in the control room just above your ship," Malkia leaned close to Rory's ear. "They can't see us right now, but in order to make it inside your ship, I will have to reveal our location. Just before we reach the craft, I will uncloak both of you, and when I do you will need to move forward without me. They aren't concerned with you two. They want me. As soon as you board your craft, leave without clearance. They can't stop the ship once you depart. When I know you two are free and clear, I can end this once and for all."

Misty expelled her breath slowly, her eyes wide with worry.

"I love you, Misty." Malkia stopped walking and lowered herself to her knees, embracing the child. "You have been my backbone, my comrade, and my knight in shining armor. We have been through the worst, of the worst with one another, and all I require from you now is to find a quiet place, away from these monsters and be a kid. No more worries. No more running from monstrosities. And no more fears. Procure your mother from Esaki, and the three of you leave for the farthest lands you can find. Don't ever look back. Please."

Misty sobbed loudly, burying her face into Malkia's hair, grasping around her neck tightly. Malkia glanced up at Rory. "Please," she implored the man.

"I promise Malkia. I swear, I will find somewhere safe for them both."

Malkia separated herself from Misty and peered into her tear-filled eyes. "You are strong. I love you with all my heart, and when I see you again, I expect you to be experiencing the best life ever."

Misty nodded, clutching onto Malkia's hand, as she used her free hand to wipe away her tears.

Straightening back up, they continued their slow walk through the drafty docking area. The air was filled with the smell of coffee mixed with engine grease, reminding Malkia of the day she left Eris. A lifetime ago, leading to this very moment.

Malkia could see dock thirty-four. There were guards placed strategically around the area, waiting for them to arrive. She pulled the two around the side of one of the ships and made their way to the check in guard. She uncloaked them just before they left the shadows of the last ship.

"Go," she ordered. She nudged them forward and then slipped to the side, racing for the guards. She glanced back to see Rory handing over his ID and Misty watching her run.

Be safe. Malkia thought.

I love you, Malkia.

The guards were after her. She could sense them attempting to match her speed, but it didn't matter. All that was needed, was to draw them away from Rory. She knew he would accomplish his part.

Dashing through the bustling crowd of workers, she caught sight of Kelsey and the mutt up ahead. Kelsey wore her typical scowl, while Balbo grinned, obviously giddy for his chance at revenge. Malkia smiled at them, just before she flipped into the air and flew over their heads, landing on the other side, continuing her course.

We are in the ship. Misty's thoughts broke through her own. *My dad is preparing to take flight. No one is paying attention to us, so it shouldn't be difficult. Be safe, yourself, and please don't forget me.*

Never, Malkia thought. *Now leave and don't you dare come back.*

We are departing, now. Thank you.

Hugs girlie. Malkia's last thought, as she tore through the corridor, away from the docking area, and through the sitting lounge.

She glanced back and could see the large group racing to capture her, all because Kelsey and her mother commanded it. Malkia zoomed forward, leaving the group behind her. She needed to find the deimos. Now that Misty was safe, she only needed Asha, and the deimos, and then she could leave. She raced through each room, her protective light creating a barrier from anything in her way.

She was nearly to the basement when she was stopped short at the end of the stairway. The door wouldn't budge, and her protective light was not allowing her to penetrate the wall. She opened her mind and closed her eyes, searching for some magic to support her to the other side.

It didn't take long to feel the magic pulsating through her body. Shifting it with her mind, she bent the energy to form a window in the wall, large enough for her to ease through. As she did, she came face to face with Emelia and several of her guards.

TWENTY-THREE
Malkia's Esaki Mother

"CLEVER GIRL," EMELIA curled her lips, with icy condescension. "Although we already planned for this scenario, so we must be slightly more intelligent."

Malkia could feel her body quickly deteriorate, as she stood in the nearly white room. The guards had her surrounded, and Emelia's grin had spread across her face. Twisting around, the bright room grew warmer, creating beads of sweat on her forehead and a tightness in her chest. She wiped the droplets from her forehead as she searched for a doorway but saw no way of escape as her powers drained rapidly.

"What is this place?" Malkia searched the space around her for any magic to assist her.

"This place?" Emelia chided. "This place was prepared, just for you." She chuckled, her nose in the air. "As you are probably feeling, at this very moment, your powers draining instantly from your body. The only magic it contains, is so intensely dark, it will terminate a person if they fight it. Now, I will take my leave and the moment we are prepared, you will be brought to Errandor, where you will choose to end his life or witness the death of your mother, all over again."

Malkia fell to her knees with exhaustion, watching Emelia and the guards depart through a raised portion of the wall. It slid back down, enclosing her. Peering frantically around the room for any way of escape, breathing in sharply when she noticed it was completely empty.

Moments later the wall to her right lit up, as if she was looking through a window into another room. A woman with long dark hair was curled up on the floor, in the far corner of the room. She moved slightly, noticing the change in the wall as well. Rising into a seated position, she peered over at Malkia.

Malkia's eyes widened with surprise. "Mom," she whispered.

The woman jumped up, running to the wall. Tears streamed down her tanned face, her familiar hazel eyes, looking through the window, as Malkia placed her hand up against the wall, matching her mother's. Her own eyes filled with tears, as she gazed at the woman who had raised her.

"Mom," Malkia cried. Her voice was louder.

Her mother shook her head and mouthed, "I cannot hear you."

Malkia mouthed back, "I will save you."

"No." Her mother shook her head again. "Save yourself."

Malkia put her other hand up against the wall and shook her head back at her mom.

The wall in her mother's room rose and the guards rushed into the room, snatching her. Malkia saw the needle in one of their hands, and the fear in her mom's eyes.

"Leave her alone you bastards," Malkia screamed, beating relentlessly at the wall.

She observed in misery, as her mother lost consciousness, reverting to the form of the deimos. The guards covered her with thick fabric, steadying her as she raised off the ground and floated out of the room. Emelia walked into her mother's room, focusing on Malkia.

"Now you know what's at stake," Emelia's voice was heard overhead. "I will be back soon, to escort you to Errandor." Emelia turned swiftly, departing the room.

Malkia watched the wall close and fell into a heap on the floor. Slamming her fist against the floor, she heard her bones crack. Pain shot through her arm, and she rolled on her back, screaming louder than she had ever before. Memories of her mother on Esaki raced through her mind.

How did this happen? How is she alive? How did Emelia know the deimos was my mother? The tears fell rapidly, and she felt the anger surging in her heart. *Why did she not return and tell me she was alive?*

Malkia jumped up and landed on her feet. An anger and pain throbbed in her chest, one that she had never experienced before. Emelia had threatened her on too many occasions. She had imprisoned Misty and used her own children to gain Malkia's trust. Now she was hurting her mother, a woman she believed dead for nine years.

That woman told me to not allow my emotions to run my decisions, but after all of this, I think that's exactly what I must do. Her skin was on fire, as she felt her blood pressure rise with the heat. She closed her eyes and searched for the dark magic Emelia had mentioned. *Who said I can't use dark magic?*

Her mind raced as she felt a darkness seep into her mind, an energy coursing through her body, unlike anything she had felt before. Her strength built on that energy, allowing it to grow inside her. Feeling the rush of ecstasy slide down her body, she noticed as the bones in her hand realigned and the pain dissipated.

Emelia has no idea who she's dealing with, she thought.

Malkia pulled her light from her body, but she noticed it was no longer purple. It was fiery red and pulsated in time with her heart. She used the dark magic to build the light and strengthen it around her body. Just as she finished, the door to her room opened, and Emelia stopped short just inside the doorway, her eyes quickly widening.

Malkia stepped closer to the woman, balling her hands into fists. "I warned you what the outcome would be if you continued to step on my toes. You built a room using dark magic, believing it would imprison me, in hopes of controlling me? Your family is nothing but animals, and my patience has faltered to a degree of no remorse. I am no longer fearful of destroying anyone who continues to keep me from finding my daughter." She peered into Emelia's eyes, hovering ominously over her. "I wish this could have been different. I truly loved your son." She hesitated, seeing the petite woman trembling. "Good-bye Emelia."

Releasing the heat from her body, the explosion rippled through the air, tearing through the woman's body. Malkia observed from the safety of her light as the body parts disintegrated, along with the glass walls surrounding Malkia. The building quivered from the detonation, and Malkia knew it would not be long before it crumbled. She flew out of the area, using the magic to lead her to her mother.

Several floors above, she found her in a cage being prepared to load into a ship. With one sweep of her hand, Malkia was able to knock out all the personnel and guards. She raced over to the cage and unlocked the door. The deimos was still unconscious. Malkia used her newfound powers to levitate the animal, enclosing her inside her protective light.

It took longer to make it to Asha, then she wanted. The warlock was packed and waiting when Malkia entered the room.

"You have made a mess of the building, haven't you?" Asha questioned.

"Don't lecture me," Malkia snapped at her friend, settling the deimos onto the ground in front of Asha. "Everyone thinks they know how this should have played out. All of you stand in judgment, while I perform most of the work. Keep your lectures to yourself, and help me rid my mother of this deimos body"

Asha pursed her lips, shaking her head as she placed her hands on the deimos head. Allowing her witch dialect to flow from her lips, Malkia regarded the light that appeared out of Asha's hands and entered her mother's head. Asha reached out with one hand and clutched Malkia's. She nodded toward the deimos back.

Malkia put her other hand on her mother's back and listened as Asha repeatedly muttered the eccentric words. The light began to course through all three bodies, and Malkia could feel the same energy she had experienced down in the white room.

"The dark magic, you have now allowed into your soul, will forever have a place in your mind," Asha spoke, eyeing Malkia with a sideways look. "You will never be able to free yourself from its grasp. You'll only be able to learn to control it or allow it to consume you. It will be what saves your mother, but it might be your downfall."

"I told you to end the lectures." Malkia closed her eyes.

"I'm only giving you a warning. I love you too much to see this magic destroy you." Asha returned to her strange utterings, closing her eyes and turning her face to the ceiling. The energy saturated the room and the deimos body began to glow, while it shifted to its human form.

Within seconds, Malkia's mom was lying naked on the floor. Grabbing a blanket, Malkia wrapped it around the still body.

"Now what?" Asha stood up, rubbing her hands together.

Malkia ran her hand through her mother's hair, peering up at Asha. "We need a safe place, where she can mend. I have to evacuate the building before Dario's family adds any more problems to my plate. I don't know what else to do but destroy their entire family and ensure everyone else is safely out of this fortress."

"Time to leave, then," Asha replied, picking up their belongings.

Malkia hoisted her mother over her shoulder and encircled them both in her now, maroon light. She could feel the dark and light energies swarming through her body, fighting for their dominance in her soul. *I'll worry about this at a later point.*

Arriving to the shipping docks, they noticed the area had been cleared of personnel as the building shook and rattled. Several ships remained, but it was only a matter of time before the remaining crowds gained access to what was left.

Malkia loaded her unconscious mother into the ship. Asha took the controls and waited for Malkia to leave.

"I will meet you at the pyramids," Malkia instructed, as she hurried over the threshold. "If I don't make it, take my mom back to Esaki."

Asha yelled after her. "You will make it. I'll see you soon."

Malkia stepped away from the ship, backing up as Asha guided it into the air and exited. The smell of the ships electric current was all that remained as she watched the sky, feeling the rumble of the building.

"Where are my daughter and grandson?" A voice behind her asked.

Malkia slowly turned, already knowing whom she was about to face.

Ginny's tall frame stood not far from her, Kelsey on one side and Balbo on the other.

"I have your grandson," Malkia replied. Her light remained strong around her body, but Ginny didn't seem to fear her.

"Malkia, I know you believe you can beat me, and your light will protect you from my family, but you don't seem to comprehend the situation." She stepped forward, her eyes intently staring at Malkia. "You have been so focused on the victory of the Enyoan war and finding a mother who was dead to you only yesterday, that you missed everything else that was occurring. Errandor and Tarance already escaped. They only allowed their favorite people to accompany them and abandoned the remainder of their people to perish in this crumbling building." Ginny shook her head, her lips set in a grim line. "Don't you see? All along you were fighting for the wrong people."

"How were they the wrong people? Are you saying you are the right people?" Malkia questioned, eyeing the woman with hatred. "Your grandchildren who lied and masqueraded as my allies, then forced me to fight a war that was not mine. Are they the right people?" Her condescending tone increased, as her eyes crinkled in disgust. "Or tell me, was it your son's wife, the woman who scrutinized and ridiculed me every chance she could. Is she the right person? You're so smart, Ginny. Why don't you tell me, who *are* the right people?"

A smile twitched on the edges of Ginny's lips, as her fingers stroked the ends of her hair. "I never claimed we were the right ones. I only said you were fighting for the wrong people. You have been played, once again. Everyone you know was strategically positioned, in order to arrive at this exact outcome. You have never had anyone on your side. And frankly, you never had a choice in the matter."

Malkia felt the heat in her face increase, as she glared at the white-haired woman. "Your daughter is dead," she shouted, wanting to hurt the old hag in anyway she could. "Was that part of your strategy? What about the scenario, where I rip you all apart, along with Dario and anyone else who's determined to stop me? You don't control me. You think you had this figured out, but you forget, I have my own mind."

The air around her was shimmering with heat and she could see her light growing stronger around her, darkening to maroon. The mutt was growling, and Kelsey's scowl had turned to anger, upon hearing of her mother's death. Ginny's expression remained devoid of emotion, just like Dario and Emelia.

Ginny took another step forward. "I knew you would absorb the dark magic. It's the natural tendency of any strong warrior. I warned Emelia of the probability, and she chose to ignore me." She shrugged her shoulders. "Her death is on herself. Do you have any idea what powers I possess?"

"Are you actually going to tell me?" Malkia screamed at the woman, hating herself for losing control of her emotions.

"No," Ginny shook her head, the same smile dancing on her lips. "But I will show you."

The trembling of the building intensified, as the walls cracked and shattered around them, just as a piercing light burst from Ginny's body. "Do you think it was the Artemisians who created the shaking and the bright light?" Her smile stretched across her face. "Or do you think I wanted you to believe it was those filthy creatures?" Ginny took another step forward, her light blinding Malkia's eyes, making her shield herself with her hands.

Without waiting for an answer from Malkia, Ginny continued speaking, "What about your father? Do you really believe he wouldn't have devised multiple plans, to force your hand? Once your mother showed her lack of loyalty, he turned to another, and now, so many years later we will finish what we started. We will destroy every single Artemisian in this system, and make every inhabitant, on every moon, fear us to the depths of their souls." She paused, taking another step closer to Malkia. "Finally, the demons have been annihilated here on Enyo, and soon, we will all leave for Eris. You will destroy what remains of them and then it will be over, and I'll be able to be with the man I love. It was never the plan to lead on Enyo, at least not for me. It was always bigger." She chuckled, her hands rising in front of her, pointing at Malkia. "See how my light is consuming yours? See how my shaking can destroy the building, and kill every person remaining inside? It's time to stop fighting and finish what you were created to do."

Malkia averted her eyes from the bright light, but she could see it absorbing her maroon glow. The building continued to shake, and Malkia knew if she didn't stop it soon, the added pressure would bring it down on top of all who remained. "What do you want me to do?"

The shaking lessened and Ginny eased her light back into her body. Balbo and Kelsey took their hands off their eyes and blinked rapidly.

"Mamu, what does this all mean?" Kelsey asked Ginny.

"Kelsey, your worry is unnecessary. Remain fighting alongside me, and you will be the victor."

Kelsey moved toward her mamu, her eyes glistening with tears. "You knew any one of us could be killed, at any time, and you never revealed to us your true reasons for pursuing leadership. Why? What about Dario? What about my mother?"

Ginny turned and glared at Kelsey. "You're about as useless as a tree stump. Stop your whining. Your mother was aware of the dangers and sacrifices to become leader of Enyo. You all were aware. What's the difference now? It's only a wider scope. You can choose to be on my side or die alongside the losers."

Hurt spread over Kelsey's face, as she listened to her mamu's words. Ginny twisted back to face Malkia, without another glance at Kelsey or Balbo.

"You need to find Errandor and Tarance and destroy them both. Once you are done, we will leave this moon and head to Eris, where you will terminate the remainder of the Artemisians and all their deimos." Ginny repeated herself, enunciating each of her words, as she eased her way closer to Malkia. "If you accomplish this, I will allow your Esaki mother and your Eris mother to go free, along with your daughter. They will be banned to the farthest moon, but they will be allowed to live. Once they are gone, I will end your life. There is only room for one goddess in this system, and it is *not* you."

Malkia shook her head, her face muscles tightening. "I'm not a goddess."

Ginny's smile had returned. "I know that. You know that. But most others don't." She placed her hand on Malkia's shoulder. "Your death will be the icing on the dessert, and I will finally be free of your shadow."

Malkia peered into the hateful woman's, stone cold eyes. "Do you at least want your grandson freed before we leave?" She asked.

"Yes. Yes, I would. Let's go do that now, and then we will be off to track Errandor."

Malkia led the way through the docking area and out into the corridor. She walked as slowly as she dared, rummaging through her mind for escape routes. She felt crushed. Her father had ensured her defeat, never giving her a chance for another life.

The walk to Dario's room didn't last as long as she'd hoped. Malkia put her hand on his chest and slowly unraveled the spell enclosing his body, watching as his body warmed and his heart returned to its normal beat. A few moments passed, and Dario opened his eyes.

"Kelsey, did we win?" Dario asked. He stared keenly at Malkia.

"We are close, dear brother. Mamu had a few surprises for all of us, but she seems to know what she is doing."

Ginny reached over and placed a hand on Dario's arm. "Of course, I know what I'm doing. This has been a moment I premeditated, for many years. Let's move on to our ship." Ginny turned to Malkia. "I suggest we evacuate the remaining people before the building tumbles. Don't you agree?"

"Yes, thank you," Malkia replied.

Ginny clutched Malkia's arm. "I'm watching you. Don't do anything you'll regret."

"I won't," she muttered, yanking her arm from Ginny's grasp, and racing out of the room.

TWENTY-FOUR
The Light Beings

MALKIA HAD LOADED the rest of the ships with people from the building before the trembling structure began to sway. She was sitting in the docking area with the last ship when Ginny and her posse rounded the corner. The shaking increased, and Malkia could feel the building shift. She opened the hatch door to the ship and waited inside for the remainder of the group.

Moments later a grinning Dario waltzed in, followed by his loyal mutt and grumpy sister. Ginny was last to board. They all took their seats after the door was secured, with Kelsey at the controls.

"Where to?" Kelsey asked. She had turned on the flying machine and was moving it out of the docking area, just when Malkia saw the building tilt to the other side.

"Hurry!" Malkia shouted.

Kelsey pulled up, as the building crumbled to the ground. She edged the ship away from the flying debris and growing cloud of dirt, barely missing a direct hit.

Ginny was the only one who remained calm. "The pyramids please. That would be the first place Errandor would seek shelter. If he's not at the large one, he will be hiding at one of the smaller ones."

"I was unaware we could enter the pyramids." Dario swiveled to see Ginny. "They found a way in?"

"You are all a little foolish and naïve," Ginny smiled, drumming her fingers on the arm of her chair. "There's a way in. Errandor has always known how to access the pyramids. He kept it to himself in the event of this exact scenario. If that building had ever been taken over by the Artemisians, he always knew he would be safe in the pyramids. He's a selfish, weak man, and I will be delighted to see his life leave his body."

Malkia eyed the pyramid as they approached and knew Asha and her mother were in a ship nearby. She hoped Asha was aware enough, to keep her distance.

She stood up from her seat and followed Ginny off the ship. The suns had set again, and she knew it would be harder to find anyone or anything at this hour. Ginny didn't seem worried as they approached the base of the pyramid.

Ginny walked to the north of the structure, picking her way carefully over the rough ground. Malkia watched as Ginny's light expanded out of her body and began to light the way for all of them.

How does she do that, and if she is so powerful, why did they ever need me? And what did she mean when she said she would finally be free from my shadow? As far as I'm concerned, she could have ended this war all on her own.

She shook her head, trying to understand her father's plan. Why had she been so foolish? Why had she not seen the possibility of her father having an ally on this moon? It seemed like a big game, and she was always on the losing end.

"We're here," Ginny interrupted Malkia's thoughts.

Malkia peered up at the giant building, looking for the entryway but not seeing it.

"Where?" Dario asked, scanning over the stones.

Ginny placed her hand on Malkia's back. "I can't make the door appear, only Malkia can. She's the only one here who can bend magic. The doorway has been cloaked, but Malkia will be able to break the barrier."

"Move over," Malkia shifted away from Ginny and around Dario. She closed her eyes, searching for the magic surrounding the pyramid.

Sensing the magic, she paused, feeling the presence of the light beings as well. Their energy coursed through her body, and she inhaled sharply, remembering the moment she had touched the etching of the feather, back on Esaki. Keeping her eyes closed, she searched for the feather with her mind, feeling the vitality stronger than the magic.

She felt a hand on her shoulder and her eyes flew open. Dario was standing next to her looking at her face. "Anything yet?" he asked.

"Seriously, Dario," she snapped at him. "I was finally adjacent with the magic, and your stupidity pulled me away."

"Dario, back off," Ginny ordered. "Let her complete the task. She's just as anxious to finish this as the rest of us, so discontinue your hovering."

Dario glanced back at his mamu, his jaw clinched. However, he moved away from Malkia and settled back by Balbo.

Turning back to the pyramid, Malkia closed her eyes again searching for the feather. *There you are.* She smiled softly seeing the symbol about twenty feet above her and slightly to the left. Leaping high into the air, she placed her hand on the feather, just as she peered back at Ginny and saw her light bursting toward her. *You're too late, you bitch.*

Malkia felt herself move through time and space. Maybe it was because she was flying when she touched the feathers or maybe she was more aware this time, but the exhilaration created a tickle in her stomach, making her laugh out loud.

She landed on the soft vegetation with a thud. It was no longer dark outside. She glanced around at her surroundings, expecting to see the beings around her, like the last time. Instead, there were tall, dark trees on every side, with a path leading through some brush in front of her. She walked cautiously along the dirt path, breathing in the deep scent of the thick tree bark, while she dodged the large branches hanging loosely in the trail.

The flowers bloomed from every nook and cranny, possessing the most amazingly, vibrant colors against the dark browns and deep greens of the trees. Malkia felt like she was in an enchantment, as her eyes took in the beauty surrounding her at every angle. The chirps of birds and insects could be heard all around, along with the scurrying of small animals in every direction. It was a wonderland of sorts, a place she had never seen or heard of before.

Where am I? Malkia asked herself.

"This is where you want to end your journey," a strong voice came from behind her.

Malkia whipped around, expecting to see a new enemy. One of the tall light beings stood back in the trees. Another two emerged from the trees, all of them gliding toward her.

"What is this place?"

"It's the one place you'll be safe, after you finish your war. You still have the means to make it here." One of the beings glided forward, its voice echoing through the trees. "You still have the chance to enjoy everything you ever wanted. Just be mindful of the bigger picture and don't do anything that goes against your intuition. You have it all inside of you. Every answer and every solution. Keep digging. It will surface, and as long as you remember what is really important, you will arrive to your final destination. The place you have always wanted to be."

"Why the cryptic message?" Malkia groaned. Even these beings were playing games with her.

Another being shifted forward, halting next to its companion. "You already have the answers, Malkia. You're capable of healing this star system and ending the bloodbath. Look deep inside and discern the answer. Discover your true and full potential."

"I don't know what you're talking about." Malkia shook her head. "Ginny has already won. My strength has been matched, if not overrun."

The beings grew in stature, their lights expanded, as their voices echoed loudly around her. "Do not play small, Malkia. Remember who you are."

The beings disappeared in an instant, and Malkia was left with the sounds of the forest life.

"Who am I?" Malkia asked, aloud. She glanced around, feeling the warmth of the suns on her skin. Following the light she walked out on top of a mountain side, seeing a whole new world in front of her.

The trees rose in every direction, with endless views of mountain tops, revealing massive waterfalls with their outpouring of never-ending water. She peered down the cliff she stood on and gasped at the roaring river snaking through the rocks below her.

The sound of the ocean waves crashing against the shore, rang in her ears. She flew into the air, looking over the overabundance of trees and breathed in deeply when she caught sight of the white sand and the clear as glass water, glistening from the suns light. The sound of the waves was music to her ears, and she knew this place was always meant to be her home.

"How do I find this place?" Malkia said, loudly. She hoped the beings would come back as she settled onto the beach.

"Go back to Enyo. You will become aware, once you accomplish your tasks," the voice was heard all around her, as if it thundered from the ocean.

Malkia glanced around, searching the trees and the beach for the beings. She wanted to know more but realized this was going to be up to her. "How long do I have?"

"Not long. Prepare yourself. Once you arrive, you will need to cloak your whereabouts."

"Thank you," Malkia replied to the wind. "Will you warn me before you send me back?"

"No. It will happen when it's meant to happen"

Malkia nodded and nestled into the sand, feeling the energy of the planet envelop around her body. The power it emanated, created a warmth and excitement deep within Malkia and for the first time since she began running on Esaki, she felt whole.

TWENTY-FIVE

Controlling the Darkness

THE SOUND OF a bomb reverberated in her ears as Malkia returned to Enyo. She crouched in the place that she landed, covering her ears with her hands, and waiting for the dust to clear. Trying not to cough, she peeked up from her position and noticed Dario standing through the trees, with his hand over his mouth and nose.

"Are you out of your mind?" Malkia heard Kelsey scream.

"It was the best idea I could think up," Dario shifted to the side, moving out of Malkia's line of sight. "Mamu said to open the door, at all costs. I didn't hear any of your notions."

"What in god's name made you think a bomb would blow open a door that is protected by magic? I might not be the smartest one in this group, but even I know that's a lame move," Kelsey hissed from her hiding spot.

"When will Ginny return," Balbo spoke up. Malkia tiptoed closer, seeing the mutt farther away, lurking behind a small building.

"I thought she would've returned by now," Kelsey replied. "From the little she said, she believed she had a way to coax Malkia back here."

The suns were up high in the sky, which meant Malkia had been gone for at least a half of a day. She cloaked herself with the magic in the air and slid away from her enemies. She glanced around for Asha's ship but could see nothing beyond the one in which they'd come.

Where would Ginny go? Does she really know how to force me to come? Really, who is this woman and how did she obtain her powers?

Malkia moved farther away, keeping her eye out for Asha as well as Ginny. As she moved around the pyramid, she caught a glimpse of something shining near the two other pyramids. She rose and floated over to that area, keeping enough distance until she knew it was safe. As she crept closer, she could see the ship Asha had taken. There was no movement anywhere around it, but the door remained closed, and the windows were obscured.

I need to take a step back. It could be a trap. They said I already had the solutions and answers inside of me, so it's time to find out what those are, before I fall into another trap. In all honesty, it is my senselessness that places me in these messes.

Malkia moved away from the craft, examining the two smaller structures. They had strange writings all over them, along with drawings of people pointing to the sky. The suns and Theia were etched in the rock in multiple places and Malkia wondered about their significance, and what the ancient civilizations were describing.

Halting abruptly in front of the middle pyramid, she recognized the symbol of the feather. She peered around, confirming she wasn't being watched. Lifting her hand she elevated toward the symbol, just as a door to one side opened. Asha walked out with her mother. They both peeked around the uprights of the door.

"It's clear," her mother whispered, glancing behind.

Errandor and Tarance moved out of the pyramid and into the sun.

They both tilted their faces up to the sky and smiled.

"Ginny will be coming soon. She won't rest until we are dead," Tarance said, his eyes closed and his face warming up from the suns.

"What about my daughter?" Malkia's mom scolded. "She has given her life for your war. You can't just leave her here."

Malkia watched her mother in amazement. Her scowl was identical from nine years ago. Her hair and eyes, reminding her of the earlier years where she would snuggle into her mother's chest, and look into her eyes while she hummed her a song or articulated a story. She thought she would never see this woman again, but there she was, standing strong while she defended her.

"Mom," Malkia whispered, waving her hand to uncloak herself.

Her mom turned her head slightly, glancing over at Malkia. Her eyes widened as Malkia tumbled into her arms. Her body shook as she sobbed into her mother's neck, allowing this woman to hold her close.

Alyssa pulled back and put her hands on both of Malkia's cheeks. "I have missed this face," she said.

"Where have you been?" Malkia asked, hiccupping from the sobs. "What happened? I buried you. I saw your lifeless body. How did you end up in a deimos body? How did all of this happen?"

"So many questions," Alyssa replied, frowning in thought. Inhaling deeply, she gave Malkia a weary smile. "Nothing has changed, I see. You are still full of life and mischief."

"I wouldn't call this mischief," Malkia whispered. "My life has been full of uncertainty and heartbreak, and you being alive has added to that list."

"I love you, my Malkia," her mother pulled her into another

embrace. "We will talk. But first, let's leave this moon and find a safe and quiet place, to enjoy a heart-to-heart."

"What about Ginny?"

"What about her?" Asha interrupted.

Malkia turned, touching her collar bone with the tips of her fingers. "She's more powerful than I was prepared for, and she's my father's lover. They had this calculated, from the beginning. The war on Enyo was only a ploy to shift my focus and force my hand against the Artemisians. Now I must finish what I started, by going to Eris and ending their feud, as well. If I don't, Ginny will kill my birth mother and my daughter."

"They have Esta?" her mother interjected.

"Yes, she's with my birth parents on Eris. I have to return there first and save them both."

Errandor cleared his throat. "If you leave before Ginny is killed, the Enyo people will only become slaves to a new master."

"What about you, Errandor?" Malkia snapped at the old man. "Why haven't you done anything to help defend these people? You say you were shot in battle, but ever since I've arrived on this god forsaken moon, I haven't seen one Enyoan pick up their sword and fight their own battles. It has been Asha, Misty, and me. Why are you sitting on the sidelines, when this woman you claim to be friends with has been conspiring behind your back, for over twenty years?"

"Don't be foolish." Errandor straightened his back and stuck out his chest. "I have been fighting against the Artemisians for years, and yes, I've battled them directly. We have all done our fair share. You're still an infant in this charade, and someday when you reminisce, you will see how senseless you sound."

"Regardless," Malkia grimaced, her toes tapping the ground. "There seems to be more to the story, than what you have revealed. You abandoned your people in that crumbling building and had no intentions of saving anyone but yourself. Why would you leave them? Why would you not ensure they were unharmed before you found your own safety?"

Errandor glared at Malkia. "How dare you question my governance? I've been running this region, far longer than you've been living. I don't need a sniveling child telling me how to be a better leader."

"Sniveling child? This is ridiculous," Malkia smirked. "You had no problems having this sniveling child, liberate your people." She stepped closer, clenching her fists. "I don't agree with you. You may be these people's leader, but your actions are atrocious. Allowing your people to be slaves to those barbarians, while you assembled in your comfortable and safe building, doesn't make you a leader. I realize you fought the Artemisians, but you never went above and beyond to free your people."

"We don't have time for you two to bicker," Tarance interrupted, blocking her view of Errandor. "Ginny thought we were in the larger pyramid, but it's only a matter of time before she shifts her focus. We require a quick departure."

"Agreed," Asha stated. "Whatever we do, we can discuss it after we have moved to a safer area."

"Where to?" Malkia questioned Errandor.

"I have no other safe house here on Enyo. We either face Ginny or start running for our lives."

"Does anyone know what abilities Ginny possesses?" Malkia asked the group.

"I do. I know what she can perform, and it's not significant." Alyssa eased forward, her hands grasped behind her back.

"What do you mean?" Asha asked.

Alyssa expelled her breath, her brows furrowing with thought. "I mean, I know what she is capable of. I met her before, many years before Malkia came to live with me. She's an Illusionist. What she possesses is nothing more than manipulating a person's mind. The shaking and the bright light are all an illusion. She can bend your thoughts, as you can bend magic."

Malkia's jaw dropped, her eyes wide with shock. "Wait. I saw her light absorbing mine. Are you telling me that wasn't really happening? She was able to intrude into my mind without my knowing?"

"I doubt she meddled too far into your mind," Alyssa touched Malkia's arm. "That is one of your greatest powers, the ability to keep people from entering your mind."

"You know what all my powers are?"

"Of course, I do," Alyssa smiled. "I'll go into more detail later, but for now let's focus on Ginny and her family. It's time to finish what you've started, if only to protect your own family."

Malkia nodded. "Okay, let's go find her."

The three women stepped forward, as Errandor and Tarance slipped quietly back into the pyramid.

They still won't fight their own war, Malkia thought.

She huffed in disgust, as she concentrated on the larger structure, walking in between the two powerful witches. She could feel their powers brewing between the three of them and the more she focused, the more her own energy stirred within her.

Reaching out, she clutched her mother's and Asha's hands. "I had no idea you were both so powerful. The energy is overwhelming to say the least, but I believe I just found our solution to ending Ginny and her family. They said I knew. They said it was already in me."

"Who said?" Malkia's mother asked.

"The light beings."

"You saw them?" Alyssa's voice climbed an octave.

"Yes," Malkia said, a grin dancing on the edges of her lips. "This is the second time I've seen them."

"You and Ginny are more alike than I realized," her mother whispered.

Malkia abruptly halted, her smile fading. "What do you mean?"

Alyssa turned to face Malkia, grabbing both of her hands. "Ginny has seen the light beings before. Years ago. Before you were born. I know she tried to return to them but couldn't enable the feather to transport her there. She felt abandoned, and many believe it was what turned her into who she is today. I don't know much about what transpired after, as I was entrusted with your life and was excluded from the network of information, but what I did witness, was turning her heart ice cold."

"I wonder why they wouldn't allow her to return," Malkia mused aloud.

"Does it matter now?" Ginny's voice seemed to be swirling around them.

Malkia whipped her head around, searching for the woman. Dario, Kelsey, and Balbo stood in the shadows of the trees that separated the smaller pyramids from the larger one.

"Where is she?" Malkia asked.

"Why would we tell you that?" Dario snickered, crossing his arms over his chest.

Malkia glared at the man she had once loved. "You're an imbecile, Dario."

Ginny walked out from behind the trio. "Malkia, you've had your last chance. I no longer have a need for you or anyone else you love."

Ginny's light burst from her body, just as Malkia encircled the three women with her maroon glow. The bright white sun bounced off Malkia's energy, but within a few moments Malkia could see it absorbing her light, once again.

"You can do this," Alyssa urged. "Don't allow her into your head. Resist her."

Alyssa and Asha took ahold of her hands, and Malkia felt the magic coursing through her body. She closed her eyes and forced her energy out farther, feeling it strengthen and rebuff the bright light.

You can't defeat me. Malkia heard Ginny's voice in her head.

Malkia opened her eyes in surprise and felt her energy weaken, as she squinted over at the tall woman. With a wide grin on her face, Ginny nudged her light forward, causing the ground to shake beneath Malkia. She released the witch's hands, as she struggled against the iron grip of fear.

How are you in my head?

I always have been. You thought you had beat me. You thought you could win this war, but no one knew what I was capable of. You will be unable to withstand my powers, and when I'm done with you, I will rip your mother apart. Then I'll go to Haltia and Esta and dismember both. This is the end of your powers, and the end of you.

Malkia cried out in anger at the mention of her daughter. Grasping her mother's and Asha's hands again, she felt the magic and energy combined into one force. She swirled it through her body and twisted it through her light. Closing her eyes, she focused on Ginny and the three others.

"Careful, my sweet angel," Alyssa coaxed, squeezing Malkia's hand. "Don't do anything out of anger. She's taunting you and desires you to embrace that dark magic inside you. It's what damaged her. I can feel it, and I can see her rage and her jealousy. Despite her wish to have never fallen for the darkness, there is no coming back and she knows. She knows exactly what she's doing to you. You'll never make it to where the light beings have promised, if you allow the darkness to take control of your soul."

Malkia opened her eyes and glanced over at her mother. "She's going to execute all of you, and Esta. How else do I stop her?"

Alyssa brought her other hand to Malkia's cheek. "I never said you couldn't end her life. I said, don't do it out of anger. Do not allow the darkness to consume your soul. She already knows she has lost this battle and her goal is to now, take you with her."

Malkia glimpsed over at Ginny and could see the madness in the woman's eyes. She slammed her eyes shut and searched for the light. The energy from the darkness continued to swirl through and around her, and as she shifted it back, she felt Ginny's energy grow in strength. Malkia focused on her purple light, envisioning how it looked and felt.

It was there, buried beneath the darkness. She forced the darkness to dissipate, sensing her purple light take control and quickly growing stronger.

You will fall to the darkness. Ginny's thoughts interrupted Malkia's concentration.

The dark magic burst through her purple light, as she stumbled from Ginny's words. Her light was smothered beneath the red light, once again, and Malkia could feel the blackness swirling in her mind, accelerating her anger back to the surface. She mentally shoved at Ginny's bright light again and opened her eyes to see the redness grasping onto her four enemies. As it twisted their bodies, she sensed the expansion and strength of her powers, her irises taking on a red glow.

"Malkia, think of your daughter. Think of Esta," Alyssa's voice interrupted her vision.

Esta's face leapt into Malkia's mind. *"Stay out of my head,"* she screamed at the white-haired woman.

Malkia's purple light erupted from her body, and as she clutched Alyssa's and Asha's hands once more, their combined force took hold of her enemy's bodies. Ginny's eyes widened with surprise, as their energy wrapped around each body, causing the mutt to howl, and Kelsey to scream in agony.

Dario remained silent, but Malkia could see the pain in his eyes. Even after all the damage he'd done, she still felt guilty for hurting him. She needed his life to end, focusing most of their powers on him. Watching him writhe in pain, she recoiled, as he slipped from her grasp and tumbled out of sight, far past the pyramids.

Gasping in shock, she focused on her other three hostages, who remained seized within her light. Ginny's face had contorted in fury and Malkia could sense her abilities pressing through the barrier. She closed her eyes and exerted all her light, snapping their bodies in half and feeling their souls retire from their shells, as she settled them back onto the ground.

Sucking in a deep breath, the darkness no longer consumed her heart and mind, and Malkia bid their souls good-bye. She felt the pain and agony they had inflicted on so many others, release into the open sky.

TWENTY-SIX
Leaving Enyo

"*YOU DID IT,*" Tarance smiled at Malkia as Errandor and he waltzed out of the pyramid, unscathed from the battle that had just occurred.

Tarance curled his arms around Malkia and gave her a squeeze, as he whispered into her ear, "He means well. He doesn't always have the best words, but he means well for his people, and for this moon."

"I differ in opinion," Malkia breathed. "He failed to inform me of Ginny's powers, knowing she could destroy me. He knew more than he was willing to divulge."

"Sometimes you have to figure circumstances out for yourself," Tarance replied. He stepped back, searching Malkia's eyes. "The war can only be won, when you become aware of what you are capable of creating."

Malkia backed up and looked at the group around her, her mother, her friend and the two older men who had only caused her grief. She could see other people walking toward them and she glanced around the area, suddenly noticing hundreds of people edging through the trees and vegetation. Women, men and children were walking hand in hand, laughing and smiling as they made their way over to Malkia's group.

"Are we really free?" a younger woman asked Errandor.

"Can we live where we want now? Can we go back to our homes?" another woman shouted from the group.

"Yes, yes," Errandor smiled at his people. "We are all free to go on with our lives, to create order again amongst our own people, and teach the ones who were enslaved to live without those tyrants. You have all been liberated."

A wave of cheers erupted from the crowd, as Errandor stood in their midst beaming with pride.

"Wait," Malkia yelled, a crimson rush of frustration sliding across her cheeks. "Wait a moment."

"What?" Errandor turned toward Malkia. "What now?"

Malkia glared at Errandor, before turning to his people. "I understand your excitement to move on with your lives. I would want to do the same. However, don't do it under the illusion that this war is finished."

"What are you implying?" the same young woman asked.

"There are still Artemisians out there," Malkia pointed up at the sky. "There are still deimos beasts roaming other moons and ships. This war is not complete. I still have so much more to do, and I don't want you to be unprepared if the demons decide to return. Back when they first invaded, you were a thriving civilization, but now your numbers have dwindled, significantly. It wouldn't take an army to extinguish what is left of your people, so stay alert and stick together. Freedom comes at a cost, and if you want to remain liberated, you have to be willing to take up arms the moment those monsters threaten you again."

"What are you going to do?" a tall man asked, hovering above the others.

Malkia glanced at Asha, and then at her mother. "What I was designed to do, finish the war. Until then, protect yourselves, and your families. Watch the sky and be mindful that we aren't alone." She paused, her eyes glazing over as her voice became a whisper. "We were never alone."

"How are you going to finish the war on your own?" another man yelled over the crowd.

"I'm not alone," Malkia refocused, standing up straighter. "I have people."

Malkia glanced over at her mother, noticing for the first time Dario's face in the crowd. His face was enflamed with fury, as he shrank back into the cheerful crowd and disappeared.

"I will finish it," Malkia whispered, staring at the spot where Dario had been.

"This makes you our warrior," another man in the front of the crowd said.

"Yes," a red-haired woman next to him agreed. "You're our warrior. We owe you our lives and our moon. You won't be forgotten."

The crowd nodded and whispered, agreeing with the red-haired woman. She moved forward and grabbed Malkia's hand and kissed it.

"Thank you," she said, gazing into Malkia's eyes.

Others moved forward, taking turns kissing Malkia's hand or touching her shoulder. Malkia stood in silence, sensing the love of the people, but struggling from the despondency of the whole situation.

After the people finished and took their leave of the three women, Malkia turned to stare at Errandor and Tarance. "Protect your moon and people," Malkia raked her hand through her hair. "I don't want to return and fight your conflict, again. You have already taken so much of me, and I really can't offer you more."

Errandor nodded, his fingers entwined with Tarance's. "We will. Thank you, Malkia. Thank you for enduring to the end and concluding what I could not."

Malkia smiled, halfheartedly. Alyssa and Asha grabbed Malkia's hands and moved away from the men, toward their flying ship. Once onboard, Malkia sat in a chair and watched as the moon grew, before it fell away from them.

"He's going to come looking for me," Malkia muttered.

"Who is?" Alyssa asked, swiveling to look at her.

Malkia breathed in deep, expelling slowly. "Dario. He escaped my grasp. I thought he was dead based on the distance he was flung, but I saw him in the crowd. He will come after me."

"He doesn't have the strength, Malkia." Alyssa shook her head, leaning forward in her seat. "His powers are insignificant compared to yours. He will require an army to dismantle you."

"Maybe," Malkia replied, biting her lip. "He might not search for me now, but he will at some point. This war will never end for me."

Malkia watched her mother and Asha exchange looks before she turned. She closed her eyes and focused on the joy of finally leaving Enyo. After so many days of being prisoner to first one, and then another, doing everyone's bidding except her own, she was finally leaving.

"I don't ever want to return to Enyo," Malkia whispered aloud, keeping her eyes closed.

"You don't have to," Asha replied.

"I mean it," Malkia said. "I don't want to ever go back to that moon again. I will never be the same. I will never feel the same. That place has changed me." The tears that she had fought to keep at bay, began to tumble down her cheeks.

"We support you," her mother's hushed voice was close. "You were never expected to do all of this. Not by the people who love you."

Malkia shook her head, her eyes remained closed, as the tears continued to fester. She leaned her head back on the chair, allowing the blackness of sleep to swallow her.

"Malkia," Alyssa's voice could be heard in her dream. "Wake up. We are approaching Eris. You might want to be awake for this."

Malkia eyes fluttered open, staring up into her mother's hazel eyes. "Mataya was taken. Do we know if she was ever found?"

"I know where she is," Alyssa replied. "At least I think I do. I'm hoping once the Artemisians are annihilated, we can find her and Esta, and go home to Esaki."

"Sounds like a dream," Malkia said as she sat up in her chair. "Esaki that is, and Esta, as well. Nothing seems real anymore. Mom?"

"What is it?"

"What happened? What happened back on Esaki? How did you escape your grave?" Malkia rubbed the tops of her legs, easing herself into a better posture. "Everything seems like a dream and I'm fighting to understand it all."

Alyssa sighed and sat down facing Malkia. "I wasn't dead. I was able to shield myself in the blast with a protection spell. I tried to block your father, Raul, and Ason but my magic wasn't strong enough. It was weak from the blow to my head, and I wasn't coherent enough to keep the men protected from the blasts."

"Why didn't we protect the house then, before the bombs came, before they had the chance to hurt any of us?" Her brows knitted into a frown.

"We could have done that. You and I." Alyssa pointed at Malkia, and then herself. "I was given strict instructions, not to reveal your powers or true identity, no matter what the cost. It wasn't until we were in the middle of the war zone, and I could see we were going to die, that I realized I should have given you the choice. I regretted that moment ever since."

Malkia leaned forward, resting her elbows on her knees and her chin in her hands. "Where did you go? Why didn't you tell me you were alive?"

Alyssa adjusted herself in her chair before answering Malkia's questions. "You said you buried me. I have no recollection of that. The spell I used to protect myself backfired, and I fell into a deep sleep. That's why you believed I was dead. My body was essentially in stasis. When I woke, I was no longer on Esaki. I have not been back since that fateful day."

"Where did you go? Did someone take you?"

"Yes, someone took me. A warlock from Eris," Alyssa glanced at Asha again. Asha nodded in agreeance, showing Malkia she knew what had happened.

Malkia stood up and looked at Asha. "Did you know my mother was on Eris? Did you know she was alive?"

"No, I didn't," Asha responded. "But I know of the warlock. I'm familiar with his abilities and I know he can be a strong ally or a fierce enemy."

"Relax Malkia," Alyssa's voice was soothing. "You're defensive and ready to strike anyone who might be against you. This is what your father and your true enemies wanted. They have used words and various settings to make it appear as if they have already won. Sit down and think about it. If they had known what was going to happen, then why is Ginny and most of her family dead? Why did your father have to create more than one plan? All these scenarios were illusions from Ginny, to create doubt in your mind. She wanted you to be with her, in the dark, forever dying of guilt and pain. Your father used everyone to accomplish his goals, including his own flesh and blood. Stop fighting with the ones who love and believe in you."

Malkia sat back in her chair, pulling her knees to her chest, and embedding her hands in her hair. "For me to trust in your logic would require me to be allies with the worst people. Dario was my lover and Kelsey was my friend. My defensives are high, and I am prepared to strike, because people I have loved, people who I thought loved me, have shown me they are actually my enemies."

Alyssa rose and knelt in front of Malkia. "I'm so sorry I abandoned you. My heart is bleeding, knowing you had to endure the pain of my passing, alongside so many other's deaths. My heart hurts for the pain you have had to overcome, learning that the man you loved, wasn't

245

who he claimed to be. I understand deception. I see your pain and if I could take it away, I would. I wished for you to have a normal life, one where you lived on Esaki, with Raul and Esta. I wanted you to have more babies and live by the ocean, just like you dreamed. I desired so many happy endings for you, and I'm at fault for not allowing you the chance to show us, you had the capability to end this back then."

"You aren't to blame," Malkia whispered, looking down at Alyssa. "You were the best mother a girl could ask for. You showed me tenderness and love. You were always there, until your perceived death. My birth parents are the ones who are at fault, and so is Asha. You were the one who kept me safe, when they threw me away."

Alyssa curved her hands around Malkia's calves, staring intently into her eyes. "Don't blame Asha. She didn't know the extent of what your father was planning to do. She also couldn't anticipate all the events that have taken place. Give her a chance."

Malkia glanced over at the warlock and could see the gleam of tears in her eyes as she kept her face turned partly away from them. "I am giving her a chance. She has been the one person I could count on. I might be angry and hurt, but I am giving her a chance."

"Thank you," Alyssa mumbled. She stood up and kissed Malkia's forehead before returning to her seat.

"What about the technology?" Malkia asked. "Asha, you said it was not the Eris people who brought the advances to Esaki. If it wasn't them, then who was it?"

Malkia noticed the approaching moon from the front window. Asha was quiet, gazing out of the window herself.

"Did you hear what I said?" Malkia asked.

Asha sighed. "Yes, I did. This is my home and I forgot how much I missed it until now."

Malkia walked over to Asha and peered at the colorful moon. She had memories of the beauty of Eris, but it no longer felt like home.

"I can understand," Malkia whispered. "I cannot wait to return to Esaki."

They flew in silence, nearing the small moon. Malkia returned to her seat and secured her seatbelt as they entered the atmosphere. The bumpy ride was quick, and the sky opened to the expanse of lush greens and red vegetation, with the brilliant blue oceans. The pops of yellow and oranges were still as awe-striking as they had been when she was a child.

"Where are we going to stay? We can't just waltz into my parent's home?"

"No, that wouldn't work. Hopefully, they don't know we are coming. I have a cottage hidden away." Asha shot Malkia a sideways look, as she steered the craft toward a large mountain. "It won't have food, because I have been gone for so long, but it has a stream nearby for water. We can sneak to the town and stock up on provisions, until we can find a way to contact Haltia."

They zoomed over a nearby river, following the twisted canyon, as they closed in on Asha's cottage. The rush of the water sent chills down Malkia's spine, and she yearned to be on the ground again.

Moments later, Asha settled into a clearing near a waterfall. "Home sweet home." Asha's grin spread across her face.

"It's a beautiful place," Malkia admired the view from the window. "Why did you have a cottage so far away from civilization?"

"This is where I lived before witches were accepted as equal citizens. It was a place to hide and practice my magic, but it was also my safe haven. This was the dwelling I came to recharge, even after I moved closer to town. I needed a sanctuary away from the madness of the world."

"Everyone should have a place like this," Alyssa joked.

They stepped out of the vessel, gazing out into the trees and vegetation, surrounding the tall grass field. Towering cliffs rose to one side, while a thundering waterfall spilled into the nearby river. There were flowers scattered in every direction, dancing in the soft breeze. Malkia removed her shoes and skipped barefoot through the tall grass, bringing her hands up to her chest in order to skim over the tops. It was a magical place.

"I can see why you would want to keep this place," Malkia said. She glanced back at the two other women and smiled. "This is a place where dreams come true."

TWENTY-SEVEN

Peace is an Illusion

THE SUNS SET, and Enyo rose in the night sky. Malkia sat on Asha's front porch enjoying the view that was so familiar, but at the same time a distant memory. Her childhood on Eris had been so long ago and although she had seen Eris from Enyo, she had never had the chance to fully enjoy the view.

The trees were swaying with the wind, and the sounds of nature surrounded her. For the first time in weeks, she felt safe. Although she knew there were Artemisians and deimos beasts on the moon, Asha had used a concealing spell to keep them hidden from any other people or creatures. The deimos beasts wouldn't even be able to track their scent.

Alyssa had used her own magical abilities to move her down the mountain unnoticed, where she was able to purchase supplies and provisions. They now had a few days leisure, to figure out their next plan of action. It would only be a matter of time before her father knew she was close.

Malkia had remained in the forest for several hours, absorbing the energy of the moon. Her connection to Eris was by far the strongest, and she knew that, although she didn't call it home, it was her true place of origin. Even many hours later she could sense the strength of the moon coursing through her body, making her feel as bright as the suns.

"It is a beautiful view," Asha interrupted Malkia's thoughts. "That's one of the reasons I picked this area."

Malkia looked up at the warlock. "What are the other reasons?"

"The waterfall and stream gave me continuous drinking water," Asha eased herself down next to Malkia. "The seeds and vegetation, along with the soft dirt, made it easy to plant my own garden. I lived off the land for many years. I don't kill animals, but if they were brought to me, I would use them for food. I had eggs from several different birds as well. This area enabled me to be on my own, disconnected from the slave owners on this moon."

"Did you ever bring my mother up here?"

Asha was silent for a moment before she answered. "I did. Many times. I brought her here when she was pregnant with you, toward the end of her term. We spent the last couple of months, living up here and infusing the most beautiful magic into your body." Asha paused, easing her hair out of her face and looking at Malkia. "You were born here."

Malkia's eyes widened when she heard Asha's words. "I was? No one ever told me that."

"That's because we always claimed you were born at your house. At the time, your father already wanted my head on a platter. We played down our alone time together." She stared down at her hands. "It was easier that way."

"I see," Malkia replied, putting her hand on Asha's leg and pivoting to face her. "Do you think she would come up here? Maybe to check on your presence, or possibly escape my father?"

"I don't know," Asha shook her head, inhaling deeply. "I don't know what is happening with your parents. Your mother was anxious to contact you and your father desired your homecoming. However, she was worried about you returning. There was so much going on, but she would never speak about it. I often wonder, what kind of grip your father has on her, because she wouldn't leave him, even though she ached to see you again. Now that circumstances have changed, I wonder if she waits for a chance to escape. There has to be a reason why she would not tell me what Thane was planning. There has to be more to the story." Asha's sentence drifted off as she gazed out into the night sky.

"Kelsey told me, 'Nothing is what it seems.' Do you think she knew something?"

"I'm sure she did. I am positive there is more happening. Look at Alyssa. Who would have guessed she was alive?"

Malkia nodded. "My thoughts exactly."

They sat in silence for several moments before Malkia stood up. "I'm retiring to bed. Thank you, Asha, for sticking with me, even after I accused you of being in league with my enemies. It has been an extremely trying time for me."

Asha twisted her head and looked up at Malkia. "I understand. You're like a daughter to me. I will always be on your side. Please know that."

"I'm trying. I am doing everything I can right now to trust again," Malkia replied. "Goodnight Asha. I'll see you in the morning."

"Goodnight, my dear."

Malkia awoke in the dawn stillness. She could see the first sun's light begin to creep golden into the cottage. Rolling out of her warm bed, she wrapped herself in a blanket before walking outside.

The air was brisk and chilly against her cheeks. She used her light to warm herself and sat down on the steps to watch the suns wake up the moon. She smiled to see that life in the forest was already moving, as she watched the various animals roam by the cottage. Some gazed at her, and then returned to munching on the tall grass. Others stole a glance and skittered off for safety.

Her smile spread across her face, as she breathed in the cold air, warming it in her lungs. This was a place she could grow used to living.

The dirt and vegetation were wet with mildew and Malkia felt the water slip in between her toes as she strolled barefoot down the path. The energy from the moon was already pulsating through her body and she wanted to laugh out loud, because for the first time in so many years, she felt vigorously and wholly alive.

This is my home more than I ever wanted to believe, Malkia thought. She moved away from the path and wandered into the trees, admiring the dark hues. The wild vegetation, and breathing the fresh air, filled her body with much needed vitality. She knew it was important to end the war, and that it was something she would have to face, along with her father, and possibly Dario. She knew the stillness and peace would end, but she also knew she could have it again.

She eased her way through the thick undergrowth, inhaling the different scents of flowers as they emerged into her view and admiring the different animals scurrying along the ground. Before long, she was near the waterfall, and could hear the rush of the water pounding over the smooth rocks at the base. She slowly followed the sound, removing her blanket and all her clothes before she slid into the bubbly water, churning around her.

She dove headfirst, the rush of the water gliding over her body, feeling more refreshed than she had in weeks. As she came up for air, her hair flipped off to one side and she giggled at her disheveled reflection in the water.

Swimming over to the waterfall, she stood in the chilly air, allowing the water to cascade through her hair and over her body. She was finally cleansed. She was finally free again. Her arm tattoo glimmered and reminded her of the day she chose to put ink on her skin. A day she had felt free and wild, just as she did, now.

"I will find my home," she whispered to herself. "This is just a detour and although it was my original home, I don't belong here." She gazed up at Theia and knew where she had to go. The answer was always there.

Standing naked underneath the waterfall, feeling the air on her body, was the moment she knew she was more than their weapon. They may have gifted her the powers, and they may have engineered her to be a certain way, but she was still her own person. She didn't have to become what they wanted her to be. She could choose another path once she had her daughter. She didn't require anyone's permission, and it was time to take back her power.

Walking back to Asha's cottage, Malkia breathed deeply as the suns dried the water with their warmth. She wandered half naked, carrying her blanket and most of her clothes, her body welcoming the occasional cool breeze. Listening to the music of nature, she felt connected as one with all the energy around her. The birds were chirping, and the wildlife was stirring. She sensed the powers of Eris, vibrating and flexing through her body and soul. She never wanted the peace to end, even though it was inevitable.

Asha and her mother were sitting on the porch as she strolled toward them. A smile was etched on her face, and she felt light as a feather. Both women smiled at her and her mother's eyes twinkled with joy.

"You look absolutely radiant, Malkia," Alyssa bubbled. "This place has done you some good."

"If you only could feel the energy of this moon," Malkia replied. "Even as a child, I never felt this free. I'm ready to have this every day, but first things first—"

"What is that?" Asha asked.

"I'm starving. Where's the food?" Malkia's smile spread wickedly across her face.

Alyssa and Asha both laughed and nodded their heads.

"Absolutely," Asha said. "Let's eat some breakfast. What else would you like to do today?"

"Do I actually have a choice?" Malkia asked.

"Today, I think you do." Asha grinned, winking at Malkia. "Today, I think you deserve to do whatever you would like. You've earned it."

Malkia smiled. "Sounds fantastic."

The women enjoyed a hearty breakfast, filled with fruits and vegetables and sweet-smelling bread. Malkia laughed at her mother's jokes and felt a joy she thought she would never feel again.

As the day wore on, she slipped away from the cottage, once again. She strode along the path for some time, coming to a stop only when she felt the warmth decreasing. Gazing through the tall branches and leaves, she saw the clouds roiling in a darkening sky. She heard the small animals racing for cover, as the birds squawked in surprise.

The tempest rolled in quickly and Malkia remained where she stood, watching the beauty of the storm. From a distance, she saw the cottage surrounded by large trees and thick vegetation that twisted with the growing strength of the wind.

She began the long stroll back to the cottage, enjoying the chaos surrounding her. A flash of lightning struck the ground, not far from Malkia, making her jump and shriek, as she felt the electricity spread through her body. Another bolt hit a large tree closer to her, and she reached out and touched the bark, feeling the light burst through her. Extracting it with her own powers, she pulled the lightning toward her.

Another lightning bolt rushed toward her, and before it hit the ground, she reached out her hand and held it still. She moved around, twisting the lights as she danced around the pathway, its energy feeding her.

I don't think my father realizes how powerful I really am. Or—maybe he does know. Maybe that is why he wants to me for himself. He has planned every move and decided every twist and turn.

She let the lights dissipate and stood in the pouring rain, her lips pursed, and her brows furrowed in thought, as she watched the storm make its way through the mountain pass and down into the valley below.

Her mother. Asha. Dario. Everyone. Her father had decided. Her father had planned all of this. He knew she was here. He was waiting for her to come to him.

Malkia focused on Damon. The vision bounced into a view as if someone had thrown it at her. She peered at Damon and could see his eyes. He was hurt.

"Damon," Malkia whispered.

He focused on her, as he sat alone on a broken boulder. "Malkia, they came," his voice shook with emotion. "They were everywhere. I couldn't save everyone. I tried. I really tried."

"Slow down," Malkia urged. "What happened?"

"The Artemisians." He paused, his face crumbling with defeat. "They were everywhere and possessed weapons far superior to ours. Most everyone perished. A few of us escaped, because the dragons whisked us away and protected us with their fire."

Malkia fell against a nearby tree, her body trembling. He had made his next move, knowing how to hurt her. He knew she could not save them. Her body shook with grief, the sobs taking over her body. "How could I be so blind?" she cried. She looked at Damon for the answer. "How could I ever think I would be able to be free of him? How could I be so foolish?"

Damon moved over toward her and although they couldn't touch, having him near her was comforting. "Malkia, this isn't your fault," he assured her, his brow furrowing. "You must stop blaming yourself for his actions. What do we need to do next?"

"I need you here," she exhaled quickly. "I need Tantiana and Parowan. Did they make it? Are they alive?"

"Yes, yes, they're both alive. They fought off the demons and killed many of them. Unfortunately, we aren't out of harm's way. Those monsters will come back and finish us off."

Malkia nodded, clutching the sides of her head. "Where's Jacob? Did he speak to the pixies?"

"Jacob is another story, Malkia. He disappeared right before my eyes." Dario's eyes crinkled in frustration, as he paced in front of her. "It was moments after the demons attacked. He was simply gone, and I haven't seen him since."

Malkia eyes widened, as she clenched her jaw. "Where would he go? Who keeps taking my people?"

"Malkia, the pixies did say something, before the attacks. They told Jacob there is a pendant they gave you. They informed you it would find honest or evil witches, but that wasn't entirely the truth. They needed you to wear the pendant to help you discover your full potential." Damon halted abruptly, examining her face as he stepped closer. "When the witches cast the spell, searching for your powers, the pendant strengthened their abilities to unbury them. The pixies informed Jacob that pendant is connected to you. It was forged out of the same magic that surges through your body. Do you have it?"

Malkia placed her hand up to her heart, remembering the pendant she had worn. "No, I left it on Esaki. It would be in my room. Why?"

"Tantiana can bring us to you. With that pendant and your connection to her and the jewel, we will be able to create a wormhole, directly to you."

"Really?" Malkia exclaimed. "Are you positive?"

"I'm not," Damon replied, clearing his throat, and glancing around him. "I'm trusting what the pixies communicated to Jacob. We need to find your pendant. You said it was in your room?"

She nodded. "Yes, it was on my bed side table, last I remember."

"That section of the castle was hit hard and is a giant mess. We will start looking right away," Damon had begun to move away from her, but appeared to have second thoughts as he gazed back into her eyes. "I'm not going to stop fighting for you. I am not on your father's side, I'm on your side. Don't forget that. Give me a little time and then channel me again."

"Thank you, Damon. I needed to hear you say those words. I'll check in soon."

The vision disappeared in an instant, and the first thing Malkia noticed was the stillness of the forest. The trees were quiet, the animals were hidden, and the rain had receded, taking the wind and the lightning with it.

She knew this wasn't peace, and that it was just another illusion. Her father was coming for her, and there was nothing she could do to stop him.

TWENTY-EIGHT
Growing Suspicion

MALKIA BURST THROUGH the front door of the cottage. Her mother and Asha, who sat in front of the fire eating their dinner, nearly dropped everything on the floor when she made her entrance.

"Malkia, you scared me," her mother exclaimed. "What's wrong with you?"

"When will he be here?" Malkia asked both women.

"What are you talking about?" Alyssa exclaimed, setting her dish onto the sidetable next to her.

"My father. Is he coming here? Did you two plan this all along?"

Asha rose from her chair and eased toward Malkia, gently touching her arm. "Are you feeling well?" She peered in Malkia's eyes, worry creasing her forehead. "You were gone for an awfully long time. Did something happen out there?"

Malkia yanked her arm away from Asha. "I'm feeling just fine," she snapped. "Is my father coming here? Will one of you please tell me what's going on? I know something is about to happen. Did you two plan this?"

Asha glanced at Alyssa, both of their expressions melting into horror. Sprinting to the back room, Alyssa came back with her bag filled with clothes and food. "Let's go," she ordered. "Grab what you can. You have two minutes."

Asha was already moving, and Malkia followed suit, grabbing some clothes, blankets, and food. The trio raced out of the door and down the pathway toward their cloaked ship, the darkness of the forest creeping in around them, making peculiar noises in every direction. As the panic rose in her chest, Malkia surrounded the three of them with her light, and flew them the remainder of the way, feeling relief wash over her when they were all inside the small ship.

The craft moved swiftly into the night sky, hovering beside the waterfall as they watched the cottage raided by a mechanical drone. It ripped the roof from its moorings and reached inside grabbing for anything it could find. A few moments passed, before the machine cocked its head to the side appearing to look over the tall grass. It stood silent for a moment before its head moved upwards and shot a beam of light right at their ship.

Asha took off into the night sky, swerving out of sight from the drone.

"You two weren't in on it?" Malkia asked.

"No, we weren't." Alyssa turned to face her. "But you knew something. You've always known when things were going to happen. Even when your powers were blocked. I knew he was coming, the moment you said you felt he was."

"Is this ever going to end?" She buried her face in her hands. "He couldn't even allow me a few peaceful days."

"It's time we faced him," Asha mumbled.

"Not yet." Malkia looked up, glaring at the warlock. "I need more time. I have an idea and possibly a way for others to join us. And weren't we going to find Mataya first? Mom? Didn't you say she was here or that you knew her whereabouts?"

Alyssa sighed heavily, as she closed her eyes and leaned back in her chair. "I have a feeling I know where she is. The same warlock who took me from Esaki." She opened her eyes, focusing on Malkia. "I believe she is with him, but I'm beginning to think Asha is right. We have to finish this first. We need to terminate your father, and any other Artemisian."

Malkia rested her head on the back of the seat. "I need to think about this. Is there any where we can hide for one more day? Just one more day."

Asha was silent for several moments before she responded. "I have one more hideout." She glimpsed over at the other two women. "It's not as beautiful or serene as our last one, but it is difficult to find, and farther from your father's grasp."

"Let's go," Malkia ordered. "Just give me one more day."

"Malkia, you don't need one more day. You know what you can create. Why do you need more time?" her mother questioned.

"Because I think my father has something far more advanced on his side, which will prevent me from doing this on my own. That machine for example." She pointed back toward the cottage. "I need to speak with Haltia. I need some guidance, and I believe she will have the answers."

"How do you expect to speak to Haltia? Your father has her locked up so tight, no one has been able to channel her in weeks," Asha said.

Malkia exhaled slowly. "I have to find a way. I must make this happen."

Asha shook her head, gripping onto the controls. "Okay, we will do it your way. One more day."

The ship leaned to the left and shot off into the air, leaving Malkia's peaceful moments behind.

The hideout was a nook, inside a cave. The ship nestled comfortably in the larger cave and the three women shared a small cavity, filled with dusty cushions, old spell books, and cobwebs from floor to ceiling. They swept out the niche, removing every cobweb and insect. It didn't take long for the two witches to create a cleaner environment. While they worked on that, Malkia took each cushion outside, shaking them off, desiring a bit of serenity before she began her work in the morning.

It was unfortunate they had picked one of the smaller ships with no beds. The few blankets and pillows that were stocked on the ship, along with the few they had grabbed from the cottage, were not as comfortable as the large soft ones left back on the bungalow beds.

Damn him. Malkia cursed her father in her mind.

She finished shaking off the cushions and surrounded them with her light, in order to move them all back into the cave in one trip. Walking through the cave entrance, she shivered from the frigid air, and quickly surrounded herself with her light, as well.

"I'm such a wimp," she whispered, as she ducked around the ship, and then into the small opening of their temporary home.

The cushions settled over into the corner of the cave. Malkia grabbed her one good blanket and one of the small ship blankets and settled onto her cushion.

"I'm beat," she said to the other women. "I need to work on my strategy, first thing in the morning. If I'm not here when you wake, I won't be far away."

"Okay," Alyssa responded. "Please don't wander off too far."

"I won't," Malkia said. Her eyes closed, thinking of her father, and loathing him even more.

Malkia woke somewhere in between the late night and early morning. The pitch black in the cave, made it impossible to distinguish. She bolted upright on her cushion and forced her light to her hand, illuminating her way through the darkness.

This is a creepy place at night.

She slid out of the doorway and past the ship again, seeing Theia's light brighten the night sky and leading her the rest of the way.

The sky was beautifully lit with two other moons, as well as Theia. Malkia sat down on the ground, shutting her eyes and allowing her body to be filled with the energy of the moon. She searched for answers in her mind, and wished to see her birth mother, but nothing came to her. Her father was doing all he could to block her.

After several moments of grounding herself, she stood up and walked back to the ship. She opened the hatch door, wanting a safe and secure place to contact Damon. The light in the ship was already on, sending a rush of unease to the pit of her stomach.

She flinched when Alyssa walked past the door. Her mother yelped, and they both fell into a fit of laughter, realizing their mistakes.

"What are you doing up?" Alyssa asked, catching her breath.

Malkia climbed into the ship and closed the hatch door. "I could ask you the same question. I woke up and couldn't go back to sleep."

"I haven't slept," Alyssa replied, easing herself into one of the chairs. "I stayed in the cave for some time, tossing and turning, but finally gave up and came in here to do some research and some of my own planning. I have an idea where we might find Mataya." She paused, as Malkia sat in the chair across from her. "Since the warlock doesn't stay in one place for long, it was hard to pinpoint his location. However, I think this last locator spell directed me to the general area. Now we can go there and see if we can narrow it down."

"That would be great. What can I do to help?" Malkia leaned forward in her chair.

"What was your plan?" Alyssa questioned.

"I was going to channel Damon again." She rested her chin in her palm, looking thoughtful. "He claims there is a way to bring Tantiana and my friends to Eris."

Alyssa's inhaled a sharp breath. "How is he going to do that? Does he have a ship that will hold a dragon?"

"No," Malkia said. "There is a pendant that was given to me by the pixies. They claimed the pendant was forged with the same magic that created my powers and will generate a tunnel that the group can walk through. I don't know if it works. I just know what they claimed."

"The pixies had the pendant?" Alyssa asked, her eyes widening as Malkia spoke.

"They did. I'm not sure who gave it to them."

"Well, you better channel him," her mother replied, her eyes glazing over.

Malkia nodded and rose from her chair. She focused on the space in front of her and thought of Damon, with his beautiful smile and dark eyes. His image jumped in front of her seconds later.

"Malkia!" Damon said, jumping to his feet. "We found it. We found your pendant."

"Thank the gods!" Malkia replied. She could see Tantiana behind Damon, along with several of her friends.

Skye was standing next to the beast staring at the empty space where Damon was speaking to Malkia. She knew no one else could see her, but relief washed over her, having the chance to see them again.

"Tell Skye that I love her, and she better bring her beautiful face to Eris, so I can give her a squeeze." Malkia grinned. "I need to have my family back. All of you." She softened her smile, as she gazed up at Damon.

Damon's smile crept quickly over his face. "We are coming to you. We aren't certain how to use it, and since Jacob is missing, we can't speak with the pixies. Any suggestions?"

"There must be another way. Bring Bella and her witch friends, to help. Someone has to know the key to make it work," she said, playing with the ends of her hair.

"Bella is on her way." He folded his arms across his chest and sighed heavily. "They've been hiding in the mountains since the Artemisians left. Most of the Domesca people who survived hid there. When she arrives, I will have her look."

Malkia rose on her toes, smiling wide again. "I cannot wait to see all of you again. This is absolute torture." Her smile creased into a scowl. "My father is a monster, and I can't speak to my mother. But." She grinned again. "The best news ever! My Esaki mother is alive! Long story, amongst other long stories, but tell Skye that Alyssa is alive. It will make her day."

"I'll let her know." A smile teased the edges of Damon's lips. "Talk to you soon." He gave her a wink, just before she let the vision dissolve.

Malkia smiled to herself, turning to face her mother. "They have the pendant, and they are searching for a way to travel to Eris," she told her.

"Did the pixies not explain how to use it?" Alyssa asked.

"No. The man who spoke to the pixies disappeared when the demons arrived. They haven't been able to find him and no one else can speak with them."

"I might have a solution," Alyssa replied, moving toward the ship's door. "Let me look through a few of Asha's spell books. I remember something from when your parents brought you to Esaki, but I can't recall the exact way to conjure up the tunnel, or if it's even a tunnel. I'll go dig up those books and see if there is a clue in them."

Malkia nodded, feeling her eyelids growing heavy, again. She watched as her mother climbed out of the ship and closed the hatch door. Settling herself back down in her chair, her eyes fluttered and eventually closed. *Just until mom returns.*

She knew she was dreaming, but she could still feel her body sitting in her chair on the ship.

This is bizarre.

She was back in the caves where she had seen Haltia. She could hear the crying of a child again, and her heart raced as she ran down the cave corridor. She had been here before and had run through these walkways. The rooms were all the same, but no one was in them.

The crying grew louder, and Malkia became more frantic. She turned the corner into the next cave area and stopped short.

Mataya was standing in the room holding Esta, as a baby. There was a dark figure behind them, its face shadowed with a dark hood. Esta and Mataya were both crying.

Mataya glanced up at Malkia and said, "Malkia please find us. Your father is going to execute us both."

Malkia woke up with a start, leaping out of her seat and peering around the ship.

"What the hell was that nightmare?" she whispered. Her heart was racing, while beads of sweat formed on her forehead.

How long was I sleeping? She thought. *And where's mom?*

She walked over to the door and eased it open, her hand shaking from the dream. Theia's light could still be seen from afar, illuminating the entrance to the cave. Malkia looked around for her mother but couldn't see her. She climbed out of the ship and shut the hatch door behind her.

I hate this place. Her hands clenched into fists, as she eased her way toward the small nook.

She climbed in their small room and using her powers, lit up the room. She glanced around for her mother and Asha, but they were gone. The books were still sitting in the same place Asha had set them the night before.

What now?

She left the niche and walked back to the large cave's entrance. She was beginning to wonder if any of this was real. She felt as if she was back in the same dream, except she reached the entrance and could see the two women standing near the edge of the cliff.

"What's going on?" Malkia asked.

Alyssa turned around, but Asha remained staring off at Theia. "Asha needed to talk for a minute. Can you give us some time and privacy? I promise I'll be back as soon as this is over."

Malkia glanced over at Asha, and then back at Alyssa. "Is this a conversation I need to hear?"

"No. No," Alyssa reassured. "We're trying to figure out some of her spell books, and some of her own misjudgments. Nothing to worry about."

"Alright," Malkia said. She hesitated one more time, taking one more look at Asha, before turning back to the cave and moving back to the ship.

There's something not right about this situation.

TWENTY-NINE

Channeling Damon

MALKIA WAITED IN the ship for some time, before her mother returned. The door opened and Alyssa climbed back in with a smile on her face.

"Did you two work everything out?" Malkia asked.

"I think so," Alyssa shut the door and approached the nearby table. "Asha returned to bed. I think she was just overly tired, but she helped me find the right spell to make that pendant work. Do you have any witch friends on Esaki?"

Malkia stood, following her mother to the table, and leaning her back side against the edge of it. "Yes, I do. What do I need them to do?"

"They will need one of Tantiana's scales to make it work. She might not want to give it to them, which is going to be the only problem I foresee. The rest is simple. Once they have the scale, they need to cover it with the blood of anyone who wants to cross over. The more people coming, the less blood they must spill." Alyssa arched a brow. "However, it is unwise to have too many people cross over, especially with a large dragon accompanying them. I would limit it to no more than five or six people."

Malkia nodded. "I'll let them know."

"They'll need to use this incantation." Alyssa handed Malkia a small book, pointing to the words on the right side. "The witch invoking the spell is required to hold the tunnel open, until she can no longer see them. If she allows it dissolve before they are through, they will be washed out into blackness, and the chances of them being rescued are slim. As well, the dragon will need to carry the pendant until they are all through to the other side." She placed her hand on Malkia's forearm. "Any misjudgments and someone is going to be swept elsewhere. It's a fragile spell, but it does work, and if your friends do it right, there shouldn't be any problems."

Malkia gave her a sideways look, her curiosity for her mother's odd behavior, spiked. "Skye will be joining us," she said. She waited for an emotional reaction from her mother, but the delay was unnerving.

"I'm so happy to hear that," her mother cracked a sheepish smile. "She was always such a sweet girl. I'm glad she survived the war, and you two are still friends."

Malkia smiled but apprehension swam in her thoughts. *Something is still not right.*

She stood in the open space and focused her mind on Damon. Moments later he popped up in her view. He had his side turned to her and was speaking to Skye and Bella.

"Glad to see Bella made it safely." Malkia's grin spread across her face.

Damon turned toward her and smiled. "She just arrived a little while ago. We've been searching for a way to cross over, and thankfully, we might have found the answer."

"I have a way as well," Malkia replied. "What are your thoughts?"

"Bella found an old spell book in Jasper's room. In it was a spell to move from one moon to another without flying. It says we have to use a dragon scale, while the dragon has to carry the pendant to the other side. However, part of the spell is smudged out. We can see something about blood, but nothing else."

"I have the same spell book. Or at least a similar one. Whoever is taking the journey must spill their blood, enough to cover the dragon scale. Do you have the actual incantation that needs to be performed?" Malkia asked, holding the book against her chest.

"Yes, it's on the next page and doesn't seem to be damaged," Damon replied. He picked up the book and showed Malkia the writing. "What do you mean by spilling blood? Do each of us have to spill blood or just one of us?"

"Anyone who is crossing through the tunnel has to add their blood to the mix. Do not bring more than five people with you, as the tunnel won't hold for larger masses. How soon do you think you can make it through?"

"Bella will begin to work on it right now," Damon turned to Bella, and handed the book back to her.

"Hi, Malkia," Bella smiled toward the area she thought Malkia stood. "We miss you."

"Tell her I'm coming home soon, and that I miss all of them, as well," she told Damon.

"I will. Give us some time to arrange everything together. I need to persuade Tantiana into giving up one of her scales, and then explaining the pendant holding task to her," Damon sighed. "It might take me longer, but I'll do my best to hurry."

"I understand," Malkia teetered on the back of her heels, a grin dangling on her lips. "Make sure you ensure everyone's safety, of who's staying behind before you leave. Parowan cannot make the excursion, so help her understand her role, while I'm gone. I have no idea how long it will take for us to return. They all need to take care of each other."

"We already have a plan for anyone who remains, and as for Parowan, she's a guard for a parentless family." He stepped forward, his lips set in a straight line. "Don't worry about what is happening back here. Now that our knowledge of these demons has been expanded, the people will be prepared if they double back."

A wary smile surfaced on Malkia's lips. "Thank you, Damon. I can't believe I'll be seeing all of you, soon. This has been the toughest few weeks of my life and I could use my friends by my side."

"Same. I can't wait to be next to you again. Stay safe, Malkia."

Malkia dropped the vision and smiled to herself before looking over at her mother.

"Sounds like it went well." Alyssa ran her hands through the ends of her hair, as she stepped toward Malkia. "So, they had a spell book on their end? When will they be able to begin it?"

"They have to retrieve the dragon scale, but they are preparing the invocation, and the people, as we speak. Hopefully before the end of the day they'll be here." Malkia released her breath slowly.

"Great news." Alyssa embraced Malkia, smiling up at her. "You'll need your friends, and your dragon to finish this. Your father is a despicable man and I'll do anything I can to help stop him, but I know my magic is not strong enough to penetrate his defenses."

"What about Mataya? You found the warlocks general location. Can we go find her, now?"

Alyssa shook her head. "I would say yes, but shouldn't we check back with your friends before long?" She twirled her finger in her, long brunette hair, as her eyes glazed over. "Staying here and waiting for them is the most important step. The more we add to the chaos, the harder it will be to bring them through."

Malkia sensed her mother was being less than forthcoming but struggled to push it any further. "I agree. We can wait until my group arrives. There is no need to jeopardize any more lives." Her eyes were dry and tired, as the insufficient sleep she had obtained was incapacitating her quickly. She walked to the ship door and opened it, before turning back to her mom. "Will you be okay if I rest? I know you haven't received any sleep, so you should join me. I feel like I've aged ten years in the past month."

"I'm right behind you." Alyssa rubbed her eyes with her fists, before giving Malkia an awkward smile. "Go ahead, and I'll be there soon to tuck you into bed."

Malkia smiled, remembering how amazing her mother had been back on Esaki. Despite her distrust in everyone, including her mother, she was happy she had her back. "I love you, Mom," Malkia whispered.

"I love you more, my dear," Alyssa replied, her smile spreading across her face, as Malkia turned back around and climbed out of the ship.

The walk back to the cave was still chilly, but Malkia welcomed the sensation. Her mind felt muddled with information, memories, and emotions. She needed some sleep.

The morning was warming up and Malkia sat on the edge of the cliff enjoying the suns progression up into the sky. She leaned her head back and closed her eyes, enjoying their warmth on her face. Her sleep had been dreamless, for once, and she had awakened feeling refreshed and focused. Asha had been awake, moving around their small cave home, while Alyssa was quietly snoring on the cushion next to Malkia.

She had decided to face the morning before contacting Damon again. She wanted to ground herself and soak in a portion of the moon's energy. It was extraordinary how much her body required the energy of nature to gain its strength. She would need to speak to Asha about that at some point. No one else seemed to need it, but for her it was essential.

She stretched her arms over her head, yawning as she pivoted and stood up. It was time to find out where Damon and her dragon were.

The cave entrance felt secure enough, as she turned her back to one of the walls and focused on Damon again. At first nothing happened, but she knew it was not always so easy. She waited for a few more minutes, keeping her focus on Damon's face in her mind.

The vision sprang forward in a peculiar burst, and Malkia awkwardly jumped. Damon saw her spooked face and smiled. She bit her lip, as she noticed he was just leaving his room, which would explain why she couldn't break through to him. Channeling only occurred, if the respondent was willing to receive.

"We are almost ready," Damon interrupted her thoughts. "I took a nap after preparations were completed, and now I'm on my way to Bella and the group."

"I had a nap myself. I needed it," She wiped her forehead with the back of her hand, stepping closer to Damon. "I'm anxious to see all of you. From what I understand, by reading the spell, you'll require the magic to attach to me. We're hiding in this cave." She pointed her thumb over her shoulder. "It will be large enough for Tantiana to come through, which is one of the reasons we haven't left. It will hide your arrival and keep us all hidden until we are ready to depart. Our vessel is cramped, but I'll ride Tantiana and the rest of you can go by ship."

"We're ready, Malkia," Damon assured her, the corners of his eyes crinkling from a small smile. "Tantiana wasn't thrilled about giving one of her scales, but Skye seems to have a connection with her. Once that was done, the rest was easy. We have our supplies, our weapons and a total of five people."

"Who's coming?" Malkia asked.

"Skye, Koleton, Justin, Bella, and myself. The other witches will be placing the spell and ensuring its strength, so we can make it all the way through. I'm not sure if they will be able to see the other side, but we are assuming it will be clear once we begin the journey."

Malkia breathed in deeply, exhaling slowly. "I hope so."

"Stop worrying so much," Damon scolded, affection glowing in his eyes. "We will make it. Just be on the other side so I can give you a much-needed hug."

She laughed. "I wouldn't miss it."

She dropped the vision, wandering down the pathway to find her mother and Asha. As she approached, she could hear hushed arguing. Hurrying to the doorway, she saw the two women staring at her, their faces flushed with anger.

"What is going on with you two?" Malkia asked, a frown creeping across her face.

"Nothing significant," Alyssa replied, turning away. "We just don't agree on all that has occurred and how to accomplish our future tasks."

Malkia stepped in the room, edging closer to the two women. "What do you mean?"

"Asha should have never allowed you to go through with the destruction of the Artemis moon or the war on Enyo." Alyssa paused, looking at Asha with icy contempt. "She should've taken on the mission herself."

Malkia's body stiffened, her face burning with frustration. "You don't decide what I do. I'm not a child. I did what was necessary to end the barbaric treatment of innocent people. Not to mention, those monsters flew to Esaki and killed our people. You have no idea what I've endured to terminate those horrible creatures, and you don't have the right to take that away from me." Her expression hardened, as the memories flooded her mind. "None of it, not the heartache, not the pain, and definitely not the victory. It's over now and the Enyoans finally have a chance to enjoy a life, free of those savages."

Alyssa frowned, glancing over at Asha before responding. "I'm not trying to take anything away from you. There had to be a better resolution. The Artemisians weren't all horrible, but now they will never have that chance to prove themselves."

"That's a difference in opinion." Malkia forked her hand through her hair, sagging against the wall behind her. "I was nearly killed by one of those monsters, just for being outside, minding my own business."

"I lived with them for months, Malkia. I know they can be barbaric and ruthless, but like I said not all of them are awful." Alyssa bit her lip and looked away. "Now their civilization is in ruins and their moon is a charred rock. I agree the ones who continue to seek violence should all be eradicated, but going to their moon, without giving any of them a chance." She paused, shaking her head. "That's what I don't understand."

"No one understands unless they have witnessed the carnage those demons created, everywhere they went," Malkia responded, her mouth setting in a hard line. "I don't know why this is an argument. Let it go. It happened. I'm finally healing from that war. The vast majority of the Enyoans despised me for freeing them. It's hard enough to know their hate, but to see your disapproval, my heart hurts all over again." She spun around and left the small cave without another word. She didn't have time for pettiness. Right now, her only focus was her friends, and her dragon safely arriving on Eris.

She waited near the large entrance to the main cave, going over her mom's words in her head and wondering if there had been another way. Would Dario or Emelia even have listened? Everyone had their own agenda, their own plans, and their own idea of how they wanted these events to end, and no one considered her, or how it was going to affect her in the end. She was beginning to hate all of them.

She needed to free her mind of all these people, and the anger that was bubbling up inside of her. She walked in circles at the mouth of the cave, but after some time that was just not enough.

Outside, she tilted her face to the suns and felt their warmth flow over her body. She turned to the right and began running along the trail, on the side of the mountain. Every few minutes she would stop and do something to strengthen her muscles, working herself harder than she had in ages. By the time she twisted her way back up the mountain and to the cave entrance, she felt a heaviness lifted off her shoulders.

Her mother and Asha had remained inside the niche. She was thankful they had left her alone, so she could have time for her own thoughts. Malkia eased herself down on the floor of the cave and leaned against the wall, waiting for Damon and the rest of her crew to come through their magical tunnel.

THIRTY
Reunited

THE SUNS SHIFTED across the sky, as Malkia waited patiently, her eyes closed, and her body relaxed. As a wind began to swirl a few feet away from her, she snapped her eyes open. She watched in amazement as the wind grew and began to take a sideways funnel shape, with the smaller end moving away from her. Moments later an opening appeared in the middle, growing as the funnel twirled faster.

They're coming! Malkia cheered in her mind.

The opening became large enough for a person to fit through, kicking up dirt, as it lengthened. Malkia could see the darkness inside the opening and searched for her friends. Once the opening was almost as large as the entrance to the cave the winds calmed and Malkia waited, her hands over her heart pleading for a safe passage.

She could feel Asha and Alyssa behind her but ignored them and focused on the entrance. It wasn't long before she saw a distant movement. She waited, her heart galloping inside her chest and her stomach somersaulting in her belly.

Then she saw her.

Skye came through first, her jet-black eyes seeing her friend and weeping, as she ran to Malkia. They embraced, holding each other tight, as Malkia sobbed into her friend's shoulder, feeling safe having her next to her, again. She pulled back just in time to see Bella stumble through, followed by Justin, Koleton, and then Damon. Malkia towed each one away from the entrance, hugging them tightly. Damon's embrace was the longest, and Malkia leaned into his chest, needing to feel the safety she knew he could provide. His massive hug eased her heart, as he kissed her on the forehead.

"We made it," he whispered in her ear.

Tantiana made her entrance known as she plunged through the entrance and grazed her head up against Malkia. She swung the end of her body through, and then the tunnel disappeared.

Malkia leapt up and hugged the dragon's nose. "I missed you."

Tantiana nodded her head in response and nuzzled her nose into Malkia's neck. The dragon dropped the pendant in Malkia's hands, and she fastened it back around her neck, where it belonged.

"Glad you two love birds can be back together, but I want my turn," Koleton bolstered. He grabbed Malkia around the waist, squeezing her tight. "It's so good to see you again. Life has been a bit of a nightmare since you flew off without us."

Malkia laughed. "I won't forget you next time."

Koleton winked at her before retreating to Skye. He cradled his arm around her shoulders and kissed her head. Skye smiled up at him, and Malkia could see they had become closer while she was gone. She smiled at the couple as she turned to Justin and Bella.

"Have you found Mataya," Justin asked.

"No, but we have an idea. Justin you never met my mother before she disappeared, but since you are courting her daughter, I suggest you go introduce yourself," Malkia nudged him toward Alyssa, giving him an encouraging smile.

Alyssa was speaking with Skye, and Malkia saw their joyful smiles. Maybe her mother's hesitation earlier was just a lapse of listening. They were all in their own worlds, trying to escape this madness, alive.

She turned back to Bella and gave her another hug. "Thank you for ensuring a smooth journey, and for not giving up on me."

"I'm always here for you." Bella placed her hands on Malkia's shoulders. "The moment I knew you were missing, I began searching for a way to find you. Damon was nearly killed. Jasper and Dario had disappeared." She shook her head and stepped back. "It wasn't the best of days, but we made it. Somehow, we survived, and now we are going to win this blasted war, so you can return to Esaki."

Malkia grinned, throwing her hands up to her face. "Ha! I cannot wait!"

She hugged her again, before walking over to Damon. He pulled her close and gave her another squeeze. Malkia let him hold her. She was in need of some physical protection, from someone besides herself.

"Dario really put you through the ringer, didn't he?" Damon asked, his breath warm on her forehead.

"Isn't that funny?" Malkia said, holding him tighter. "All along I thought you were the savage. He had us all fooled, no one the wiser to his deceit. I'm still kicking myself for trusting him and Kelsey so easily."

Damon leaned back, his eyes wide. "Kelsey was in on this?"

"Yes! Did I not tell you?" Malkia frowned, holding onto Damon's arms, as she looked up at his face. "They're siblings. You have no idea how psycho their family is. They all steamrolled me, along with the Artemisians. It has been a hellish month."

Damon held her close, again. "I can only imagine. I knew that man had something wrong with him. He hated me with a passion. I know I did some horrid things, but his dogs instilled the ideas into my head. He had planned it all along, so how could he hate me for something he wanted me to do?"

Malkia pulled back, reaching her hand up to his cheek. "Everything he did, was an act. He was a master of deception. I honestly believe he was still in his acting persona, all the way to the end. I wouldn't hold any merit for his hatred for you. He hated me as well, just for existing, and I had no idea he felt that way until after he drugged me and took me off of Esaki."

"I still don't understand him," Damon said, shaking his head. "The whole charade seems such a big effort, without the guarantee of success."

Malkia nodded. "I agree. Not much makes sense when it comes to Dario."

"Malkia?" Alyssa interrupted.

Malkia pulled away from Damon and looked over at her mother. "Yes?"

"Have you tried contacting Haltia?"

"I attempted to reach her a few times today, but I'm not making it past their blockade. I can try again." Malkia stepped in front of Damon, wringing her hands together.

"We need to leave this place." Alyssa touched Malkia's arm. "I know everyone just arrived, but we are running out of time. Your father knows you're here. Your mother and Esta are already in danger, and Dario might have made his way here, in order to hurt you."

"I agree," Malkia shifted around her mom, moving toward their niche. "I'll do my best to reach Haltia. If you want to run our plan by everyone, we can leave as soon as I am done."

Alyssa nodded as Malkia walked away. She followed the path into the small cave and sat down on her cushion. Taking a few deep breaths, she focused on her birth mother's face, again.

Instantly, she felt the block preventing her channel. Shaking her head, she searched for the magic in the air, and focused harder on the block. Within seconds it formed into a shape in front of her eyes, enabling her to encircle it with her purple light. She could feel the resistance of whatever spell was preventing her penetration, but she knew she was stronger.

She tightened her light around the block, squeezing it with her mind, and feeling it pulsate around her. It wanted to break through her light. She focused even more, using her mind as a muscle, and thrusting back at the block. It resisted even more and broke out of her light, emerging even stronger than it had before.

Malkia sighed, releasing the vision of the block. She closed her eyes and allowed her mind to settle for a moment.

As her eyes flashed open, she focused again on her mother's face, feeling the block mounting in strength. In her mind she called upon the spirits of Eris and asked for them to take hold of the spell that was barricading her. She could feel a mysterious force move through her and shoot out of her body at the dark block before her. It wrapped around the darkness, and tightened its grip, as Malkia added her light to the force. She could feel the block fighting underneath, but she held it tight, feeling the energy of Eris race through every inch of her body.

Her powers were growing more resilient, instead of weakening like they had in the past. She watched in amazement as the force strangled the dark blockade, and moments later the darkness shattered into the air.

Haltia jumped into focus as Malkia watched the dark fragments disintegrate around them.

"Mom!" Malkia called out.

"Malkia! You found a way through," Haltia quietly exclaimed, shifting toward her. "I can't believe you succeeded. I mean, I can believe it, but I really believed I would never see you again."

"What's happening?" Malkia asked, as she reached her hand out in longing. "Why can no one reach you? What is father up to?"

"Malkia, he's going to execute me, along with your sister, Mataya." Haltia wiped away the tears in her eyes, as Malkia's face burned with fury. "She's here. I don't know how, but he has captured her. Dario showed up today, and your father is planning on killing us both, and leave with Dario, Palma, and Esta. You must stop him. I can slow him down, but I can't halt his departure. If he can't exterminate you, he will leave, and we will never see Esta again."

"Why is Palma comfortable with this?" Malkia cried, her face turning scarlet. "She was my best friend. Why would she allow this to ensue?"

"Just like most people who know your father, she wants to be his favorite. She wants his love and acceptance and is on his side, because she is weak. She was never the strong one. It was always you, and your father resents you and me both for that."

"I don't know how to find you," Malkia whispered. Tears had welled up in her eyes, and she couldn't prevent them from spilling onto her cheeks. "Alyssa and Asha have been searching for your hideout, but their progression is slow."

Haltia eased forward, closing her eyes as she ran her hands through her golden hair. "We are cloaked. Have Alyssa do a locator spell on Dario. He hasn't been protected yet, and your father is so focused on finding and killing you, that he has forgotten." She turned, suddenly, checking the door. "He will be back soon. I can't talk much longer, or he will know you broke through his barricade. Have her perform the locator spell and come save us. Please."

Malkia nodded. "I'm coming mom. You stay alive. Promise, you will stay alive."

"I will do my best, which is all I can promise. I'll protect Mataya, but if you don't arrive soon, we will both be dead." Haltia inhaled a sharp breath, pivoting to face the door. "Go now. Hurry. He's coming."

Malkia dropped the vision and felt the darkness fold back into place. Its fragmented pieces had rejoined, and she was aware her efforts would have to double, in order to break through again.

Her long legs moved her swiftly through the nook, bending as she eased through the doorway. Asha was waiting only a few feet from the small entrance, and Malkia nearly toppled right over her.

"Asha, you frightened me," Malkia exclaimed, gripping a rock in the wall to steady her shaky legs. "What are you doing in the dark?"

"I was waiting for you. I heard you talking, so I knew you were channeling someone," Asha smiled sheepishly. "I was trying to give you some privacy."

Malkia grabbed Asha by her shoulders, her smile spreading across her face. "I broke through my father's barrier! Asha, it was amazing. I spoke to my mom. She looks worn and tired, but she's alive." She stepped back, a frown melting down her lips. "However, my father has captured Mataya. He's going to execute them both, if he can't find a way to kill me, first. On top of that—"

"Whoa there, Malkia," Asha interrupted. "Slow down and rewind. Your father has Mataya? I thought Alyssa said the warlock has your sister."

"I know! Unless the warlock is working with my father, Alyssa lied." Malkia paused, breathing in deep, as the notion sank deep. "I hope she isn't lying." She shook her head, looking off to the side. "I don't know. What I do know is that my mom says Thane captured Mataya." She glanced back at Asha. "And Dario is there. He arrived today and I can only imagine the garbage he is filling my father's brain with. We have to leave now, before he hurts anyone else I love."

"I'm right behind you," Asha replied.

Malkia raced toward the others, relieved to see her friends and dragon again. Alyssa was standing with the group, speaking about the plans to find her father.

"My father has Mataya," Malkia yelled, as she neared the group.

Everyone turned toward her, Alyssa being the first one to speak out. "How do you know? Were you able to channel Haltia?"

She stopped short, as she entered the groups circle. "Yes, I did. He has Mataya, and he's going to murder her and Haltia, if he cannot find a way to kill me. He also has a new sidekick, named Dario. We really are running out of time. What did you all decide was our final strategy?"

"Well, we might have to rethink a few things," Damon said. "We were planning on finding your sister first, but now that is pointless."

"Mom," Malkia turned to face her mother, her jaw clenched tight. "Haltia says you should do a locator spell on Dario. As of a few moments ago, he wasn't protected by their spell."

"Brilliant thinking," Alyssa whispered. "I'm on it right now. Asha or Bella, will one of you please assist me?"

"I will," Bella volunteered. She followed Alyssa away from the group and back to their niche.

"Once we have their location, we should leave," Malkia said, once the two women were gone. "We need to surprise them, but the way my father has conducted himself, I don't believe anything will truly catch him off guard. They know I'm here, and they know I have Asha and Alyssa with me. The only surprise we possess, is Tantiana and the five of you." Her foot tapped on the ground, and her fingers rubbed across her lips. "Alyssa or Asha could approach alone, finding any spells and breaking them down. Once that has been completed, I'll move in, with all of you coming in at different angles, ready to pounce when the moment arises. Any thoughts on who does what?"

Asha spoke up first. "I think I should go in first. Surrender myself. He will know it is a distraction, but he will believe it is just you and Alyssa remaining. After I'm captured, show yourselves from afar, and have Alyssa and Bella breaking down the incantations around the house. He will be distracted by your presence. Once the spells are down, Tantiana can seize Dario and remove him from the situation."

"What if he has additional attackers?" Koleton interjected. "Dario is going to be the least of our problems."

"I agree," Malkia nodded. "What about the mutt's mother? I remember her from when I was a child. She could be another enemy we will need to watch out for." Biting her lip, she looked around at the group. "What about any others who are waiting for me to arrive, particularly the Artemisians? My father is not injudicious. As soon as I betrayed him, he made allies with everyone who hates me. We have to be prepared for all scenarios."

"Yes, the Artemisians. They would be a perfect ally," Damon added. "He might desire their death and vice versa, but right now they share a common enemy. I wouldn't be surprised if they joined forces, just to ensure your execution."

"I hadn't thought of that." Asha breathed in sharply, her eyes wide. "You're right. He most likely has an army of them, protecting the boundaries of his fortress. They could possess ships and weapons, which would outnumber us."

"The Artemis demons don't scare me." Malkia placed her hands on her hips, standing up straighter. "They aren't as durable as I am. What scares me is his capability of using my daughter, or Mataya as a human shield. There has to be a better way to lower his defenses, without endangering them."

"I think sending Asha in first, is a start," Skye responded. "It seems to make the most sense. He won't kill her, right away. It will provide Asha with the time she requires to protect herself. She can link herself to him or Palma, creating a new problem he will need to solve, before he can exterminate her," She threw a look over her shoulder, then stared back at the group, her eyes shifting around to everyone. "While they're distracted, you can confirm your presence from a distance, and give him a reason to worry. With these two distractions, the remainder of our group can move in, searching for a prime spot to strike. I vote Tantiana stays with the ship, just until we know the Artemisians are dead or not present. They could focus on her and she would lead them away, but it wouldn't take them long to slaughter her."

"I'm with you on all of this," Malkia nodded at Skye. "Tantiana can be used, but we have to wait until we have the Artemis problem under control and have an idea of what and who we are facing. She can't go in and char up the fortress, because there are three lives we have to rescue, first. Tantiana stays back with the ship."

The rest of the group nodded.

"So, it's decided," Asha spoke. "I'll go in first. Once I'm able to link my life to your father, make your presence known. Create enough havoc to scare him out of his mind. If you and I can keep him occupied, then maybe the rest of the group can clean house."

"We found him," Alyssa exclaimed, from behind.

Everyone in the group quickly revolved to see her. The two women were standing only a few feet away, their faces beaming with happiness.

"Haltia has saved us," Alyssa spoke up again. "The locator spell worked, and we have Dario's exact location. We can depart whenever the group is ready."

Malkia stepped forward, moving toward Tantiana. "We are ready now," she said, glancing back at the group. "Let's gather up whatever we need from the cave. Tantiana and I will follow the ship. Once we near their location, let's land, and hide the ship and the dragon. The remainder of the way, can be trekked on foot."

"What are we waiting for?" Kolton boasted. "Let's go surprise the schmuck."

THIRTY-ONE
Her Father

BEING BACK ON Tantiana made life wondrous again. The rush of the wind swirled around her, as she howled at Theia. Soaring through the sky on the dragons back, was far more exhilarating than on her own.

They followed behind the small ship, zooming through the clouds and over mountain tops. Her father had done his work well. He had moved his family to the far outreach of the Erebus Forest. Whatever fortress he had built there, was not only to deny her access, but barricade all the dark creatures of Erebus.

Malkia had asked how they would hide their ship and keep Tantiana from falling prey to these creatures. Asha described a rugged mountain not far from the forest, which had the height to safely enclose both the dragon and the small ship. In her many travels, she had used the Erebus Forest to hide, in times of desperation.

Half the night slipped on by, as they finally approached the mountain. Malkia watched the ship disappear between two cliff sides and directed Tantiana to follow suit. A few moments later they were snuggled up against the mountain side, protected from the evils in the forest.

"Are you ready for this?" Alyssa asked, walking down the ship plank.

"I have to be," Malkia jumped off Tantiana's back. "I want this over with just as much as the next person. I can only hope it will end quickly, and my father and any Artemisians will be slayed." She shivered as her eyes scanned the skyline. "I'm afraid of my own movements if the fight is drawn out for too long."

Skye had walked up next to Malkia, and she put her arm around Malkia's shoulders. "We can do this. Somehow, we'll make it work."

"I hope so," Malkia whispered, closing her eyes, and breathing deep.

Malkia gave her instructions to Tantiana, making sure she understood that she had to stay back, even if the battle becomes unconquerable. The dragon pouted, but after coaxing her into being aware of how dangerous it would be, she relented. "I will call for you as soon as I know it will be safe for your assistance. Let me destroy the horrid demons first, and then you can help with the rest of the monsters," Malkia whispered into her ear, as she scratched just above it.

Tantiana nodded her head and settled in next to the flying machine.

The group gathered, each armed with several weapons. Damon's powers had intensified since his return to Eris. His speed had increased, along with his strength. His mind manipulation was amplified, which created tension in the group, however Malkia was confident in his desire to bring peace to Eris. The mind manipulation would be handy when they drew closer to her father's fortress.

The trudge down the mountain was complicated. Malkia didn't want to take the chance of being seen, so her light was out of the question. The jagged cliffs were the most difficult, but once they were down, they moved slyly through the trees, heading into the Erebus forest.

The shadows of the forest swayed around the group, making them secure themselves into a circle formation. Creeping slowly through the trees and vegetation, they eyed their surroundings, keeping each other and themselves safe. It wasn't a far walk to the perimeter of the fortress, and Malkia knew the group would need to be careful until they were able to make their move but watching the forest and the fortress was going to be a chore.

She halted just inside the forest's shadows. "Asha, it's time to make your move," she whispered, placing a hand on Asha's shoulder. "We won't have the luxury of time initiating this plan if the creatures notice our presence."

Asha nodded. "I'm heading in. It won't take me long to link myself, so stay alert."

The group watched as Asha moved in on her own. Several feet in, she cloaked herself, creating a safe passage to the fortress, although she already knew her cloaking wouldn't work once inside. Malkia waved her hand, signaling for everyone to move into position. Alyssa and Bella remained the closest to Malkia, with Bella cloaking herself, as well.

It was Malkia's job to display Alyssa and herself, just out of her father's reach. Alyssa and Bella were well into their incantation, attempting to break down the protection surrounding the fortress, and the rest of the group shifted out of her line of sight.

Here's to hoping this goes smoothly. Malkia cheered them on, in her mind.

Asha's scream sliced the quiet, early morning sky like a knife to the heart. Malkia enclosed herself, Alyssa and Bella inside her protective light and strengthened it to shine as bright as the suns. Seeing her father's figure move outside the main doorway, her muscles tightened, and her face flooded with heat. He stood on the molded rocks around his home, with Asha on her knees in front of him.

"She's going to perish, Malkia," Thane bellowed, through the darkness.

Malkia reached for the sky and imagined the clouds darkening and the lightening gathering force. Within seconds, the winds cut through the forest and moved swiftly toward the fortress. The clouds blew in, their menace darkening as they lowered. The first arc of lightening, smashed into the rocks halfway between Malkia and her father, sending fragments rushing through the air. The next one, she grabbed with her hands and stirred through the sky, directing it to strike anything that wasn't human that was hidden around the fortress.

The lightening shot out of her hand and impacted five different concealed areas. She heard the grunts of the Artemis demons, as their bodies died.

Her father eyes flashed around, crinkling them to narrow slits as he brought out a large knife, and slid it in front of Asha's neck. Malkia watched, as Asha fervently whispered to Thane, causing him to ease his knife back in its sheath. He shoved Asha and glared at Malkia, surrounded by her light.

"How dare you?" his voice thundered. "You're my flesh and blood. You are supposed to be on my side. How dare you defy me?"

"Just like you were on my side so many years ago?" Malkia

screamed. Her light grew stronger and brighter as her fury mounted.

"What about Alyssa?" Thane shouted. "After all she has hidden from you. After her place in this plan, why do you allow her to be by your side?"

Malkia paused and stared at her father. She slowly turned to face her Esaki mother and saw the fear in her wide eyes.

"She didn't tell you, did she?" Thane laughed. "Amazing. Are you really that gullible, Malkia? Are you really so trusting that you never questioned why your dead mother was really alive? What about the pendant you wear around your neck? Did she disclose its secrets? Did she inform you, she has been searching for it, for many years? At least I've never pretended to be something I'm not. I have always been clear with you, about how I feel and what I want. What about her? What about Haltia and Dario and Palma and even your sweet, delicious sister Mataya?"

"What did you say?" Malkia hissed, her face crimson with fury, facing her father again. "If you hurt even a hair on my sister's body, I will gut you while you're still breathing."

Thane's laugh grew as he watched Malkia's light change from purple to maroon. "I can see even you have a dark side. Maybe your mother should have been more forthcoming."

The first blow didn't phase Malkia, but she wasn't sure where it had originated. The second one shook her light, just enough for her to withdraw and tighten her light. She moved next to Alyssa and Bella and relocated them.

The third hit sent shockwaves through her body and with half-closed eyes she searched the ground and sky for whatever it might be.

Her father had dragged Asha back into the fortress, and she could see small ships emerging from behind the fortress, as the morning light began to pour into the sky.

"The Artemis creatures are coming for us," Malkia whispered to the two women. "There are too many. We'll have to fight our way out."

The women nodded, shifting away and beginning to use their individual magic. Malkia flew into the air, grabbing hold of the first vessel she came in contact with, and twisting it into a pretzel mid-flight. The demon's inside shrieked in pain, as Malkia tossed the hunk of metal into the next approaching craft. Bursting into flames, they both tumbled to the ground, just outside the boundary of the fortress, creating a massive explosion.

Malkia was struck again by another ship, as more of their small fighter vessels surrounded her. She could see their strategy. They had been instructed to exterminate her first. The remainder of her group would be easily eradicated, once she was gone.

Her light wasn't weakening as it had in the past, but the assault caused her to produce an even darker glow. She could feel the fury inside her increasing, and she didn't want to be consumed by the darkness.

She frantically searched for a way out, but could only see more ships whizzing by, shooting at her from every angle. Her rage was strengthening, along with her fear. She could feel these two emotions were creating a lethal amalgamation, and she was afraid Tantiana would insist on rescuing her.

She recognized this sensation, and just like on Enyo, she was struggling to reign it in. Her face was flushed, the sweat beading excessively on her forehead and neck. The energy was building, and she desperately grasped onto it, begging it to not detonate.

As her light escaped her body, she felt her powers move through the air and spread in multiple directions. The explosion was as bright as the sun, disintegrating the closest ships on contact. As the air cleared, she witnessed the remnants of the ships tumbling toward the ground, and realized her friends had no protection from her wrath.

Her panic rose out of her stomach, not paying attention to the plethora of flying vessels, once again, surrounding her. The ground crawled with deimos beasts and Artemis creatures, while the sky was bursting with their ships. Her friends were doomed, and her father was winning.

She shot down to the ground, plowing through the deimos and demons. The explosion she caused slaughtered everything in her path, but it didn't stop them from advancing. They were completely focused on her every move. She could feel a warmth on her chest and glanced down to see the pendant glowing like a black onyx rock, pulsating heat as it grew in strength.

The pendant is keeping my light strong. What is it about this thing that my mother didn't disclose?

Losing her focus, she was struck by a powerful blow. She flew through the air, colliding violently against a large boulder, just on the outskirts of her father's fortress. Her light flickered as she dropped to the ground with a thud, feeling a large hand clasp her foot and drag her through the tall grass. She could see the stature of the Artemisian and was well aware of what he was about to do.

She yanked her foot away and jumped back into the air,

surrounding herself with her dark maroon light. The pendants power was creating a fire inside her, and as the demons continued to shower her with their weapons, the fire moved outside her body and engulfed her light.

Malkia lifted her hand, aiming the fire at each vessel. As the inferno made contact, the ship burst with an instant explosion, striking other ships nearby. The sky filled with smoke and the ground raced with flames. The advances decreased, and through the smolder, she could see several of the ships turn and fly away. She continued to throw the fire and light at any ships left in the vicinity, and watched as they tumbled to the ground, blossoming flames against the dark forest.

The deimos beasts were running and the demons on the ground, had all but receded into the forest. She could feel the heat of the fire around her and sensed the darkness filling her heart, as she peered around at the damage she had created.

She couldn't allow them to escape. The Artemisians would only return later if she let them live. Flying off the ground, she followed the path of the ships that had flown off. Within moments she caught up to the five of them, yanking the first one back with her energy and throwing it into the nearby mountain.

The next two she collided together and listened joyfully to the screams of the creatures, as they tumbled to the ground and exploded on impact. The last two were shooting at her. Their blows were actually strengthening her light, but it grew darker as well.

Balling up her light in her hand, the loathing she felt in her heart, ached throughout her joints and muscles, as she released her energy at the nearest vessel. The explosion rocked the air around her and smashed against the other ship, knocking it off course. The creatures inside attempted to correct it and flew straight into the closest mountainside.

Malkia stared at the mess, feeling a pain in her heart for her lack of control. The darkness was consuming her soul. She flew back to her father's fortress, seeing the large fires as she grew closer.

Where are my friends?

The terror shook her body, as she searched the ground for all the people she loved and cared for. She called for her dragon and a moment later Tantiana landed on the ground below. Malkia settled next to her.

"Do you know where they are?" Malkia asked her dragon. "Do you know where our friends have gone?"

Tantiana nodded. She leaned her head down and Malkia jumped on her back. The dragon shot into the air and over the fortress to the other side. The forest was not nearly as damaged on that side and Malkia could see her friends gathered against a rock wall just outside the fortress.

The dragon landed, and Malkia raced over to her friends, seeing they had been injured. Koleton was lying on the ground unconscious, his left leg charred from the fire. His pant leg was melted into his skin, while his feverish body emitted a sweltering heat.

Skye was next to him, begging him to hold on. Damon was limping toward Koleton, his leg barely able to hold any weight and his shirt ripped off his body.

Justin and Skye both appeared to be unharmed, but Alyssa and Bella were nowhere to be seen.

Malkia positioned her hands on Koleton's chest and used the

energy of the moon to heal his wounds. She could feel the powers moving through her and into his body, as they visibly moved down his torso and into his leg.

"What happened up there?" Skye whispered. She was staring at Malkia as if she were a foreigner.

The burn of the tears, flooded Malkia's eyes and rolled down her cheeks. "I don't know. It isn't the first time this has happened. It's as if I lose all control of my body and powers. I can't explain it and I don't know how to regulate it."

"You could have killed us all," Justin snapped. He stood a few feet away, his eyes burning with disgust.

"I know," Malkia whispered. "I might have murdered my mother and Bella. I haven't seen either one of them since we separated. I'm so sorry." Her body trembled, the pain of what she had done thundering through her. "I don't know what happens to me, but when it does, it's a flood of ferocity escaping my body."

"We all saw it," Damon interjected, placing a hand on her shoulder. "We all saw your light go from purple, to maroon, to nearly black. Then the fire, it was if you were a ball of fire in the sky."

"I was a ball of fire in the sky," Malkia replied, shaking her head. "I'm dangerous. My father wanted a weapon and now—" She paused, hanging her head in defeat. "Now, I'm exactly who he wanted me to be."

Koleton stirred and barely whispered, "You, Malkia, are *not* a weapon. Don't let that monster force his way into your head, any more than he already has. We are your family, not him." Koleton's eyes remained closed, but he gave Malkia a sly smile, as his body continued to heal.

Damon knelt next to Malkia. "We *are* your family," he said, cradling his arm around her shoulders. "Koleton is right. Your father is trying to turn you into the weapon he wanted. He's playing you and playing all of us. Don't give into him."

Malkia watched Koleton's leg repairing itself, thinking about the idea that her father was turning her into his weapon. *What did he mean about the pendant?*

"Malkia," Bella screamed, breathing heavily from a few yards away. "Alyssa—your mother—she went in by herself. She has gone in to confront your father."

THIRTY-TWO
The Ugly Truth

THE RACE TO the fortress felt like an eternity. She heard her mother scream before she reached the outer doors. Without waiting for the others she shot through the wall and into the first room. It was dark and cold, but she could see a light through one of the corridors. Maneuvering quickly down the large hallway, she entered a sitting room similar to the one she remembered as a child, before living on Esaki. Over on the far end stood Alyssa, frozen in place.

Malkia rushed to her mother, but before she reached her, she caught sight of Mataya's dark hair haloed by pooling of blood.

"*No*," Malkia cried. She dashed to her sister's body and pulled Mataya into her lap.

Malkia wiped Mataya's hair away from her face, and could see her once rosy cheeks were waxen. She placed her cheek next to Mataya's mouth, checking her breathing, as she touched the side of her neck, searching for a pulse. Not feeling either one, she laid her sister's body down and began to pound on her chest, trying to restore her heartbeat.

"*Don't you dare leave me*," Malkia pleaded. Her cheeks began to flush, as her anger for her father increased. "I'm not allowing you to disappear from my life again, do you hear me? I am not going to stop until you take that breath, so breathe *now*."

Malkia heard sobs coming from her mom and the loathing slithering down her gut frightened her. "Go find my daughter!"

She heard her mother's footsteps quickly disappear, as she continued to push on her sister's chest. After a moment, she placed her hands on Mataya's stomach and drove her powers through her hands and into her sister's body.

She didn't know how much time had passed before Damon sat next to her and curled his hand over her shoulder. "She's gone, Malkia. Stop torturing yourself and let her go."

Malkia's lips curled with icy contempt, as she shook his hand from her shoulder. "I'm not giving up. Go help my mother find Esta and Haltia."

Damon rose and she focused back on Mataya, alternating between pumping her chest and feeding her the light. Just as he was walking away, Mataya inhaled sharply.

Breathing deep, Malkia moved her fingertips back to Mataya's neck. "She's alive," Malkia whispered, feeling a faint heartbeat. "She made it back." She curled her arms around Mataya's body, lifting her from the floor and then laid her on the couch. "Damon stay with her. Don't allow her stop breathing. I'll return after I find the others."

Damon sat next to Mataya and put his hand on her stomach. "I won't leave her side."

Malkia hurried from the room and ran through each room, searching for Esta. As she neared the end of the first hallway, she collided with Justin in the dark. Grabbing his arms, she forced him to look at her. "Mataya is alive. Go to the other end of this hallway and turn left. She's inside the sitting room, just on the other side of the foyer." Justin turned to leave, but Malkia clutched his arm, obliging him to twist back, "I'm sorry, Justin. I truly am."

"I know you are." He nodded, as she released his arm and he raced down the corridor.

The next room was pitch black and Malkia had to use her light as a candle. She noticed a body on the far end draped over a chair. "Please don't be Esta or Haltia," Malkia prayed to whatever or whoever was listening.

She ran over to whoever it was and breathed a sigh of relief when she saw the face of the short old woman, who had the sharp teeth from her childhood. The mutt's mother was dead.

Good riddance, Malkia thought.

She tore out of that room and onto the next ones. After finishing the first floor, she flew down the stairs to the underground floor. On the way down, she ran into Asha, hobbling down the corridor.

"What happened, Asha? Where are my daughter and Haltia?"

"I'm looking for them," Asha croaked. Her voice was shaking and as she turned toward Malkia, she saw her swollen eye and bruised face, as well as her arm dangling loosely next to her side.

"What happened to you?" Malkia rushed to her side, placing her hand on her back.

"Your father handed me over to the Artemisians. He told them not to kill me, but they had his permission to come close. I don't remember much after the first few blows." Asha closed her eyes, wincing from the pain. "I blacked out."

"That bastard," Malkia hissed, allowing her light to enrobe Asha and ease her pain. "I can't wait to strangle that monster. Did you see my daughter or Haltia before the beatings?"

Asha relaxed, as the pain slowly dissipated. "I did see Esta. She was frightened, but Palma was with her. I told her you weren't the enemy, that your father was and then Palma told me to shut up. At that point, your father had me removed and handed me over to the demons."

"We have to find her. Let's check this floor. If they aren't here, then all we have left is the upper floor."

The two women searched every inch of the sublevel, coming across old machinery and newer models of robots and drones. There were large torture chambers and dungeons, and Malkia wondered how much he had tortured Haltia in the past few months.

"I've never felt this much hate in my life," Malkia told Asha, running her hands down the iron cell in front of her. "The madness building inside me, is frightening. I have never felt anything more intense and powerful as this dark energy swirling through my body. I need your direction and guidance." She turned to face Asha, her lips quivering. "Please don't allow it to consume the good I still possess."

"I'm not leaving you," Asha replied. "But you have to learn to control yourself. I can't be here forever, and I don't think you need an old woman attached to your hip for the rest of your life."

"If it stops me from creating the destruction I performed outside, then maybe I do need you attached to my hip," Malkia said, a wary smile surfacing on her lips. She turned in a circle, inspecting every inch of the room. "There's no one down here. Let's go check the upper floor."

The two women eased their way up the stairs. The upper floor was quiet, but the light from the suns brightened each room. The fortress was huge. Malkia could only hope Thane had left Esta and Haltia unharmed in one of the rooms, and hopefully Alyssa or Bella had found them already.

It wasn't long before they ran into Alyssa who was searching all of the rooms but had started at the other end. "The only rooms I haven't searched are on the East side. Every other room is empty," she told Asha and Malkia.

The three of them headed in that direction, checking each chamber carefully. As they opened the doors to the last room, Malkia was assailed by the copper stench of fresh blood. Edging their way in, all three gasped from the scene before them. Haltia hung by her feet, the blood from her slashed back and legs dripped down her body, oozing through her hair. As the stream reached her hands, it fell quietly to the ground, creating a crimson puddle.

Malkia sprinted to her mother and flew into the air, pulling Haltia into her light. She cut the ropes holding her mother's feet, and dropped to the ground, easing Haltia's still body to the stones. Malkia pressed her fingers to her neck, searching for a pulse and sighed with relief from the weak heartbeat.

"Her heart is beating," Malkia breathed, closing her eyes.

Asha cried and rushed to Haltia's side. Malkia placed her hands on her mother's stomach and began the healing process again.

She glanced over at Alyssa. "Go be with Mataya. She's alive and will need you."

Without another word, Alyssa raced out of the room. Malkia turned back to Asha and her mother and smiled as she saw Asha holding her mother's hand and kissing it tenderly, while tears streamed down her face.

"You really do love her." Malkia's tired face beamed with approval.

Asha nodded. "With all my heart. She's my everything. It has been torture to be apart for so long."

Malkia continued to heal Haltia but glanced around the large room still searching for Esta. "We have searched every inch of this place. Where's Esta?"

"I don't know." Asha looked up, surveying the room as well. "There has to be somewhere we missed."

"My father departed in such a hurry, there has to be some clue that remained, pointing us to her whereabouts. He wouldn't let her die, would he?" Malkia eyes glazed over, as she stared past Asha. "He may despise me, but he doesn't hate Esta."

Asha touched Malkia's forearm. "We will find her. Focus on Haltia and when we return to the sitting hall, we can see if they've found her or have any ideas where she might be."

Malkia nodded. Haltia's wounds were severe, her legs cut deep, with a sword slash across her side and back. With Malkia's powers, they were healing fast, and color was returning to her face. It hadn't been long, when her eyes fluttered open, and she looked up at Malkia and Asha.

Haltia cried out, seeing her daughter, as she attempted to sit up, but stopped short from the pain. "Malkia! You're here." She winced, reaching to touch Malkia's face. "You're finally here!"

"Mom," Malkia whispered. "I've missed you so much." She leaned down and pulled her mom up into a sitting position and gave her a tight hug. "Don't ever scare me like that again."

Haltia chuckled, grimacing again from the pain in her torso. "I've missed you, my baby girl."

Malkia pulled back and Asha eased her arms around Haltia's back, cradling her softly. They embraced, kissing tenderly, and whispering to each other, as they touched their foreheads together. After another long kiss, the two women laughed and smiled at each other before turning back to Malkia.

"Let's go find your daughter," Asha said, helping Haltia to her feet.

"Wait," Haltia interjected. "You haven't found Esta yet? Has your father left? Was he killed? What did I miss?"

Malkia shook her head. "I don't know where Father is. If he is dead, we haven't found his body. We have searched every inch of this fortress and we have yet to find Esta." She reached over and curled her arm around Haltia's back, easing her toward the door. "That's what we will do next. Let's go downstairs and regroup."

As they entered the sitting room, Mataya's eyes widened, as she propped herself up on her pillows. "Malkia, you found me." Her voice was barely a whisper, but a smiled danced on the edges of her lips as she closed her eyes, snuggling into the pillow.

"I would have never given up on you, dear sister," Malkia replied, as she sat down next to her. She ran her hands through Mataya's hair, and then kissed her forehead.

Malkia looked up at the rest of the group. Skye and Koleton had hobbled into the fortress and were sitting on a couch across from her. Bella was settled on the floor, her back up against a cushion, and Justin was on the couch with Mataya, her legs over his lap. Asha and Haltia had taken a seat next to Alyssa, and Damon stood behind Malkia.

"No one has seen Esta?" Malkia asked.

The group shook their heads as one, and shaking her own head, Malkia lowered her face in her hands. Damon put his hand on her back and Mataya reached over and touched her leg.

"We will find her," Mataya whispered.

Malkia sat up straight, flashing her eyes across the group, desperation rising in her expression. "We have to find her. We have to know what my father did with her. He must have left a clue."

"Let's start searching, then," Damon spoke up. "Is there anything in the lowest levels that might lead us to him or point to her hiding spot?"

Malkia shook her head. "No. I didn't see anything. I wasn't searching for a clue to show me the way, but nothing stood out to me either."

"Alright, what about out in the grounds? Did anyone notice anything out there?" Dario stepped to the side of Malkia, crossing his arms over his chest and looking down at her. "How did your father leave? Was there a ship that departed from the fortress? Was there anything out of the ordinary while the Artemis ships were flying around?" He paused, kneeling down in front of Malkia and clutching her hands. "By the way, your father knew the perfect distraction for all of us. While we were attempting to confuse him, he had his own diversions up his sleeve. We knew there would be those dirty demons here, but we weren't prepared for how many."

"No we weren't," Koleton said. "I've never seen so much chaos and fire in my life. Malkia, I know why you did what you did, and I don't blame you for any of it, but good hell, that was like seeing into the eye of darkness. You were literally on fire."

Malkia shook her head. "I realize this. The darkness was consuming my whole body and it was powerful. I felt powerful. That is a place I want to avoid, but if I have to continue to fight these Artemisians, and my father, I don't know if I will be able to stop it."

"The pendant," Alyssa spoke up. "The pendant makes you more powerful. I constructed it and gave it to Asha to create you. Whatever emotion you feel, the pendant will utilize them to amplify your powers."

Malkia glanced at Alyssa and Asha, feeling confused by what her Esaki mother was saying, and then she peered down at her pendant. "No more secrets," Malkia whispered. She could feel a painful rage inside her. The deceit and the lies was too much for her heart to bear. "What is wrong with all of you? Especially you three?" She was glaring at the three women, whom she had thought were on her side. She snarled, raising herself from her perch. "Why all these mysteries, and why didn't you just let me be who I was, from the beginning? And what about Enyo? I exploded there, as well, but I didn't have my pendant. Why is that? Why don't you all quit with the games, and finally divulge your lies? I'm tired of living under everyone else's thumb. Stop lying to me!"

The group shrank back, as Malkia moved toward the three women. The light in her body broke through and her pendant, turning ebony, again. "Alyssa, who are you? What have you not been telling me?"

Alyssa's wide eyes glanced at Mataya, still lying on the couch and then back at Malkia. "Malkia, please. This is not the time to start anything."

"Tell me who you are?" Malkia shrieked.

Alyssa paused, glancing over at Asha who nodded back at her.

"Stop it!" Malkia sobbed. "You two know something. Tell me now."

"Malkia," Alyssa started, her voice shaking. "There was never a warlock who seized me from Esaki." She paused, her eyes flashing, as she looked over at Asha. "I'm the warlock. I healed and protected myself in the grave, until I could safely emerge. Once I was free, I returned to Eris in a ship I had used to transport myself to Esaki, many years before. You see, I'm not from Esaki, either. I'm from Eris, and Asha is my sister."

"What?" Malkia yelled at the two women. "You two are sisters?"

Asha spoke this time. "Malkia, I didn't know she was alive. So please don't think this was one giant plot against you. We all had different plans and different reasons. You need to relax and allow us to discuss this calmly."

"What about my pendant. What about Mataya? Who procured her?"

Alyssa glanced at Justin, and then Mataya, who was now completely alert and listening for the answer as well. "I apprehended Mataya," she responded. "I posed as an unknown warlock and taught her how to use her magic. I didn't want to scare her, by showing her my face, but I needed her to learn her magic. All the things I should have taught her years ago instead of buying into this plan of Thane and Haltia's."

Mataya began to sob and Justin pulled her into his arms. He shot Alyssa an icy stare, before turning back to Mataya.

"How did my father steal Mataya from you?" Malkia hissed at Alyssa.

Alyssa's face flushed deeply. "Malkia, I tried to keep her safe. Don't act like you're the only one who can preserve other's safety. We have all made mistakes, and we've all failed in one way or another. You had your motives and we all had ours."

"You're right," Malkia murmured. "You did try. You only tried. You had the opportunity and the knowledge to direct this story down a different path, and you chose your greed over the love of your children."

"That's not fair," Alyssa started, sitting up straight.

Malkia turned to Haltia, ignoring her Esaki mother. "Mom. What about you? What happened with you? Why did you abandon me on Esaki? I remember it was your idea to hide us there. Why?" She shook her head, urging her anger to dissolve. "I don't understand any of this. It all started with you."

Haltia glanced down at her hands, before looking back at Malkia, tears festering in her eyes. "It did begin with me. At least when it came to you, but all of this," She hesitated, wiping the tears from her eyes. "All of this began long before I even met your father. There is so much more to the story than what you have seen or heard. I left you on Esaki because I trusted Alyssa. My idea to hide all the gifted children there was a way to remove you and Palma from your father's grasp. I needed you both to grow up, away from his power hungry plots." She closed her eyes, breathing in deep, before slowly opening her eyes and continuing. "By articulating the importance of hiding you away, I was able to coerce him into believing it was his idea. I had no knowledge the Enyo people would share their technology with the Esakians. I was distraught that the Artemisians followed the Enyoans there and massacred all those people. I'll forever regret my decision to place you in a habitation, where I could not protect you."

"What about you, Asha?" Malkia turned to her friend, and in her eyes, another mother. "You told me on the ship you knew about the warlock who captured my mother. You told me *he* existed. Was this just one more lie to protect your sister?"

"No, Malkia," Asha shook her head. "It wasn't a lie. I did think she was speaking of a warlock that has hunted my family and yours for many years. I thought that was who she meant. I should have waited to agree with her, but your anger has spiraled. You never had the chance to learn to control it, and for that, we three, are to blame."

"You are all despicable," Malkia hissed at the three women. She felt an ache gnawing deep inside her gut, making her wish she could disappear into thin air. "Not one of you are any better than my father. You had the chance to resolve this years ago, but instead your greed and selfish needs were your main focus." She raked her hands through her hair, squeezing her eyes shut. Exhaling sharply, she flashed her eyes open, freezing contempt surfacing on her face. "Asha, you're correct. You three are to blame for all of this. If you had given me the chance to know who I was, instead of springing it on me when a war was on my heels, maybe, just maybe, it wouldn't be the mess it is today. Maybe, I wouldn't have to be searching for my daughter, wondering if I'll ever have the chance to hold her in my arms, again." She stepped backward, unwanted tears spilling onto her cheeks. "I'm done with all of you."

Malkia glanced around at the group, before pivoting on her heel and racing from the room. She walked toward the outer doors and opened them the old fashion way to let in the dimming sunlight.

The day was already ending. She had fought another war and saved her sister and mother in the process. She had destroyed more of the demons and their pets, but the only thing she ached for was her daughter.

Tantiana landed next to her on the rocks surrounding the fortress. She nuzzled Malkia's face, and then turned her head to the sky. Malkia searched for whatever Tantiana was looking for, and just before it disappeared out of the atmosphere, Malkia eyed a large ship.

"Who is that?" She stepped forward, placing her hand on Tantiana's chin, her hands shaking uncontrollably. "Is that my father's ship? Was my daughter on that ship?" Malkia asked Tantiana.

The dragon nodded her head and spoke in her head a simple, *I believe so.*

Malkia turned back to the doors and ran straight into Damon.

"We found something," Damon told her. "You need to come see it for yourself."

Malkia sprinted after Damon, into the fortress and down to the sitting room. There was a strange machine, sitting on the table in the middle of the room. Malkia watched as Justin waved his hand over its top and a hologram of her father stepped out of the machine.

He smiled at the room before speaking. "Well, my dear Malkia, this is the end. You have made your choice, and now, your sister and your mother have paid for your sins. I have Dario with me, and he and I will be taking Palma and Esta to another moon, and maybe an entirely different star system. I will raise Esta as my own, and Dario and Palma will produce their own children, who will be raised to know you as their enemy. As the years pass, Esta will forget all about you. I will ensure she only knows you as the woman who destroyed her family's lives. You had an opportunity to decide whose team you desired, and now you must live with this decision. Until we meet again."

"No," Malkia whispered. She felt someone's hand on her back, but she ignored it.

The hologram disappeared and Malkia slammed her fists on the table, watching it shatter beneath her. "No!" she cried at the machine, as it tumbled to the ground near her feet.

Stunned by her father's words, she stared at her friends and family, noticing the shock on all of their faces. Her light felt like fire in her soul, causing her skin to take on a crimson glow. She quickly turned away from the group and ran back to the outer doors, flying through their wooden particles.

Racing out toward the rock walls at the edge of the perimeter, she stopped short in the middle of the stone walkway and scanned the clouds that had swallowed the ship. Her eyes searched for any signs of life, silently pleading to the Gods to bring her daughter back to her. Tears flooded down her face and her heart pulsated like a drum in her head, with a whirlwind of emotions spinning within her.

Losing all sense of reality, she sank to the ground, her knees crunched against the rock as her anger boiled out of her skin. She wiped the beads of sweat from her forehead, ignoring the hot tears streaming down her cheeks. Tilting her face to the darkening sky, the wind raged past her, and the rain drenched her skin, as she screamed her daughter's name.

The End.

Follow Malkia on her journey in the next installment, *Protectors of the Stars*. Available on Amazon.

I love to hear back from my readers!

If you enjoyed this book, please leave a brief review on Amazon.

Thank you for reading!

The adventure is not over!

See what befalls Malkia and her friends in Protectors of the Stars!

MALKIA COULD SEE his eyes staring at her through the darkness. She knew who he was and had known he would come, but she was not prepared for the robust energy he brought with him. She felt it pulsating through the trees, as he advanced to her position.

"How did you find me?" Malkia asked, stepping backwards, as he closed in.

His eyes narrowed and she saw his brow furrow, as he stood still several feet in front of her. "You can't hide from me." His voice was a knife to her stomach. "You have failed to be the warrior you were designed to be, and for that I am here." His hands clenched fiercely at his sides.

"What are you talking about?" Malkia questioned, shaking her head. She surrounded herself with her purple light, her chest tightening with the same fear that had consumed her the moment she had lost her daughter again.

"That won't stop me." His energy squeezed her light, snuffing it out, right before her eyes. Startled by her nakedness, she quickly stepped back, balling up her energy and directing it at him. Her eyes widened and her pulse quickened, as he grasped her energy and increased it in size, barreling it back toward her.

The blow felt like a hundred bees had stung her all at once, as her body flew backwards, colliding with a large boulder. Gasping for air, she struggled to inhale fully, and faltered to stand.

I have to disappear. He's going to kill me. She glanced around, eyeing his shadow edging toward her through the trees. Her heart was racing, as she staggered back up and floundered blindly through the trees and brush. Sensing her light again, her body began to heal, and her legs sprinted faster, while she surrounded herself with her protective energy.

Lurching high into the sky, she frantically searched for a safe place to hide from the monster chasing her. Malkia felt the impact before she made it more than forty feet into the air. Her light flickered and then disappeared altogether. Her heart dropped into her stomach, as she tumbled rapidly toward the ground, screaming as the jolt of the collision sent jarring pain throughout her body. Her twisted form lay broken and bent, blood trickling from her nose and mouth.

Malkia willed her body to heal and waited while it mended all the broken pieces, praying the man wouldn't find her before she was able to fight. *Who is this man?*

I'm the one person who can destroy you.

She cringed when she heard the voice, but quickly realized it was in her head. *Please leave me alone. Why are you after me? I've never done anything to you.* Malkia pled with the man.

How do you know you haven't done anything to me? The only person you ever think about is yourself.

Malkia glanced around at her surroundings, but with the tall grass, she was unable to discern the shadows. Squeezing her eyes shut in frustration, she willed her body to heal faster. *That's not true. You don't know me at all, if that's what you think of me.*

Then, who are you? His voice echoed in her head.

Her hair was matted against her cheek, as the gummy blood continued to seep from her forehead. Twisting her head back, she struggled to find her pursuer. *Why can I not live in peace? Why are you tormenting me? I'm not here to hurt anyone. I just want to live my life alone.*

Malkia knew she didn't want to be alone, but she needed this man to know she wasn't his enemy. Asha and her Esaki mother had warned her about him. They had said if she stayed on Eris, he would come for her. She thought back to that moment and wished she had listened more, instead of choosing to be difficult.

Why did you stay here, Malkia? Why have you not gone after your daughter?

"What do you know of my daughter?" Malkia screamed into the chilly air.

"I know more than you would want me to know." His voice was close. She sensed his presence beside her, as a hand eased onto her stomach. The silence was deafening, as she breathed in deep, opening her reluctant eyelids, and staring at the warlock who haunted her dreams.

His hand remained on her torso, as his dark face turned toward her, a smile playing over his lips, "Did you know?" He pressed down firmly, staring at her pointedly. "This one will surpass your abilities, bringing a force into this star system, no one has ever known."

Malkia's eyes widened, her heart accelerating, as she edged her fingers toward her stomach. Her hand rested in the spot the warlock's had been, directing her energy into her own body and searching with her mind. Inhaling sharply, she gulped, her eyes darting back to his face, just as the blackness enveloped her sight.

Acknowledgements

LIFE THROWS CURVE balls. It's inevitable. And sometimes, we forget how bright our light shines within, while dealing with the madness of our lives. Distractions. People who don't have our best interest in mind, tugging us away into the drama and chaos. Addictions. Wolves in sheep's clothing. *And so much more.*

These external and internal battles can be exhausting, but we all have the power to choose how we respond. We can change our stars. Shift our attitudes. And evolve to a higher frequency. It's within us all, just like Malkia is painfully learning. And more often than not, it's our own torment that brings us to an evolved vibration if we choose to grow instead of allowing the darkness to swallow us whole.

Easier said then done, but regardless, it is possible. This story reminds me to be better every day. Do better for my family and those I will leave behind when it is time to transition back to the light.

Thank you to my life partner, Steven. The man who holds me steady when I'm on the verge of faltering. I would have plummeted in peril while working through all the edits of this book without your words of encouragement.

And to all my friends and family, who have supported, loved, and endlessly cheered me on. Thank you for not abandoning me. Especially Crystal, my friend and mentor. Thank you for showing me how to find the calm within the storm and providing the tools to discover it on my own.

To my Editor, Erin Sandlin. From the bottom of my heart (yes, all that gushiness), I am thankful, for your constructive criticism, your audacious sense of humor, and your continued assistance. As well, thank you for holding me to my highest excellence, expecting nothing but the best from me.

I couldn't have found a better cover designer to recreate this book cover. Thank you, Niki Ellis Designs, for working with me on my many questions and ups and downs through this project. Your patience and understanding will not be forgotten. I am deeply grateful for your compassion and endless desire to create the best cover possible for this story. It has been an honor to work with you!

And Brandon Burgon, the Illustrator of the previous cover. The design is beautiful and will be used in the future for special projects. Thank you for seeing my vision and using your gift to produce such a dazzling book cover. Your creation far surpassed my expectations, and I am thrilled to have worked with you. To see more of his work, visit his website at:

www.burgonartworks.com

More by the author

About the Author

International Bestselling Author Niki Livingston writes tales of epic and dystopian fantasy worlds filled with magic, mysticism, and mystery.

When she's not busy writing enchanting stories of diverse women rising in their power and strength, she spends her time walking her rescue puppy, quieting her mind with meditation and yoga, diving into the newest books of Veronica Roth and Laurie Forest, and binge-watching The 100 and The Wheel of Time.

For all her latest releases and updates, subscribe to Niki Livingston's newsletter!

www.NikiLivingston.com

www.ingramcontent.com/pod-product-compliance
Lightning Source LLC
Chambersburg PA
CBHW020402260626
47156CB00007B/2205